T0194364

Author Diane Nielsen was born and raised in the Nebraska. She has been entertaining others with her stories since the age of nine.

Besides her passion for writing, Diane loves spending time with her two sons, rock hunting and the Nebraska Cornhuskers.

This is Diane's fourth published book from: The Guardian Series.

Other Fictional Romantic Drama Books Published by Author Diane Nielsen

"WISH ME DEAD"
Book #1 in The Guardian Series

"DARK WHISPERS"
Book #2 in The Guardian Series

"DARK SECRETS"
Book #3 in The Guardian Series

OMEN LAKE

BOOK FOUR OF THE GUARDIAN SERIES

DIANE NIELSEN

Order this book online at www.trafford.com
or email orders@trafford.com

Most Trafford titles are also available at major online book retailers.

Print information available on the last page.

ISBN: 978-1-4907-6210-4 (sc)
ISBN: 978-1-4907-6209-8 (e)

Trafford rev.   07/30/2015

 www.trafford.com

North America & international
toll-free: 1 888 232 4444 (USA & Canada)
fax: 812 355 4082

This book is dedicated to my sister, Cathy, and her husband, Jim. Thank you for letting me lean on you every day. Your strength and support means more to me than I could ever tell you. I love you guys!

And to Dee Daugherty, the talented children's author and my friend, and also to Hunter Arterburn, the radio D.J. that kick started my mornings better than caffeine. You guys rock!!

And of course to Kathy Larson for being a truly wonderful editor. Thank you so much!!

Prologue

The mighty Immortal Guardian, Saul, stood before the Window to the World, watching his human charges. He had many. It was his job to oversee them as they faced the daily challenges that made up their lives.

He flexed the mighty wings on his back, spreading them out to their full length, as he contemplated a problem that weighed on his mind.

A new baby was to be born and it was up to him to decide which soul would be best suited to be reborn as this special human. "Ah yes," he said aloud, having come up with a choice that he considered a perfect match.

Saul went in search for the soul of Abigale Mathews. He found her hovering quietly in a secluded garden, enjoying the peace and beauty of the spot. Her spirit glowed as she watched the daughter she had left behind in life, sitting under a tree doing her homework. She was preparing for her high school graduation in just a few weeks.

"Abby," Saul said, coming to stand beside her, "I have to speak with you."

Abby turned her head and smiled up at the handsome Immortal. "Hi Saul," she said, peace and contentment radiating from her ghostly form. "What is it?"

"Come with me," he said and took her hand, leading her away from any distractions so they could talk.

When they had traveled up into the clouds and were alone, Saul let go of Abby's hand and smiled down at her. "It's time, Abby," he said.

"Time?" Abby questioned. "Time for what?"

"Time for you to go back," he said. "Back to earth to live life as a human again." Abby became agitated, as the news Saul had given her sunk in.

"But I won't be able to watch Peyton any more, will I?" she declared, more than asked. She knew this day had to come eventually.

"No," Saul said with compassion, "but there is a new baby to be born, and you will have a new life. A special life."

"Special?" Abby questioned.

"Yes," he began, "this baby will be born to a woman named Hannah Priest. Hannah was also born with a special gift. As you grow with her, you will learn what her gift is. She will be able to guide you as your powers become apparent."

"What kind of powers?" Abby asked, interested in the turn the conversation had taken.

"You will see," Saul said, smiling. "But before you begin this journey, I think you might like to meet someone."

Saul closed his eyes and lifted his face upward. Without speaking, he called out for the Guardian Hunter, Jaxon, to come to him. He opened his eyes as the sky rumbled and a black form came speeding towards them.

As Jaxon came to a stop beside Saul, lightning bolts cracked and thunder boomed with the power this Immortal carried with him, inside him.

"What's up, Saul?" Jaxon asked his dark hair flying around his handsome face. "Is there trouble?"

"No," Saul said, smiling wide as he greeted his friend. "I want you to meet someone. Abby, this is Jaxon," he said, turning aside so she was visible to the Hunter. "And, Jaxon, this is Abby. Your daughter."

"My what?" Jaxon barked, his tone disbelieving.

"I never told you," Saul began, "but when you died, Hannah was pregnant with your child. It is now almost time for your daughter to be born. I thought you might like to meet her before she begins her human life."

Jaxon's eyes grew stormy as he looked from Saul to Abby and back again.

"You never told me about Hannah carrying my child before. Why not?" he asked.

Saul began to doubt his decision as he watched the pain grow in Jaxon's eyes, until it was a full blown storm. Dark and angry, with memories of loss adding fuel to its fire.

"Easy, my friend," Saul said, laying a hand on Jaxon's shoulder. "I wanted the two of you to meet so Abby will know her father in the next life."

"She won't remember!" Jaxon said, finally coming out of his shock.

"Not the details, but she will always have a sense of you because of this meeting. She will know she is loved by her father, and not just because her mother will tell her so."

Jaxon moved to stand beside Abby, taking her fragile hand in his.

"Hello, Abby," he said, with such feeling in his voice that Abby could do nothing else but smile at him.

"Do I call you Dad?" she asked, mischief in her voice.

"Just once," Jason said quietly, no joking in his voice. "I want to hear it, just once."

Abby moved into Jaxon's arms and stood still, her head on his chest. She could feel the love he had for this Hannah Priest and, in turn, the love he had for her as his daughter.

"Take care of your mother," he said, stroking her hair. "You won't remember to tell her, but I still love her, so much," he murmured, "So very much."

"I love you, Daddy," Abby said, as she began to fade away, her voice becoming that of a young child. "I love you." And then she was gone as Madison Riley Priest was about to be born.

Jaxon the mighty Immortal Hunter, his arms once again empty, fell to his knees and wept

Chapter 1

Saul kept the promise he had made to Jaxon and stayed close to Hannah for nine months giving her strength when she needed it, taking the pain as his own when her loneliness threatened to buckle her knees and drop her into an abyss of darkness. He gave her peace when she could not find any on her own and he made sure Roman and his dark minions stayed far away from this human and her unborn baby.

Saul knew Hannah would be okay with time and he had all the time in the world to give her. He would be patient until the baby came to give her a piece of Jaxon to care for and to love. He would do this until her human existence had direction again and her love a place to go with someone to lavish it upon.

To keep Jaxon from going rogue, Saul shared what he could with him and even though he knew it caused his Guardian Hunter pain, Saul could not deny him the scraps of information he could give him. He never revealed Hannah's condition until the last few days of her pregnancy approached.

When the time came for the baby to be born, Saul stayed with Hannah and when her muscles quivered with exhaustion, he gave her the strength to continue until her daughter took her first breath and greeted her new world with a loud cry.

"Jaxon," Saul said quietly, "come and see your daughter." Saul knew Jaxon would not be far away and he was right, as a rush of wind brought the Hunter to his side. Saul backed away to make room for the father of this special baby and he mourned the path of fate that took him away from her.

Saul stood forgotten as Jaxon bent over Hannah and his daughter, unfurling his great wings and wrapping them around the two humans giving them his protection and whispering his undying love into Hannah's ear and into the ear of the new born.

"I will always love you," he said. His deep voice was solemn with the oath he gave. His lips left a kiss on his love's forehead and another on the downy soft cheek of his daughter before he straightened to stand beside the bed.

"Watch over them, Saul," he said. Jaxon did not ask, as nothing less than the Guardian's promise would be accepted.

"I will," Saul said, resting his hand on Jaxon's powerful shoulder. "I will watch over them until you are all together again."

"Can I check in on them once in awhile?" Jaxon asked, unable to leave them without at least the solace that he could peek in on them from time to time.

"It is not allowed," Saul began, before the growl that Jaxon emitted woke the baby and made her 'mew' in distress. "But I will let you know when something important is happening and you may come with me to watch."

Jaxon calmed down as he knew he was getting more than most and more than Saul should allow.

"Thank you," he said and gazed one more time on the resting pair that he loved more than life.

Before he left, Jaxon turned to Saul with his eyes burning with promise. "Should you ever need me, if the Dark ever dares to threaten them, you have only to call and I will come."

Saul looked into the dark eyes and he knew if anyone or anything dared to harm Hannah or the baby, Jaxon would not rest until he had hunted the offender down and made him pay, before granting him a very painful death.

"I will," Saul assured him. "I will."

With this, Jaxon nodded his head and vanished from sight, but a deep growl of warning trailed behind him letting the Dark know that his protection had been extended.

"Stay away," it warned "or I'll come hunting and if you are too stupid to heed my warning, I'll come hunting for you!"

Chapter 2

Hannah fought the sleep that her body needed as she waited for them to bring her daughter to her. The pain she had gone through to bring her daughter into this world was but a distant memory, as anticipation drove all else from her mind.

She did not have long to wait, as her nurse Hillery brought her the pink bundle and placed it in her arms.

"Your daughter is beautiful," Hillery said, standing by in case she was needed. "You should be very proud."

"I am," Hannah said softly, "I am." as tears of joy and sorrow streamed from her unusual eyes and down her cheeks. The pain of losing Jaxon was dimmed as she held a piece of him in her arms, close, oh so close to her heart.

"I have some paperwork for you to fill out," Hillery said. "So if you will be okay for a few minutes, I will go get it and we can get it done together."

"We will be fine," Hannah said, beginning to unwrap the blanket so she could get her first look at the baby.

"Okay, I'll be right back." With that, Hillery left, quietly closing the door to give the new mother and her child some privacy.

Hannah barely noticed, so intent was she on her task. She touched the soft skin as it was exposed to her and marveled at the perfection in her arms. Hannah gently pulled the tiny pink cap off the head and gazed at the deep dark head of hair, so like Jaxon's in color and softness. A smile bloomed on her lips and her eyes glowed as she saw Jaxon in their daughter.

She stroked the petal soft cheeks until the tiny eyes opened and looked up at her. The tears that had hovered in her eyes fell to her cheeks as she gazed at the rich brown orbs and she hiccupped a giggle as she noticed shards of red mixed in, glad that each parent was represented in their daughter.

A tiny hand waved in the air until Hannah caught it and held on as the fingers wrapped around her own finger with a strong grip and the bond of love forged for all time.

"Look what we made, Jaxon," Hannah said. She was hoping that wherever Jaxon was he could hear her and see this miracle. "I think we did good."

"Here we go," Hillery said, as she came back into the room after lightly tapping on the door. "This should only take a minute."

Together they filled out the information for the birth certificate and when it came to listing the father's name a familiar pain wrapped around Hannah's heart as she gave the information.

"Will he be in to sign the paper?" Hillery asked.

"No," Hannah said quietly. "He died before we knew I was even pregnant."

Hillery reached out a kind hand and touched Hannah's arm. "I'm sorry," she said, "but we can add his name anyway."

The paperwork was finished and tiny foot prints were added before Hillery stepped back smiling. "And what are we going to call this little angel?" she asked as she waited for the name of the newborn.

"This is Madison Riley Priest," Hannah said.

"Nice to meet you, Madison Riley Priest," Hillery said, reaching out a hand and laying it on the cap of dark hair. "Welcome to the world. My wish for you is that you have a long and happy life." As she spoke the words, a soft light traveled from her hand to the baby in Hannah's arms.

Hannah flashed questioning eyes up to the face of the nurse and, using her powers, tried to see what kind of being stood beside her bed. All she saw was a golden aura and felt the warmth that radiated from this woman. She could detect no evil.

"Thank you," Hannah said, as the hand was withdrawn and the nurse stepped to the door.

"Take good care of her," Hillery said before exiting the room. She walked to the nurse's station and handed over the paperwork before heading down the long hallway. The farther she walked the dimmer she became until she faded from sight. With her blessing delivered, her job was complete.

Chapter 3

Hannah closely watched her daughter, Madison, known affectionately as Dee, to see if she had inherited her abilities, but years passed with no signs of monstrous images appearing and she was relieved.

Everything appeared normal until Dee turned six, a day Hannah would never forget.

Hannah had taken Dee shopping for her birthday present and had dragged her dear friend and employee Regina with her. They had spent the morning browsing in and out of stores and when Dee had expressed interest in a toy Hannah had secretly slipped Regina money to purchase it as a surprise. She did not spoil her daughter but she did try and give her the things she wished for, within reason.

Every year since Dee could talk the little one had been asked what she wanted for her birthday and every year it had been the same, "I would like to see my daddy."

Hannah had explained with a heavy heart, over and over again, that Jaxon had died before she, Dee, was born. But that someday, if she was very good, she would be able to see him.

"I have seen him," Dee said that day when her dark eyes met her mother's eyes with seriousness and total intent.

Hannah had stopped what she was doing and had lifted her daughter up in her arms, bringing her face even with her own.

"Honey, you know that your daddy died before you were born. I've told you that, remember?" Hannah explained gently once again.

"Yes, mommy," Dee said with complete seriousness. "But I think I met him in heaven before I came to you."

"Why do you think that?" Hannah asked with a strange feeling in her stomach that things were about to change.

"Because when I touch Daddy's things I see a face that I have seen before. So I think I got to meet Daddy before I was born. He said he loved me."

Hannah's heart beat hard in her chest as she studied the innocent face before her. She needed answers. "When you touch your Daddy's things you see him?" she asked.

"Uh huh," Dee said, nodding her head until the dark hair swung about her face.

"Do you see other people when you touch things?" Hannah asked, hoping she was wrong.

"Yes, mommy," Dee replied. "Sometimes they are doing good things, but sometimes they are doing things that scare me."

"Like what?" Hannah pressed.

"Well," Dee said, "sometimes they are having picnics or doing fun things but sometimes when I touch things,

I see people doing things that make others cry or that hurt other people. I don't like those things."

"No, of course you don't, sweetie," Hannah said, her heart heavy. Her daughter had not inherited her powers but it seemed she had been given ones of her own.

Hannah had begun to relax thinking her daughter, even though her eyes were scored with red shards, had been spared the pain of having a gift that let her see the ugly side of human nature. She had been wrong.

From that day forward Hannah had watched her daughter slowly withdraw from touching things, and from allowing others to touch her. She had given into Dee's request for little gloves to cover her hands which she wore everywhere but at home. And she tried not to make a big deal of it when Dee would sit for hours holding one of Jaxon's shirts, smiling at the memories she could see.

Hannah packed away the clothes that Dee would drop after holding for only a few seconds, not knowing what she had seen, but knowing it was not good. She never let Dee touch the military uniforms that Jaxon had brought to her apartment with him, nor would she let her touch the personal effects they had given her when Jaxon had been killed. These items had never seen the light of day, and they never would.

She would protect her daughter as best she could. She would help her understand her abilities and to live with them on a daily basis. For the most part she succeeded, but sometimes she saw the pain and the horror that would come over Dee's face and she would know that something bad had gotten through.

Dee had learned to never touch money with her bare hands, as images flew through her mind about those that had touched it before her. Too fast for her to dwell on any one event, but long enough to see the blood and pain that humans could cause as they fought over the bills they wanted, needed, stole for and killed for. Money had blood on it and Dee could see it all.

When Dee was little she would shriek with the visions, but as she grew older she worked at keeping them to herself as she could see how they upset her mother and freaked out those around her.

She grew and learned, until she graduated from high school and against her mother's wishes, moved out into her own apartment. She enrolled in college and did well taking on part time jobs to meet her expenses. Her mother had given her plenty of money to live on but she wanted to earn her own and stand on her own two feet.

She, like every other young adult in the world, thought she was invincible and would live forever.

Mortality meant nothing to her, had not touched her, but that was all about to change

Chapter 4

Saul spent what time he could with Hannah and Dee but he had other charges that needed him as well. He had assumed that since Jaxon had let it be known Hannah and his daughter were off limits, the two humans would be safe. Both had been sadly mistaken.

True, Roman had promised to leave Hannah alone but he had said nothing about leaving the daughter untouched. Thus moaning in glee, he had called one of his Minions, Daniel, to him and told him he was to target Dee Priest and make her life as miserable as he could.

Daniel, thinking he was earning favor with Roman, left to do his bidding. He was to discover Dee's special talent and he almost danced with the ease of his duties. He made the images Dee saw so horrific, as he threw in her path every vile object he could find, letting her see the truth behind the most evil of mortal actions.

Daniel thought he would be able to quickly break this human, but her will was strong and it took months before she reached the point of screaming in terror.

Those screams became music to his Dark ears. He relished the idea of being her constant companion and never missed an opportunity to create mischief. Yet, the thrill of his victories was not to last as Saul found out the Dark's plan and, without a second thought, called Jaxon to him

"What is it?" Jaxon asked, coming to rest beside his friend.

"I need you to take care of a Dark Being that is causing problems with one of my charges," Saul said.

"Why do you need me?" Jaxon asked as his interest was aroused. Saul was more than capable of dispatching Dark Beings that messed with his humans, so Jaxon was sure this was something special.

"I just thought you might like to handle this one on your own," Saul said slowly. He was dragging out the time when he would divulge all to the Immortal Hunter.

"Ok," Jaxon said. "What is the name of the person I need to help?"

Saul braced himself for the storm he was about to unleash and then he looked Jaxon straight in the eye and told him. "It's your daughter."

The dark eyes that had been interested before turned to ice and the handsome face became stone.

"Say it again." Jaxon ground out, his voice low and gravely.

"You heard me correctly," Saul said. "The Dark has sent one if its own to mess with her life."

"How?" Jaxon demanded.

"They have turned her gift into a curse," Saul said, "by forcing her to see the worst acts that humans have committed. This Dark Being, Daniel, has not let up and your daughter is on the verge of breaking. She is strong but the human mind is fragile and she has seen too much. I have just found out about this meddling and thought you might like to send a message of your own to Roman and his followers."

Jaxon's hands turned to fists and the growl that came from his throat caused the ground to heave and the air to tremble.

"Do you need me to tell you where she is?" Saul asked, knowing the question was only a formality.

"I know where to find her," Jaxon said, as he opened his wings and, with a mighty leap, took flight. Fire surrounded him as he flew to where his daughter lived and he had no trouble finding her as she sat huddled in a large chair in her small living room. Jaxon had been able to check in on her on occasion as she grew up and the young woman he saw before him now was a shadow of what she had looked like the last time he had seen her.

Jaxon knelt before her chair and raised his hand to brush the soft hair that fell over her cheek. As he touched her, Dee sighed and felt an easing in her mind. She had been afraid of late to leave her apartment; so horrible were the things that she saw. Everything she touched had fired images into her head that made her scream in the night, as they crept out and haunted her dreams.

Jaxon spent a few precious moments stroking the long dark hair, so like his own, before he whispered into her ear. "It's ok to sleep now," he said. "I will make it all better."

He waited until Dee relaxed enough to slip into a dreamless sleep before he stood and sniffed the air. He could smell Daniel and, because he could, he knew the

Dark was close. Now that Dee was asleep, all he had to do was wait and the Dark would come to him. The smile that covered his face was anything but beautiful. It was a bearing of his teeth and he clenched them in awful rage.

No one and nothing threatened his own flesh and blood. Jaxon faded from sight and began his wait. Before he was finished, his daughter would once again be safe and the Dark would think twice before messing with her again.

Oh yes, the Dark had problems, for the Hunter had been let loose and he had a hunger in his belly.

A hunger for revenge!

Chapter 5

Daniel had been hanging around the street, watching from the shadows, causing what chaos he could until he sensed Dee slipping into a dreamless sleep.

'Now we can't have that,' he thought and rubbed his bony hands together in anticipation of the dreams he would give her. Dreams of blood and murder, of hate and crime was her nightly menu and tonight was not going to be any different.

Daniel did not proceed with caution as he entered Dee's apartment, so sure was he that he had nothing to fear. He forgot about the Guardians in his haste and misplaced confidence, and he bent over the sleeping human. He reached out fingers that became long and pointed, aiming them at his victim's head, meaning to insert them and the dreams they carried into Dee's sleeping brain. Black drool drenched his chin as he was almost dancing with the ease of the task his master had given him. He was going to drive this mortal mad and he would be given rewards from Roman for a job well done.

"Oh, let's not wait for Roman," a deep voice whispered behind him. "Let me give you the rewards you deserve now."

It took a few seconds for the implication of a voice at his back to sink in, but when it did, Daniel squeaked in fright and tried to escape.

"Going some where?" Jaxon asked as he grabbed a handful of darkness before it could disappear.

"I'm just doing what I was told to do," Daniel groveled up at the Hunter who held him prisoner.

"By whom?" Jaxon demanded. Jaxon wanted desperately to wring all information at once from this dark creature, like he was some old soaking dishrag. Struggling to ask questions one at a time was almost impossible.

"I told you." Daniel squirmed harder, trying to get loose. "It was Roman himself who told me to make her life miserable. I'm just doing what I was ordered to do. Let me go!"

Jaxon raised an eyebrow as he looked at Daniel, and the laugh that escaped his throat was anything but humorous. "Do you seriously think I would just let you go after the pain you have caused my daughter?" he asked in disbelief.

Daniel twisted like one possessed when he learned that he had been messing with an Immortal Hunter's daughter. Not just any Hunter but the most feared one of all.

Jaxon had not been in the game long, but he had built a reputation amongst the Dark as being fierce and showing no mercy. The Dark took extra care not to be caught by this Hunter, for the ones who were did not live to see the setting of the moon. Although their screams of pain echoed when they were vanquished, echoed in the dark places where mischief did its work and left no one feeling safe from this Guardian Beast.

"Let me go," Daniel begged. Dark rivers ran from his nose as he tried to escape death's grip. "It's Roman you want. He was the one who wanted your daughter tortured, not me. I was just following orders."

Jaxon could not hear the pleas that Daniel gurgled out as he was gripped with an anger that consumed him. How dare these foul creatures target his own flesh and blood! Did they think for one moment that he would not find out, that he would let them go on their merry way after causing pain to his daughter?

"Thank you for telling me about Roman," Jaxon crooned. "But it does not change the fate that I have planned for you."

Daniel screamed again, this time in agony as fire from Jaxon's hands consumed him. Jaxon held on until the flames from his hands had no more to burn. Holding on until the dark figure in his grasp turned to ash and was carried away on the heat waves from those flames. He dusted off the residue and threw back his head to roar his victory. "Stay away from my family!" he shouted.

Saul appeared at Jaxon's side and laid a calming hand upon his shoulder. "It is finished," he said, calming his Hunter until he raged no more. "I think the Dark will think twice before coming to visit Hannah or Dee again. Your message was clear."

As Jaxon looked at Saul, the anger he had felt at being ripped away from his family banked within his eyes.

"I have to go," he said. His voice was low and deep. "I can't stay here."

"No, I know," Saul said as he felt the pain Jaxon lived with every day.

Jaxon turned and, kneeling one more time at his daughter's side, laid his hand upon hers. "I love you, Madison," he whispered into her ear. "You're safe now. Daddy will always keep you safe." He kissed her cheek and swallowed the lump in his throat as a smile came to her resting lips.

"I love you too, Daddy," she sighed and snuggled down deeper into her chair. "Thank you."

Jaxon's heart ached.

"She heard me, Saul," he said with awe in his voice. "She spoke to me."

"The sleeping mind can be reached," Saul imparted. "Your daughter is special."

"Yes," Jaxon agreed with pride expanding his chest. "Yes she is."

Chapter 6

It was several hours before Dee roused herself from the first good sleep that she had been able to get in weeks.

She stretched her arms above her head and pointed her toes as her muscles quivered with the hard stretch she put them through. Relaxing back into the chair, Dee became still, as a dream she had experienced surfaced.

She remembered dreaming that her father had come to her and told her everything was going to be okay and he would take care of her. Tears filled her eyes and her hand rose up to touch her cheek where Jaxon had rested his hand a short time before.

It had seemed so real Dee mused, real enough that she could feel the ghost of his touch still on her cheek.

"Are you here, Dad?" she whispered. "Can you hear me?" Silence was the only answer she received to her pleas.

All her life she had longed for a father, her father, to be by her side to share her life with her and to take the sadness from her mother's eyes. But it had only been her mother and herself as she grew up. No matter how old she got, she still felt the little girl inside her waiting and wishing for the man she could see when she held his possessions. It was the closest she was ever going to get to her dad and it left her feeling empty.

Letting herself wallow for a few more minutes, Dee finally pulled herself together and rose to her feet. She walked into the bathroom, flicking on the light, even though it was still light out, she felt the need for more light to chase the shadows away.

She stopped in front of the mirror and stood still as she looked at her reflection. Her skin was pale and her eyes held shadows that no amount of light could hide. The last month or so had been hard on her and it had left a mark.

Dee turned away and peeled off her clothes, letting them drop in a forgotten pile on the floor, before stepping into the shower and under the hot spray.

She relaxed for a few precious moments under the beating water before getting down to business and washing herself from head to toe. She wanted to stay under the warm water that let her forget her problems but she had things to do and she knew, she just knew, that she did not have to worry any more about leaving her apartment.

Dee shut the water off and reached past the curtain, grabbing a big fluffy towel, and proceeded to dry the cooling moisture from her skin. She soaked the excess moisture from her long hair and before dressing, pulled a brush through her tresses until the tangles were eliminated and the wet mass hung straight down her back. She then went in search of clean clothes and, choosing a cool tee shirt of white and a pair of lightweight lime green shorts, pulled them on and retraced her steps back to the bathroom.

Dee turned on her blow dryer and, hanging her head down, she worked the warm air through, until the dampness was no more. Turning off the dryer, she stood up, tossing her hair until it fell in a dark blanket around her face. She brushed it again and when she was finished, she looked in the mirror and was satisfied with the deep, dark and rich shine that was mirrored in her eyes. Her mother had always told her that she got her hair color from her father and she took it as a compliment, never once wishing for the blonde color that was rumored men liked the best.

Dee smiled, more than happy with the looks her parents had passed on to her. Dark brown eyes with veins of red marbling, the irises were rimmed with unusually long thick lashes, tilted under brows that delicately arched above them. Her nose was narrow, also a gift from her father. Her cheeks, since her warm shower, carried the slight blush of heat and her mouth was more likely to smile than not. She did not hide her smile and flashed it often even though her incisors, top and bottom, tended to be a bit longer than normal and her friends told her she had puppy teeth. Dee liked being different and resisted changing, even though she could to conform to the way everyone else looked.

Very few people knew of her gift and she guarded her secret, letting the ones who did not know think she was just a little off for not wanting to touch or be touched. She could live with that.

Hannah had told Dee that her father had been tall but she, Dee, shared her height with her mother, standing five feet seven inches, lean and muscled like her father. Giving herself one last look in the mirror, Dee added just a touch of dark pink to her lips before nodding her head and calling it good.

Grabbing her purse and keys, she opened the door and stepped out. She had been in a bad place for a while now, but that was over and she needed to go see her mother.

Her small SUV started up with a growl and she pointed its nose west and gunned the engine. Dee made one stop to pick up her mother a cold strawberry treat before pushing the speed limit on the fifteen minute drive to her mother's shop and the apartment that she had grown up in over it.

Not bothering to knock, Dee climbed the stairs and opened the door to familiar surroundings.

"Mom," she called out, dropping her keys and purse by the door. "Where are you?"

Hannah poked her head out of the kitchen and her face was bathed with delight as she confirmed it was her daughter who had come to see her.

"Well, hi, Sweetie," she said, wiping her hands on a dishtowel. "How are you?" Moving across the living room, Hannah gathered Dee in her arms and gave her a hard squeeze before letting her go and stepping back for a closer look. She knew by looking that times had been hard for her only child and she wanted to pry for the cause. But she didn't.

"What a wonderful surprise," Hannah said as she led the way into the kitchen where wonderful smells were originating.

Dee's mouth watered as she smelled and spied the chocolate chip cookies on a cooling rack on the cupboard.

"Oh, mom," she said, reaching for a treat. "Can I have some?"

Hannah laughed, as her permission was not needed for the cookies to find their way into a waiting mouth.

"Here, this is for you," Dee said around a gooey bite and handed the drink to her mother.

Hannah smiled and sighed as she took her first sip of the cold drink her daughter knew was her latest obsession. "Ahhh, that hits the spot," she said as she felt the icy liquid slide down her throat. "I have one more batch in the oven and then I'm done. Sit down and talk to me." She invited her daughter to sit at the kitchen table, as she put on an oven mitt and bent to take out the tray.

Dee swallowed the last bite and licked her fingers, as she pulled out a chair and got ready to do just that.

Chapter 7

"I'm sorry I haven't been by for a while." Dee began, clutching her hands together between her knees. "I've kind of been having a hard time," she confessed, "and I guess I wasn't in any shape to go out. I should have told you."

Hannah turned off the oven and placed the cookies on the rack, giving herself time to think before responding to her daughter. Her heart had picked up speed with the words Dee spoke and Hannah ached for the pain her daughter had to endure. She knew what having a gift could do to you and wished, with all her heart, she could have spared her baby the pain of it all. Even though their gifts were different, each had to find a way to live with what they saw plus retain their sanity.

"I could have helped," Hannah said, "even if it was only to listen to what you needed to talk about. Saying things out loud sometimes makes them better. I would have helped."

"I know, Mom," Dee said. Her eyes locked with her mother's. "But you know how I hate to lay all my mess on your shoulders. You have your own issues to deal with and really don't need to have anymore dumped on you."

Hannah could keep still no longer, as she reached for Dee's soft hands and gripped them tight in her own. "I'm here for you," she said softly, trying to keep the desperation from her voice. "We're all we have, you and me, so when we have problems we need to know that we can go to each other with anything and everything. You know that, right?"

"Yes, Mom," Dee said with regret in her tone, feeling as though she had made things worse with her words. "I did not mean for you to think I would not or will not come to you when I need someone. You're my best friend. Remember?"

Hannah patted the hands she still held and sniffed back the tears that wanted to fall. She wanted, so desperately, to keep her daughter safe and for her to have a normal life that she tended to overprotect her. She had chided herself many times for not letting her grow and learn on her own. "I remember," Hannah said, putting a smile on her face. "I've lived with my gift longer than you and would give you all my experience if I could."

"Don't worry so much, Mom," Dee said, pulling her hands away and, not being able to stop herself, reached for another cookie. "I'm ok now, really."

"What happened this time?" Hannah asked, reaching for a cookie herself.

"I had some pretty bad nightmares," Dee said as she was licking gooey chocolate from her fingertips.

"From what?" Hannah asked.

"Well, it seemed that lately everything I touched had a bad image attached to it. It sort of built up and got me down. But then today something changed and I feel pretty good right now."

"What changed?" Hannah coaxed carefully, fearing the worst, but hoping for the best for her daughter. Hannah watched her daughter fidget in her chair and knew that what was to come was not going to be pleasant.

Dee took a deep breath and dove in. "Okay, I was sitting in my apartment and I was pretty stressed out and I guess scared with all the things I had been seeing and stuff. But all of a sudden I got this feeling. It was this warm feeling and it sort of calmed me down and took away all my fears. I fell asleep and it was the best sleep I've had in weeks."

"And, what else?" Hannah asked. She knew there was more by the way Dee was looking everywhere but at her.

Dee swallowed hard and answered her mom. Hannah always knew when she was hiding things from her and delaying the inevitable would not make it go away or get her mother off the subject. "It was Dad, Mom," she said softly. "Dad was the one who helped me."

"What?" Hannah whispered as the blood drained from her face, leaving it pale and her mind frozen.

"I know it sounds totally unbelievable, but it's true," Dee rushed on. "I swear Dad talked to me and told me everything was going to be okay and it was safe for me to sleep. I could feel his hand on my cheek and I think I told him I loved him before I went to sleep. Dad's watching over us Mom and, no matter how strange it sounds, I believe it," Dee said. She leaned forward and stared intently into her mother's glazed eyes, trying to convince her that what she said was true.

The red irises that Dee had grown up with were unfocused and she was seeing something that she was not allowed to share.

"Mom! Mom, are you alright? Mom?" Dee was worried that she had pushed her mom over the edge by telling her that Jaxon was still in their lives.

Hannah heard her daughter talking to her but it was far away and pushed aside as the images of Jaxon that she had locked away in her heart and mind came flooding out as if the gates of a dam had been opened wide. With the memories came the pain of loss and love that hurt as much today, as it had the day she had been told he had died protecting her.

Hannah had wished every day that Jaxon would talk to her, come to her, just let her know that he was with her and had not left her altogether. But he never had. All she heard was silence. All she felt was emptiness.

No. That was not true. It was not true that all she felt was emptiness and loneliness. Anger was taking root and beginning to grow. Anger at Jaxon for not coming to her and anger at her daughter for getting something she so desperately wanted.

Roman laughed.

Chapter 8

Roman laughed at his little bit of mischief. Oh sure, he had promised he would leave Hannah alone, but really! Did Saul and his cohorts forget with whom they were dealing? Did they really expect him to keep a promise? Him, Roman, the leader of the Dark!

He had only tickled Hannah's mind a smidge and had no doubt that she would squash the seeds of anger before they were allowed to grow further. But he really could not resist this bit of fun.

Roman had not been idle while Dee had been growing up. He had caused as much chaos as he could, and his minions had been working nonstop making the world as miserable a place as they could. Sure, the Guardians had interfered whenever trouble was detected, but Roman was satisfied with the results his forces were producing, keeping for himself a few special humans. Hannah was at the top of his list.

It still rubbed him raw when he thought of the failed attempt on her life and the loss of Jaxon's soul bit deep into his pride. But he was wise and he let time go by, giving the Guardians and their Hunters time to feel safe and to relax their guard over Hannah and her daughter.

Roman had come so close with the minion he had set upon Dee to drive her insane that he had almost started celebrating. But Saul had found out his plan and Jaxon had ended his minion's existence. Not a big loss for Roman, as his army was bloated and growing each day. The human race was becoming more corrupt and evil with each passing day, and Roman could almost see the finish line on the horizon.

Leaders of nations were egomaniacs and were only concerned with power and feathering their own nests. The humans were being lied to and before long wars would be fought and the numbers on earth would dwindle. But not Roman's! His numbers would swell until there would be no denying that the Dark would be the controlling force.

Roman did nothing to hide his greed for this end and worked hard to bring it about. All he had to do was keep the good humans to a minimum. Unfortunately, Saul and his Guardians were just as set upon bringing back the goodness to humans. A war between good and evil was being waged behind the scenes, with each side betting on themselves.

Roman gave one last little giggle before retreating from Hannah's home, not wanting to be around when Saul checked in and discovered his interference. It was a good day and Roman was happy to once again bide his time. He, after all, had all the time in the world. However, Hannah did not, and he was going to make sure she was reunited with her lover before destiny's plan could be carried out.

Roman had his own plan and to hell with what Destiny had written. The drums of war had begun to beat a deep and dark warning of the fight between the Guardians and the Dark. The louder they boomed the closer the conflict came to becoming reality.

Roman couldn't wait!

Chapter 9

Hannah swallowed hard, frightened by the feelings of anger that had welled up inside of her. Anger at the two people she loved the most in this world. Never in her wildest dreams or worst nightmares would she hurt her daughter or stop longing for the man she would never get over. So why had she felt the rush of betrayal when Dee had told her Jaxon had come to her when she needed help? She had wished, since the day their daughter was born, that Jaxon could be a part of her life and now it seems it had come to pass. Well, sort of. Hannah should have been feeling gratitude and relief that Jaxon had stepped in to save Dee from the pain of her gift, not anger. What was happening to her? Hannah began to shiver with the fight going on inside her mind, trying to expel the negative emotions that had no place there.

Dee rose from her chair, never taking her eyes off her mother. Kneeling down beside her, she gripped the hand that was clamped down on the chair's arm and spoke with urgency. "Mom, what's wrong? Mom, what's wrong?" she questioned even louder.

The hand was cold to the touch and Dee felt a rush of fright when her mother did not respond to her questions. "Should I call an ambulance, Mom?"

Dee was about to rise to do just that when she felt warmth surge back into her mother's hand and the eyes that had, but seconds ago, been on fire, dulled and refocused on her own face.

Hannah pulled her hand from under Dee's and, with only a slight trembling, touched her forehead in confusion. "I'm sorry," she said with embarrassment, "I don't know what happened to me. I'm fine now," she said, giving Dee's concerned face a gentle pat. "Really, I'm fine."

"Can I get you anything, like a glass of water?" Dee asked, unwilling to take her mother's word that everything was ok

"Yes, yes that would be good," Hannah responded to get her daughter away for just a few seconds, so she could finish collecting herself.

Dee moved quickly to the sink and filled a glass with cold water from the tap. "Here you go," she said, setting the glass down on the table within easy reach.

Hannah lifted the glass and took a sip, giving Dee a small smile to try and erase the worry still there.

"What happened?" Dee asked again, hoping her mother would tell her the truth.

"I'm not sure," Hannah said, giving her daughter the only answer she could. She really did not know what had happened so she had no other explanation to offer. "Don't worry because what ever it was has passed now. So sit down again and stop worrying."

"Let's go sit on the couch," Dee suggested, reaching for her mother's arm to assist her.

Hannah rose with ease, ignoring the hand Dee held out, and stepped around her to enter the living room. She fluffed the pillows before taking a seat and looked back at her daughter in expectation. Dee shrugged her shoulders and moved around the other end to take a seat close by her side.

Seeing that her mother had no intentions of talking further about what had happened, Dee asked a question she had never asked before. "Mom, when you look at me have you ever used your gift to see what kind of person I am?"

Hannah's unusual eyes opened wide at the startling question that Dee had just asked her. "I've never had to use my gift to see what you are deep down inside, "she said. "I know that you are good and kind. I feel it."

"Could you look now?" Dee asked, facing her mother intently.

"Why?" Hannah asked with hesitation.

"I just want to know what you see. Please." Dee pleaded with her mother.

Hannah's brow creased as she wondered what had brought on this strange request, but she could see nothing but her beautiful girl.

"All right," Hannah agreed with a shrug. She too turned to face her daughter full on before letting her gift out and waited. Hannah's eyes glowed molten red until she could no longer see the face of her daughter. The room grew quiet and nothing moved except for her eyes as they traveled unhindered over the face and body so dear to her. When she was satisfied that she had seen all she could, Hannah took a deep breath and focused on her daughter. But she did not speak.

Dee paled slightly and swallowed hard. "What did you see, Mom?" she asked. She was beginning to regret having asked at all. "Was it that bad?" she asked in a whisper.

Hannah smiled softly and brushed back a strand of rich dark hair until Dee's face was open to her gaze. "No, it was not bad, darling," Hannah said, breaking her silence.

"Tell me," Dee said, slightly less anxious.

"You know that when I look at someone I can see their inner soul and all that they are inside. Nothing is hidden from me. Sometimes they are so evil that it is hard not to scream with the picture I see. The awful thing that we humans hide within us and what we are capable of is beyond anything you could imagine."

"I know this, Mom," Dee said. "Why are you telling me this again? Just come out and say what it is you saw in me. Please!" she begged her mother.

"The only thing I could see was an aura around you. It was a rainbow of colors pastel blue, soft pink, golden yellow, and light shades of purple. All of these are good things," Hannah assured her. "There was only one small ribbon of deep, dark red woven through the colors. If I had to guess I would say this represents your gift. I can't tell you anymore than that," Hannah said, sitting back with a sigh. "Why was it important for you to know now?" she questioned her daughter.

"I just was having such a hard time lately that I wondered if my gift was good or bad." Dee replied.

"It is up to you to decide how to use what you were given. But you have been raised to see the good in others and to use your gift to help bring peace to those in need if you can."

"Thanks, Mom," Dee said, giving her mother a hug for the staunch support she gave without being asked.

"You're welcome," Hannah replied, giving back the hug she received.

"How about we go out to get something to eat and lighten the mood a tad?" Hannah asked, getting up to snatch her purse and keys before holding the door open in invitation.

"Lead the way," Dee said, smiling at the idea and following her out the door, closing it in her wake.

Had she looked back she would have been shocked to see a handsome man standing in the living room in a red polo shirt, jeans and sporting the most amazing pair of wings on his back. And she would have trembled at the growl that came from deep within his being.

Saul had come to get answers.

Chapter 10

Saul had no warning that anything strange was happening with his charges, neither Hannah nor Dee. He had only popped in to check on them and listen in for a while. He liked doing this, as then he would have news for Jaxon, even if it were just to tell him all was well.

But he had arrived in time to find Hannah battling the anger that had been planted in her mind by a Dark being. Saul could smell it, this stench left behind by the Dark.

Saul had laid his hands upon Hannah's shoulders and taken the negative feelings into himself, leaving her at peace once again. But it filled him with a need to exact revenge on the one who had done this deed. It had taken him only a moment to rid himself of these urges, but it left a sour taste in his mouth for far longer.

Saul had stayed with the humans, listening to their conversation and was slightly surprised when Dee had made the unusual request of her mother. He did not know what had brought about her need to know, but he, too, had been interested to know what Hannah could see in her daughter. He was pleased that all she showed was an aura of basic goodness and agreed with Hannah's assessment on the dark red woven through it. It was not possible to be the bearer of a gift without it adding some slight darkness to the mix of things. Had Dee chosen to use her gift for evil, the red would have taken over and the image Hannah had seen, when looking at her daughter, would have been enough to make her scream, even as seasoned as she was.

Saul roamed the apartment checking every corner and peering into every shadow but the doer of the mischief was nowhere to be found. The coward had hit and run.

Saul was satisfied that there was no more danger and prepared to leave. He had a decision to make and that was whether to tell Jaxon and alert the Immortal Hunter or to keep the information of the attack to himself and handle it on his own.

The latter seemed to be the best way to keep things under control. So Saul nodded his head in satisfaction and shimmered away.

Saul reappeared before the Window to the World and waited for his friend to find him. Jaxon always seemed to know when he had paid a visit to his loved ones on earth and today was no different.

"How was Dee?" Jaxon asked, not wasting time.

"She was good," Saul said, as he gripped his friend's rock hard shoulder. "Hannah and she just left to go eat and they both seemed happy."

Jaxon nodded his head in satisfaction and relaxed slightly under Saul's touch. "Good," he sighed. "That's good."

"I have a favor to ask you," Jaxon said, looking at something far away or maybe nothing at all.

Saul forgot for a moment, his dilemma, about telling Jaxon that Hannah was a target once again. He knew his Hunter did not ask for things very often.

"What is it?" Saul asked. Jaxon remained silent.

Jaxon swallowed hard as he turned towards Saul and took a breath to speak. "I would like you to make Dee's abilities more manageable," he said.

"By this you mean what?" Saul countered.

"If you could concentrate her gift into one spot, I think her life would become much easier and she could experience it more fully." Jaxon replied.

"By one spot, you mean what?" Saul asked, a frown marring his smooth brow. "I don't think I am quite following you."

"Instead of anything that touches her being able to give her flashes of the past, I think if you could shrink down her exposed sensitive areas, things would be more manageable for her."

"To what?" Saul asked, beginning to follow where Jaxon wanted him to go.

"How about say her left hand," Jaxon provided. "If her powers only worked in her left hand, let's say, her life would be manageable and she would be able to at least have some semblance of normalcy."

Saul thought about Jaxon's request for a few moments and decided the granting of this father's request would not change the course of Dee's destiny.

"Very well," Saul said in his deep voice. "I think this we can do." Saul held up a hand, before Jaxon could say anything, wanting to put all that this entailed on the table.

"It will take some doing," Saul continued, as Jaxon listened. "I will have to make Dee believe she willed this change herself. That she has control over her gift and that she has found a way to make her life better and living with this power will not be so bad."

"How do you accomplish this?" Jaxon asked.

"While she sleeps, I will put the idea in her head that she needs to focus her powers into one spot and be able to contain it there. When she wakes up, she will attempt this and she will be successful. I will already have put it into this place and she will feel in control and much happier." Saul concluded.

"Thank you, Saul," Jaxon said, offering his hand in gratitude and in friendship for the Immortal to clasp and shake, sealing the bargain.

"I will meet you tonight outside Dee's home," he said, twitching his wings open, preparing to take flight. "I will meet you," Jaxon said again, with steel in his voice, as he read the doubt and refusal in Saul's eyes.

Saul witnessed the determination in his warrior's eyes and knew nothing would keep him from his daughter's side this night.

"I see nothing I say will dissuade you," Saul said. "So very well, you may stand by my side while I help your daughter," he conceded.

Jaxon could live with that, so he nodded his head and let the hardness in his eyes soften, until they returned to the deep brown of normal.

"Till tonight," he said, and leaped into the air.

"Tonight," Saul repeated, as Jaxon disappeared from his sight. "Yes, tonight."

Chapter 11

Jaxon waited for Saul to arrive, just across the street from Dee's. He had come early, not being able to stay away any longer. He felt excitement as he waited, knowing his daughter's life was going to be much better from now on and that he would have a hand in the changing. He watched the groups of humanity walking the dark streets and listened unknowingly to the conversations as they passed by. Each human believing that what was happening to them was of cosmic importance, when really it was not much more than a blip on his radar.

Jaxon peered into minds, looking for the presence of the Dark. Jaxon could not lay down his work, even on this night, but he found nothing and was glad for it. He had other things to do and did not want to be distracted tonight.

After a short time, Jaxon felt a rush of wind and beneath his feet the ground shuddered, as Saul joined him. Jaxon's mouth twitched as he looked at the Immortal. "Nice entrance," he said, giving Saul a slap on the back.

Saul let a smile stretch his beautiful mouth, accepting the compliment and finally laughing out loud. "You're not the only one that can cause a stir," he replied. "I just felt like airing out the dramatic a little, is all."

"Nice," Jaxon repeated, before dropping his hand. "Shall we?" he said, stepping back to allow the Guardian to go ahead of him

Saul nodded his head and took the lead. In the blink of an eye, both were standing beside the soft bed that held one half of all that was precious to Jaxon.

Saul sat down on the side of the bed in which Dee's sleeping form was facing and reached out his hands to bracket the sleeping face. Her cheeks were soft and warm in his hands and he felt the peace that only the sleep of a mortal could bring moving up his arms and settling in his chest.

Taking a deep breath, Saul closed his eyes and concentrated on the human before him. He could feel the power that moved through her and he willed it into submission, into a mass that pulsated with each beat of her heart. He wrapped his mind around it until it moved when and where he wanted. Harnessing the power, he moved it until it settled in the delicate left hand as Jaxon had requested. He anchored it there, pulling back only when he was sure it would stay there, waiting to read objects that it came into contact with.

"Half way home," Saul thought, as he gently planted a dream, an idea in Dee's sleeping mind, letting her believe she could control her gift and free herself of it, everywhere except her one hand. He gave her the concentration that would allow her to keep it in check and to believe it was all due to her will, that her life would be different.

Saul opened his eyes and slowly removed his hands from the delicate face. "It is finished," he said. "I hope this makes things easier for her and for you," he said, turning to look at Jaxon.

"Thank you, Saul," Jaxon said, as he watched his daughter slumber. "All I have ever wanted for her was to be happy and to be able to find love. A love like her mother and I had...have."

"This will give her a fighting chance," Saul assured him. "I will keep watch and help where and when I can. We should go now."

Jaxon stepped closer to the bed and leaned in to stroke the dark fall of hair on the pillow and to place a feather light touch on her cheek. "I love you, Dee," he whispered, hoping she would hear him in her dreams. "I'll be watching." With that he stood back, and together, Saul and he turned and left the apartment to its occupant.

Jaxon went back to his hunting but a weight had been lifted from his mind. The guilt he carried with him at having created a life that was filled with pain and horror lessened until he could breath easier. He knew that when he was able to hold his daughter in his arms again he would do so with happiness and not regret, no apologies would be needed, nor tears shed.

That sounded good to Jaxon and he smiled in anticipation of that time. Till then he had a job to do, a purpose to fulfill, and he looked forward to it.

He caught the scent of a Dark Being and his eyes caught fire. As he folded his wings and plummeted down a thought came to his mind, '*it was a good night*.' Yes, indeed, it was a good night!

Chapter 12

It was past ten when Dee finally stirred, coming awake to peek at the clock and smile in pure pleasure as she wallowed in the knowledge that she had finally gotten a good night sleep. She lay still for a moment and then stretched her arms above her head, arching her back and curling her toes. As she lowered her arms, her gaze focused on her left hand. A thought entered her mind and held on, as she stared at her hand almost feeling as if it was foreign to her, different. *"What if?"* she thought. *"What if I could put all my power into just my hand?"* The wishful thought sent a shiver through her body at how much simpler things could be for her if she really could do this.

Sitting up in her bed, Dee brushed the dark hair behind her ears and took a deep breath. No harm would come from her trying she thought. If nothing changed, then she would be no worse off for having tried. Dee had no idea how to go about this, but she followed her instincts and closed her eyes, concentrating. She concentrated hard, willing her powers to move to her one hand and one hand only. A light sweat beaded her forehead with her efforts and after what seemed like forever, she opened her eyes and breathed deep.

Had it worked she wondered? How would she know? *"Pick something up, stupid,"* she thought. So she did.

She jumped out of bed and crossed the room until she faced her dresser and, opening a drawer, let her eyes wander until they found what she was looking for. A shirt of her father's lay folded neatly in the corner. She had kept it because when she touched it, as she did often, she could see him laughing and could feel his total happiness. It was a shirt he had worn when he had spent a day with her mother. That he loved her was so apparent that Dee loved to share the moment of their happiness over and over again, never tiring of the love she felt when she touched the softness of the material. Dee knew exactly what she would see if she held the shirt and it would be a good test to see if her will had been enough to contain her gift to her hand or not.

Dee extended her right hand and pulled the shirt from the drawer. She felt nothing, could see nothing. Transferring the shirt to her left hand, her mind was filled with the familiar images and she smiled. Because of the images and because her first experiment had been successful, she put the shirt back and went in search of another object she could try. She stopped in the middle of her living room as her eyes had fallen on a ball that rested in the corner.

A red ball the size of a baseball but made of rubber. Dee remembered having found the ball outside in a ditch and she remembered picking it up and bringing it inside with her about a week ago. When she had entered her apartment and shut the door, she had laid the ball on her counter while she took off the gloves that she wore when she was in public. This done she had picked up the ball and immediately images of a small dog entered her mind. She had smiled as she saw the dog chasing the ball as a boy threw it for him to fetch.

The smile had turned to horror and tears, as she watched the ball roll into the street and the little dog followed. She gagged as the car hit the dog and she felt the pain of the animal as it lay broken and dying. Dee had thrown the ball away from her, letting it stay where it had come to rest, vowing to never touch it again. She had meant to get a dustpan and throw it into the garbage, but she had not.

Gathering her courage, she now bent down and picked it up with her right hand, ready to fling it from her again, if the images came back. But she felt nothing, she saw nothing. Letting out the breath she had been holding, Dee walked to the garbage and stood over it as she slowly transferred the ball into her left hand. Again the images started to flood her mind, but she dropped the ball into the trash before she could see the accident again.

"It worked, "she said out loud, "It really worked!" She felt the smile on her face and it felt good. "*I can deal with this,*" she thought, her whole being lighting up with her new discovery.

"*I won't have to wear my gloves outside these walls any more,*" she thought. "*I can learn to use my right hand, mostly and when I need to I can just wear one glove.*"

Dee felt like she had just been given the most special Christmas gift ever! The best birthday gift ever, everything all rolled into one.

She stood in her kitchen with her arms around her stomach feeling like she might burst with the happiness that she was feeling. Spinning on her heels, she dashed for the bathroom and the shower, meaning to clean up before heading straight over to her mother's to share the good news with her. She paused in front of the mirror to look at herself to see if she looked different because she definitely felt different.

The smile was still on her face and grew just a little bit bigger as she stared at it. Dee cocked her head to the right as she stared into her eyes in the mirror. She leaned closer to the mirror until her nose was almost touching the glass. She stared at her eyes.

The deep rich brown irises with the shards of red in them were different. The red glowed now, turning the shards into molten veins of lava. As Dee watched, a trickle of fear crawled up her back and she knew. She knew that this was the trade off for controlling her gift. Her powers were now concentrated and held in her left hand, but her eyes had changed. Dee swallowed hard and straightened back up, pulling back to normal distance from the mirror.

She thought of her mother's eyes and the way she had always had to hide them, the stares she had to live with because she was different. She had never really had to deal with this issue because her gift was not visible.

Until now!

Until now!

Chapter 13

The pleasure and excitement Dee had been feeling dulled as she stared at herself. Maybe her eyes would return to normal in a few minutes or maybe they would while she took her shower. No use freaking out over nothing. She reasoned that it was not really such a bad deal. She could live with this as she now had control over her gift.

"Get in the shower," she told herself. When she got to her mother's house, she would talk to her and she would help her put things in perspective. Figure everything out. Hannah was good at not letting Dee blow things out of proportion.

Dee got cleaned up and hustled her butt over to her best friend's house. When she walked in the door, she was met with hugs and happiness from Hannah and it soothed her mind to just be loved.

"What brings you here today?" Hannah asked, not really caring, just glad she was getting to see her daughter twice in just a few days

"I just thought I would come and hang out for a while," Dee lied, keeping her eyes downcast.

Hannah knew she was not telling her the truth but she let it slide, giving Dee the time she evidently needed before the truth came out. "Well, come on in," Hannah urged, waving her hand towards the kitchen. "I was just about ready to make me a salad. Want one?"

"Sounds yummy," Dee said, accepting the invitation to join her mother.

Dee sat at the table after having her offer to help rejected. She watched her mother move around the kitchen and kept up the idle chatter until the delicious, homemade chef salads were on the table and Hannah had taken a seat across from her. "This looks great Mom," Dee said, as she dug in and took her first bite of the crisp lettuce. She closed her eyes as she enjoyed the taste, opening them as she swallowed, and then met the dark red eyes across from her; another compliment froze on her lips, as she saw the look on her mother's face.

Hannah's fork stopped midway to her mouth and the bite she had just chewed stuck in her throat. "Talk to me," she said, placing her fork back in her bowl.

Dee did not pretend to not know what her mother was talking about. She knew that tone of voice and it meant nothing but the truth would satisfy her and get her off the hook. She dove in. "When I woke up this morning, I had an idea that I might be able to control my powers."

"How?" Hannah quickly fired at her.

"Well, I closed my eyes and concentrated really hard and kind of got it to just work in my left hand." Dee replied.

"You have no other places that if something were to touch you, there would be no images for you to see?"

Hannah asked, making sure she had the tale perfectly correct

"Nope, none," Dee confirmed. "How great is that?"

"That's wonderful," Hannah replied. Hannah was surprised, but truly happy for Dee. "So, now, explain what happened to your eyes."

Dee dropped her eyes and shrugged her shoulders. "I don't know," she admitted. "When I had sort of tested it out, I decided to jump in the shower and come tell you the good news. When I looked in the mirror, I noticed them right away. I don't know what happened. I was sort of hoping you would be able to help me figure it out."

Hannah cupped her hand under the beautiful chin and looked into the eyes that used to be deep brown with a few sparks of red mixed in. The eyes she looked at now were scared. The red, so subdued before, now made deep valleys from the black pupils to the outer edge of the dark brown irises that she had inherited from her father. She was reminded of the pictures she had seen of a lava flow, dark and burnt on the top, but hot and molten underneath. The fierce heat was just waiting to emerge to devour all in its path. Hannah wondered what the change meant for her daughter and hoped with all her heart that the change was only cosmetic. But she doubted it.

"Ok," Hannah said out loud. "It may just be nothing so I think you should not worry about it or let it control who you are or what you do. There is no use borrowing trouble when there is no need. Agreed?"

"Thanks, Mom," Dee said, feeling comforted by her mother's confidence that all would be okay.

"You're welcome, sweetie," Hannah said, as she picked up her fork again, even though her appetite had died when she had looked into her daughter's eyes.

She changed the subject and listened with half an ear to what Dee was telling her. She was glad she had told Dee to not worry because she was able to worry enough for both of them. Only time would tell what, if anything, this change meant for her daughter. Hannah only hoped that good would be the result of this change, because if it wasn't, she had no way of protecting her from what was to come.

She had been given a protector and had known love because of Jaxon's presence in her life. She was not so sure Dee would be so lucky.

Chapter 14

Every day Dee got up and every day nothing changed. Not her eyes, not her gift, nothing. With time she relaxed and took her appearance in stride until she thought of it no more.

But Roman did. He thought of it often and he snickered every time he did. He had watched from the deep shadows of night as Saul and Jaxon had made Dee's gift easier to live with. He couldn't have that now, could he? There had to be consequences for the Guardians helping a mortal. Especially one that had the ability to see actions committed in the past. Actions that sometimes had been directed by the Dark.

So far, Dee had not caused too much damage to the Dark's plans, but Roman planned on keeping a close eye on her to make sure he was aware if and when she did. After all, she had the ability to see deeds that the Dark's puppets had committed, and to get them caught for it. All she had to do was tell.

A little redirection on his part, when she was about to come into contact with a damning object, was all he needed to do for the time being. And it had worked. A few thoughts that made her want to stay away from using her gift was all he needed to plant in her head, and he had done just that.

He looked out for his own and those that could hinder them were taken care of. That is until Hannah had escaped his grasp and Dee had fallen under the protection of her father, the Immortal Hunter, Jaxon.

Roman treaded lightly when it came to crossing him. Jaxon was fierce, just as he, the leader of the Dark, knew he would be.

"Oh, the things they could have done together," Roman thought. The fate of the human race would have been sealed had they paired up together to defeat the Guardians.

The dark, twisting form of Roman grew agitated with the thoughts of loss and defeat. The bitter taste on his tongue, usually so welcome, now made him want to spew black vomit from his belly, burning every human it touched until their souls moaned in agony and the goodness in them died a terrible death. He needed to do something to take his mind off his own demons. Only then would the black lump in his chest stop tormenting him and grieving over the past.

Roman faded from sight and sought out the first soul he sensed with any amount of blackness in it. He turned it, without a second thought, and laughed out loud when an innocent being met its death before its time.

"Better," he thought, *"but I think I need a little more. Yes, yes,"* he thought, sticking out his dark tongue and licking the drool from his thin lips," *More!"* And, he went hunting for another victim.

Chapter 15

Dee hung up the phone and did a little dance around her apartment. She had filled out an application a few weeks ago for what she considered the perfect job and, having not heard back from this place, considered it a bust. Until just now! She had answered the phone and agreed to an interview for tomorrow. She was a bundle of nerves at having to wait the few hours until she could get herself ready and out the door.

She cleaned her apartment until there was not a speck of dust to be found and then she actually cooked a meal of homemade macaroni and cheese and German ring sausage. Her home smelled great and she actually took a few bites before her nerves kept her from eating any more.

Once again she cleaned up the dishes and finally gave up and got ready for bed. She wanted to call her mother to share the news, but did not want to jinx the possibility of her getting the job. Silly, of course, but still the way she felt.

The night drug on and Dee was just barely dozing when the alarm sounded the next morning. Her heart jumped as she opened her eyes and had to hold herself back from jumping up and racing out the door. Pacing herself, she ate a small breakfast and got her shower taken before she figured it was safe to head over to her interview.

She got in her car and, turning the key, fired up the engine as her pulse rose to match it. In less than thirty minutes, she was leaving the city behind and it took only a short twenty minutes more until she pulled into a graveled parking area and shut off her car. She sat in the quiet for a few minutes, letting her eyes wander and her breathing slow, as the fresh air filled her lungs and relaxed her nerves.

This was going to work, she thought. It just felt right.

It was not what she expected though. There was no ornate archway with the name, 'Omen Lake Cemetery,' showing the way to the final resting place of those souls who had come to be there. There were no rolling hills of green grass and no pretty benches where visitors could sit for a spell and commune with the dead. Instead there were tall weeds and overgrown bushes as far as the eye could see, with weathered head stones peeking through the chaos, fighting for the right to be there with nature.

Dee would never have found the place if she had not been given detailed directions and, even now, she wondered if she was in the right place. She had sort of expected to be met by the man who had called her yesterday, a Mr. David Tower. But so far she could not detect another living soul around. Not quite sure what to do, Dee opened the car door and slid out, standing for a moment before shutting it. She had barely swung it closed but the door made a sound louder than a gunshot. It made her jump with guilt at the intrusion of noise.

"Can I help you?' a deep, raspy voice asked from behind her.

For the second time in as many seconds, Dee jumped. She had not heard any footsteps approaching and she swallowed hard, trying to find spit in her mouth to wet her dry throat. Turning around, Dee made a grab at the dark hair that blew across her face, fighting with it before she was able to get her first look at the man behind the voice.

"Are you Mr. Tower?" she asked, waiting to extend her right hand until he nodded the affirmative.

"I am," the man said, "and you are?"

"Dee. I mean, Madison Priest," she said, leaving her hand out so her prospective boss could finish the introductions.

"Which is it?" he asked. "Dee or Madison?"

"Both," Dee replied. "My name is Madison, but everyone calls me Dee."

"Dee it is then," David said. "Did you have any trouble finding the place?" he asked, as he turned to walk away, expecting her to follow without an invitation.

"No, your directions were excellent." Dee replied and walked quickly to catch up with him.

David snorted in response and kept walking, leading the way until they rounded a clump of old cottonwood trees that effectively hid a small cabin and a shed.

"Come on in," he motioned, having walked up to the door and opened it without bothering to unlock it.

Dee moved past him, as she entered first, and stopped a few steps inside. Her eyes did a quick sweep of the interior. She fell in love with it right then and there. The outside had been aged and weathered but the inside was polished, warm and welcoming. "This is beautiful," Dee said, not meaning to let the surprise she felt leak out into her tone, but it did.

David raised his bushy white eyebrows. "Glad you like it," he said," Because this is where you're going to be living if I offer you the job."

It was Dee's turn to raise her eyebrows and she didn't know what to say. She had not expected this, so was at a loss for words.

"Come sit down," he said, taking off his old cowboy hat. The brim of which had kept his features in shadow, until now.

He turned to face Dee and she got her first good look at him. His hair was thick and white with what looked like a permanent ridge from his hat circling the back of his head. His face was tanned from hours in the sun and the wrinkles etched in it came from squinting into the sun and, she hoped, from laughing at life. His eyes were sea green and deep, as they locked with hers and held secrets she could not read.

He was a good head taller than Dee so she was forced to tip her head back to keep the eye contact. He wore old, soft jeans that showed wear from many washings and a faded green and white plaid shirt rolled up to his elbows, exposing still strong arms and work hardened hands.

Dee guessed him to be in his mid seventies or so and blinked a couple of times in mild surprise when he smiled and almost blinded her with straight white teeth.

"Sit down, young lady," he said, and waved her into an overstuffed recliner. "What can I get you to drink?' he asked, not waiting for her answer, as he turned around and headed for what Dee assumed was the kitchen.

"Water is fine," she called to his retreating back.

David came back and handed her a frosty glass with clear, cold water in it and, to Dee's amusement, a coaster for her to set it on.

"Now," David said, as he took a seat across from her at a low end table, "tell me why a beautiful young thing like yourself would want to take a job maintaining a grave yard. And don't lie. I'll know if you are lying."

Sea green eyes hardened and dove into deep brown ones.

Dee shivered.

Chapter 16

"I need to be away from crowds," Dee gave as an explanation as to why she wanted the job.

"Why?" David asked her with hesitation.

Dee looked at the worn face across from her and fought with herself, trying to decide if she should tell him about her gift or take her chances with telling a half-truth. *"Really?"* she thought. *"How would he be able to tell if she told some but not all of the truth?"*

"I'll know," he said, guessing as to what she was thinking.

"You might not like it," she warned him. She was trying to give him a chance to back down before she had to spill her guts to him.

"You in trouble with the law?" he asked, cocking one bushy eyebrow.

"No," she said quickly, a little surprised at his question.

"You into drugs and stuff like that?' he asked.

"No," she said, with a shake of her head. Her eyes were beginning to glow with amusement, as he guessed all the obvious choices.

"You meaning to hide from someone, boyfriend, family or such?" he continued with the interview questions.

"No," she answered again.

"Then, what?" he asked. "Spit it out."

Dee took a chance and dove in. "I was born with a gift that makes being around people and things hard on me."

"Go on," David prodded, when she fell silent, leaning back and looking at her.

"If I touch people or things, I get flashes of past events that have happened and, as you can probably guess, not all of them are pretty." She offered a quick explanation to his questions.

"Fair enough," David said, nodding his head in satisfaction with her explanation. "I can guarantee you not too many things around here have a past. Headstones don't get recycled and most of the equipment and this house have only known me. I don't have anything to hide so whatever you would learn about me by touching things would not be giving you any nightmares."

Dee smiled in relief. She had been wondering how many people had been here and had left part of themselves behind.

"Have you heard anything about this place?" he asked, twitching in his chair.

"No," Dee answered, shooting off a question of her own. "Why, what is there to have people talking about?"

"Now most people would not be hearing this from me, but I figure with all you've seen and know, it's safe to tell you the truth." he continued.

"Spit it out," Dee said, throwing his own words back at him.

"Let's take a walk while we talk," David said, wanting to be out in the sun as he talked.

Dee rose and took a big drink of cold water before heading out the door with David at her back.

For the next two hours, David took her on a tour of the cemetery, showing her the boundaries. Showing her the shed and all the equipment she would have to use if she got the job. Explaining to her that she would have to cut the grass, trim, water and generally take care of grooming the grounds. Make it look nice again. He stalled when he had no more to tell her.

"Are you finished yet?" Dee asked, as they came to a stop under a stand of aspen trees.

David took off his hat and mopped the sweat that he had worked up walking and talking. He liked this girl. He liked the way she took in what he told her and liked how she asked intelligent questions when she did not understand something. He didn't want to scare her off. He needed her to take this job. He trusted her to take this job.

His time was running short, running out.

Huffing out a breath, David jammed the hat back on his head and nodded his head in agreement.

"Did you wonder why this place is called Omen Lake Cemetery?" he asked her.

"The question crossed my mind," she told him.

"When I started here and the story was told to me, I doubted it," he began. "But I will tell you right off that it is the honest truth, what I'm about to tell you. Let me get finished with my story before you ask any questions," he said, raising his hand slightly to stay off her interrupting him.

"Okay," Dee agreed. "Go ahead." She leaned back against a thick silvery trunk and crossed her ankles and arms getting as comfortable as she could.

David reached down and broke off a long stem of pasture grass, sticking it in his mouth to worry the end for a few seconds before speaking.

"Did you notice any water on the property as I was showing you around?" he asked, looking off into the distance, instead of at her.

"No," Dee said, wondering what this had to do with anything.

"There's a lake here," he said. "Right over there," he informed her, pointing towards the south with the wet end of the grass he had been chewing on.

Dee looked and saw nothing. "I don't see anything," she said, thinking he was stalling for time.

"That's good," he said. "That's really good."

"Why?" she asked, her curiosity peaked.

Looking her straight in the eye, his face paled before he could answer. "Cause if you see the lake, if it appears to you, you or someone you know is going to die. And it's never wrong!"

"Never?"

Chapter 17

"Excuse me?" Dee asked, thinking the old man had fallen off his rocker.

"You think I'm crazy?" David asked, getting a kick out of shocking Dee. "Do you think I could really make this up?"

"Well, yes and yes," Dee said. She was sure the old man was pulling her leg.

"I'm not," David said. "This place is special. It has been since way back. The story goes just like I said. A beautiful lake appears to certain people and it is an omen of death. Now whether it is your own or someone close to you is something each person has to figure out. But everyone who has seen it, and is still alive, will swear that it is never wrong in its predictions. The stones here in this cemetery are of people who have seen the lake or of their loved ones who died right after it appeared. It only seems right that this should be the place where they come for their final rest."

Dee remained silent, watching David to see if he started laughing or even smirking. She hoped to see if the tale he was telling was on the up and up. No smile broke his face and the eyes that locked with hers were dead serious. She hugged herself tighter with arms that crossed her waist. The air around her had become still and the birds that had been singing just a moment before fell silent until the only sound to be heard was the wind moving through the tall grass and stirring the leaves over her head. It sounded like whispers and hisses of voices that were just beyond Dee's ability to understand. As if it was all something Dee should listen to but was unable to grasp its meaning.

"Do you believe me?' David asked, a familiar chill creepily crawling up his spine.

"I don't know," Dee answered honestly. "I believe that you believe," she said, staring the old man straight in the eye, the hot lava streaks in her own eyes beginning to grow brighter, as her confusion deepened.

"You claim to have a gift that lets you see what normal people can't, right?" David asked.

"I don't just claim," Dee said, sitting up straighter as her word was questioned.

"I have no reason to doubt you," the old man said. "Even though I have seen no proof or evidence to prove what you say is true. All I am asking is that the same trust that I'm showing you be given to me and what I am telling you."

Dee didn't want to believe what she had heard. It would mean that there were even more weird things in the world than what she knew already. But he did have a point; she of all people should not question anything odd or unusual. After all, her mother and she were both 'odd and unusual.'

"I can't offer you any more proof than my word," David said. "I can't call up the lake and make you see. It just doesn't work like that."

"Have you seen the lake?' Dee asked.

"Twice," David said, nodding his head.

"What happened?' she asked, wanting more information.

"The first time was about three years after I started working here. I was doing the grass, mowing it and things, when I was stopped dead in my tracks. The grass had turned into water and I can tell you now I was scared beyond my wildest fears." His reply was serious and his eyes didn't waver.

"Who died?" Dee wanted to know.

"My wife and son," David said. A liquid sheen covered his eyes as he looked back into the past. He turned and walked a few steps into the tangled grass before stopping and resting a hand on each of two headstones that stood side by side. "This is them, Barbara and David Jr."

"I'm sorry," Dee whispered, seeing the pain David's memories caused him.

He nodded his head as his hands caressed the cold stone slabs marking the graves.

"At first I didn't believe it because it took almost a week before the accident happened. As each day went by, I had almost convinced myself that the story told to me was just that. A made up story. But it happened just like I was told it would. I saw the lake and someone close to me died. I never doubted again. I prayed every day, when I woke up, that I would not see that awful, dammed lake again."

"But you said you saw it twice. What happened the second time?" Dee asked, even though she was not sure she wanted to know. The telling of the first time gave her goose bumps up and down her arms and the air that had been warm, almost hot, just a moment before, now blew cold across her skin. Shadows that should have offered relief from the sun now seemed suddenly deeper, darker and menacing. Again Dee shivered.

The silence drug on and Dee was beginning to doubt that David was going to answer her question. He finally moved to stand behind a headstone that appeared to her to be newer than the two of his son and of his wife. It stood beside Barbara's and when he did not move again, Dee dropped her eyes to read the information carved into it.

Her stomach heaved and her knees shook before she could get control of herself. She raised wide eyes to stare at the old man standing with slumped shoulders behind the stone.

With a voice quiet and resigned, he nodded his head and said," It's mine. The next one to die is me."

Chapter 18

"Are you serious?" Dee's voice seemed to come from someone other than from herself.

"I know," David said. "No question in my mind. I just know. I had this made not that long ago." He continued tapping the rock slab with his fingers. "Cause I was pretty sure the next time I saw the lake, it was going to be coming for me. I put an ad in the paper a couple of weeks ago, meaning to retire when I found a replacement, but a couple of days ago, I saw the lake again and I knew my time was about up. That's why I called you, to have you come out for an interview. I'm going to offer you the job right here and now. I would like you to give me your answer today before you leave. Everything else is in order but this."

Dee didn't know what to say. She had wanted the job before she heard David's story, but now she was scared. Scared about what she had heard, about what he said was true. Scared too for what he believed and was asking her to believe.

"If you take the job," he said, coming to stand beside her, "you will be in my shoes one day. Telling this story to the next one you choose to take care of this place. Asking someone to believe you and take you at your word. Be the caretaker of these souls and the keeper of this secret. We can talk about wages and living arrangements when we get back to the house, but I would like an answer before we move on," David said, remaining by her side.

Dee's head had stopped spinning and her mind seemed to accept what she was seeing and hearing. How strange, she thought, that she had gone from being scared and confused to this feeling of acceptance. Dee uncrossed her legs and stood up straight, letting her hands hang at her sides. She didn't want to look at the old man's face; not wanting to look at a person she knew was going to be dead in a short while. But she did.

Taking a deep breath she again held out her hand and waited for it to be taken and held in a work roughened grip. "I don't know why but I'm going to take the job," she said, feeling David's relief as if it were her own.

His smile was sad as he gripped her hand before letting it fall. "Let's go back to the house," he said, turning to head back. "We have a few details to work out and some papers to sign before you leave to get your stuff and move in."

The walk back was made in silence as David tried to soak up everything in what, to his way of thinking, was going to be his last time.

For Dee, it was trying to see everything for the first time and not let her mind think too far ahead.

For Saul, it was a time to purge the feelings of fear and disbelief that he had taken from Dee. He had stood behind Dee, taking her feelings of fear and denial from her so she would be able to follow the path destiny had written for her. Some humans were chosen to take on difficult and unusual tasks and Dee was one of them. She was strong, stronger than she could ever imagine, and if she should falter Saul would be there to help her. For now he would stay by her side, stay until she became used to her new life. And he would keep the lake and death hidden from her sight for as long as he could.

For as long as he could.

Chapter 19

Dee and David finalized the paperwork and David gave her a ring of keys before she got in her car and headed back into the city. David had told her he was already moved out and she should move in as soon as possible.

Before Dee got in her car she touched his lined cheek with her left hand and saw flashes of a beautiful woman, a dark haired boy and a younger version of the man she had spent the afternoon with, all of them running and playing in a field of grass and flowers. She could feel the love this family had for each other and the grief that she felt for the life that was ending was lessened, as she knew they were all going to be together soon.

The drive back to her apartment was over before she knew it and Dee walked on stiff legs until she reached her door. She unlocked her door, entered, and then locked the door behind her. She looked with eyes that assessed her belongings and wondered if she took a very long time to gather her things if David's death would be delayed. Deep down she knew it would happen as scheduled. Nothing she could do would change the outcome.

Dee thought about calling her mother and telling her what had happened, but she decided to get the packing done and be moved in before she told her. She could take her for a ride, drive her out to the cemetery and introduce her mom to her new home. She didn't think she would be telling her about the lake anytime soon so it would just be a new job and a new home that her mother would just have to like.

Nodding her head, satisfied with her choice, Dee dug out boxes and totes, beginning in the bedroom and working her way through her apartment until she was packed and ready to go. It didn't take long as she tended not to collect things the way normal people did. They carried too many memories of the previous owners or if new, they carried details of the workers who made them. Dee just didn't need that in her home. Her safe place.

Dee stretched her tired muscles and made herself a cup of hot chocolate before crawling under the covers of her bed. The sun was just beginning to peek over the horizon but the hot, sweet drink had done its job, making her feel relaxed and drowsy.

She closed her eyes and fell asleep, never giving a thought to any dreams she might have.

She had slept well into the afternoon before her one and only dream began. It felt like she was watching a movie that was playing for her alone. She saw herself pulling weeds and doing what needed to be done in her new job. She could feel the sun on her back and the sweat that the hard work produced, working its way from her hair line down to her chin, before the fat drops fell to the dirt and were soaked up by the thirsty earth. She felt contentment with her work and enjoyed the dream as it played out behind her closed eyelids.

The dream was so real she could smell the fresh scent of the grass and of the wet dirt that clung to the roots of weeds she'd pulled and heaped into a pile to be picked up when she had gathered a load. She could feel herself enjoying the physical labor and she had no regrets taking this job. She stopped for a moment to get a drink from a thermos that kept the ice water freezing cold even in the warm sun. She tipped her head back, letting the water slide down her throat and she could feel the cold go all the way down until it hit her stomach. She sighed with happiness.

Dee's sleeping form smiled and she snuggled down deeper under the covers. The dream continued as she poured some of the icy water onto a hankie and wiped her face and neck to cool down before tucking it back into her back pocket and bending down to work again. She loved the fact that dirt got under her fingernails and she didn't care. She didn't have to worry about touching things or wearing gloves to protect herself from images that made her shiver and hide from the world.

Life was good. Or was it? Something was different. The dream that had been, just seconds before, all bright and wonderful was now darker, colder and not such a nice place.

Dee stood up and gathered her tools together, meaning to get back to her home and stay there for the day, but the wind picked up and she heard voices. A lone voice said, "You are all alone. You always have been and you always will be. All you have is your mother to tell your news. She is the only one with whom you can share. She is the only one that will ever be there for you. You know that, because of your gift, no one is ever going to love you. Once you have shared your secret, no man will ever look at you with anything else but fear and disgust. You belong here, here in this strange cemetery. With all these other lost souls that were marked and taken because of their curses."

"I don't have a curse!" Dee shouted into the wind. But her words were whipped from her mouth and flung back into her face. The wind blew against her, making her back up against its strength. She stumbled until her back cracked against an unyielding tree trunk. She stood still as if invisible ties held her in place. Her chest heaved as she found breathing had become a chore. "I don't have a curse!" she repeated. Her hands clenched into fists to give her strength and anchor her.

"Really?" the voice asked. Its tone was sly and secretive.

"I have a gift and it is good. I will use it for good," she vowed.

"When?" the voiced queried. "You are too scared of what you will see to do anything but hide from what you could see. Admit it. You are weak and unworthy of the powers you were born with."

"Shut up," Dee whispered, covering her ears with her hands to muffle the voice that put words to the feelings she could not admit to herself.

"Why don't you open your eyes? Open them and see what is in store for you." it challenged her.

She didn't want to obey the voice but she had no power not to do as it said. Slowly she raised her bent head and lowered her cold hands from her ears. Her eyelids, ever so slowly rose until she was looking out at a scene she did not want to see.

The lush grass that she had so lovingly been nurturing had disappeared and a lake appeared in its place. Not a beautiful body of water with waves that lapped at its shores, but instead white caps rolled across its surface that was dark and menacing. Faces of those buried underneath dirt, boiled in those waves, each one moaning in pain at being held. Arms of the dead rose out of the water and a plea for help rode every face.

"You see?" the voice asked. "You see the souls that this lake has claimed? They will be the only friends you will ever have. The only ones that will accept you for what you are. They're waiting for you, waiting for you to join them. Walk into the lake," it crooned. "Why prolong this lonely life any longer? All you have to do is take a step and then another. So easy, so simple."

Dee felt tears slide down her cheeks and her soul could find no hope for her future. Against her will, her foot moved forward a few inches, taking a step, then another followed, continuing until she felt the cold water rise above her ankles. She struggled against her actions and fought against the control the voice had over her mind. But she was loosing as she moved farther out into the dark water.

As she moved closer to her death, Dee found one slight thread of hope and she did not even know why she thought of it as a solution to her dilemma, but it was all she had to cling to. "Help me," she whispered into the fierce wind. "Help me, please," she implored. She repeated the plea over and over until the water reached her waist. Taking a deep breath, she mustered all her strength, tipped her head back until she stared at a pitch-black sky, and she screamed. Screamed for the only person she could think of that could help her, save her. She filled her lungs and screamed.

"Daddy!"

Chapter 20

Jaxon was a half a world away when he heard the plea. It arrowed into his body and made him double over as if a bullet had been fired into his no longer human form.

He stayed hunched over trying to figure out what had happened, trying to zero in on the mortal that needed his help. The Dark had to be responsible for the pain this soul was in and Jaxon felt a fire begin to burn in his belly, as his nostrils flared trying to pick up the stench to follow to the source.

The plea had been garbled, giving no clue for him to follow. He stayed still, waiting for the cry of help to come again. When it did, it flung his body into the air, his back arched, and he burned. He knew the voice and did not hesitate. The black wings on his back unfolded and lunged down with power as he took to flight. He flew with magnificent speed until he landed beside the bed that held his daughter.

He heard her cry again as she called for him, her father, to help her, to save her. Jaxon did not know how to enter her mind and help her, so he sent his own plea out for the one Immortal he needed now. Raising his dark head, Jaxon used his power to call his friend to his side. "Saul!" he bellowed. "I need you!"

In a fraction of a second, the Immortal Saul appeared by his side and placed a hand upon his shoulder. "I am here, Jaxon," he said, his voice trying to calm the hunter. "What is it?"

"She needs us," Jaxon said, and his muscles corded under the hand, letting Saul know the situation was urgent.

Saul sat beside the rigid mortal and prepared to enter Dee's nightmare, but was stopped as he now felt a hand on his own shoulder.

"Take me with you," Jaxon said.

Saul opened his mouth to deny the request, but before he could Jaxon's fingers dug in and he did not ask. "Take me with you. She called for me," he said, "and I will come to her aid. I will help her. Now take me with you."

Saul saw the steel in Jaxon's eyes and he felt the need roll off this father. The need to protect and save his daughter. Saul nodded his head in consent and again turned to Dee. "Hold on to my shoulder," he said, as he closed his eyes and focused until he brought them both into the nightmare in Dee's mind.

Jaxon saw his daughter being pulled into the dark water and he jumped into action. "I'm here, Dee," he said softly; as he moved upon the water reaching down to pull her up into his arms. The water was like tar and it clung to her, not wanting to let its prize go, but Jaxon would not be denied. Power radiated from him and he growled with anger until the hold was broken and Dee clung to him. She gasped for air and sobbed as her arms clung to the father she had never met in life.

Jaxon moved with his daughter until they stood beside Saul. The water that had been so dark and foul before was now calm and docile, no longer being controlled by the Dark. Jaxon's dark eyes met the equally dark eyes of Saul over his daughter's head and the Guardian could read the relief in them now that Dee was safe. But it didn't last. Relief turned to rage as the crisis had passed and the Hunter could now think about who had caused this. "It was the Dark," Jaxon said. "They are still coming after her even though they know they will have to answer to me if anything happens to her."

"Yes," Saul said. "The Dark needs to be dealt with. But we are too late to find the one responsible this time."

"This time," Jaxon ground out. "I'm not giving up. Dee needs protection."

"Again, I agree," Saul said. "But this is not the place to discuss what needs to be done." He lowered his eyes to the human still clinging to her Immortal father.

Jaxon placed a kiss on his daughter's head and stroked her dark hair. "You're safe now," he said softly. "This was all just a nightmare and it is over now."

Dee stopped shivering and relaxed as the deep voice soothed her, took away her fears.

"I know this isn't real," Dee said. "Thank you, Daddy," she said into his strong shoulder. "You came when I needed you, just like I knew you would."

"I'll always come when you need me," Jaxon said sadly, knowing it was time to leave her.

Saul moved to stand behind the pair and laying his hands upon Dee's shoulders, he took her memories of the nightmare, until Dee no longer remembered any of it and would not remember when she woke up.

Jaxon found himself standing beside the bed again with Saul and he dropped his hand to his side. "We need to find her a protector," he said to Dee's Guardian.

"Yes," Saul said. "I will look for one."

"Like you did me?" Jaxon asked.

"Yes, as I did for you, for Hannah." Saul replied.

"I have a better idea," Jaxon said, not sure his idea would be accepted, but he was sure it was the only one.

"Come," Saul said. "We will discuss this idea of yours, but just not here."

Jaxon moved to bend over Dee's now peacefully sleeping form and touched her cheek. "I always seem to be leaving you," he whispered. "But I will find you someone to keep you safe. I love you." He placed a kiss on her cheek.

Dee's eyes fluttered open as the touch of the Hunter's lips brought her slowly from her sleep. She smiled and stretched before opening her eyes to the waning day.

As much as she felt another presence in her room, her eyes found no one there.

She was, as always, alone.

Chapter 21

"Now what is this idea that you have?" Saul asked when he and Jaxon had once again left the mortal behind. "Having me go find another mortal to protect Dee sounds like a good plan to me. It is, after all, tried and true."

Jaxon shrugged his mighty shoulders. "I agree that it worked before, but I have issues with the way things turned out."

"It was the way fate wanted it," Saul said, leaving no room for argument.

"The past is the past, "Jaxon said, "but it is the future and the safety of my daughter that we have come to talk about now."

"Agreed," Saul said. "So tell me this idea you have."

Jaxon remained silent but raised his head and stood still as he sent out a call. After he opened his eyes, he smiled and waited. Not for long.

The air around the two Immortals rumbled and stirred, announcing the eminent arrival of another.

Saul raised his eyebrows in surprise when the Immortal Guardian Hunter joined them. Not a Hunter like Jaxon, but an Immortal Guardian, like Saul.

In mortal life, Hunter Gunn had been a good man. His life had been cut short when the Dark had enlisted a human to ambush him and steal the many years he had left to lead humanity towards peace and unity.

"I don't think I have to introduce you two, but to make it official, Saul, this is Hunter. Hunter, this is Saul."

"What can I do for you?" Hunter asked Jaxon. It was not unusual for an Immortal to call on another for help, but it was out of the norm for a Hunter to call a Guardian, unless there was a threat to one of the humans that the Guardian was watching over.

Hunter had detected no problems with his charges, but out of curiosity he had answered the call of this Immortal Hunter. Jaxon not only carried a fierce reputation with the Dark, but the same exact reputation with the Immortals. They did not fear him, but none doubted he was the one to call if the Dark got out of hand. Now it seemed Jaxon needed him for something.

Saul had nodded his head and smiled when Jaxon had introduced the two Guardians to each other. He already knew Hunter and, in fact, had been the one to bring him to his new life as an Immortal. He had been the one to train him and he had found Hunter still carried a love for the human race, making him an excellent Guardian.

Saul looked him over with new eyes, assessing his ability to protect Dee. He stood six feet three inches tall, had dark brown hair, green eyes and a smile that had inspired both love and lust when he was alive. He still wore the traditional robes of the Guardians, but the wings on his back made him stand out, as they were as golden as the sun. His body was toned and muscled but carried no bulk. Instead, he looked lean and fit.

"Does one of you want to tell me why I am here?" Hunter asked, tired of waiting.

"I have an assignment for you," Jaxon said.

"Assignment." Hunter repeated, wondering what was going on.

Jaxon forgot he was not dealing with one of his men. "Sorry," he said, smiling a little. "I guess it would be more of a favor."

Hunter hid his surprise well, as he drew in a sharp breath. "Okay," he said," lay it out for me."

"I need you to protect a human for me," Jaxon said. "A special human."

"Special, how?" Hunter asked.

She was born with the gift of seeing the past of objects and of even bodies. She is on the Dark's list to be taken out, if they find her to be a threat. It seems the Dark is taking an interest in her and we, I, need her to be kept safe."

"Sounds like a good cause," Hunter said. "What else?"

Saul let a little smile play about his lips as he stood back and listened to Jaxon try and get Hunter to help without giving him all the information. And Hunter was digging for everything that he could get before committing.

"Two reasons I picked you," Jaxon said, giving in. "One is the human who I need protected is my daughter, and Two," he continued, ignoring Hunter's open mouth, "is the fact that you are uniquely qualified for this favor."

Hunter closed his mouth, regaining his composure before clearing his throat and saying, "Go on."

"You have knowledge from your human life that will help you and my daughter stay safe." Jaxon continued.

"Just tell me, will you?" Hunter said, beginning to itch with Jaxon's stalling.

"Very well," Jaxon said, taking a deep breath and diving in. "You know about the Omen Lake and what it involves."

Hunter stiffened as if he had been struck. "What do you know about that lake?" he asked.

"I know that my daughter, Dee, has taken a job at the cemetery and the Dark has decided to invade her dreams, giving her nightmares about the Lake, trying to scare her off. If Saul and I had not intervened, she would have died in her dream and in real life. I need someone I can trust to watch over her and keep her safe. You know about the situation and I think you would do a good job keeping her alive. If the Dark gets into her head and tries it again, you can be there to fight them off."

"Is that all?' Hunter asked, his voice grim.

Jaxon locked eyes with his choice of protectors and said," No. I chose you because your headstone is in that cemetery. Because Omen Lake chose you, and because the Dark set it all up. I'm offering you a little pay back."

Hunter growled.

Chapter 22

Jaxon smiled at the sound coming from the Guardian, but it was a cold reaction. Nothing warm and comforting was going to be given from the fierce Immortal hunter, Jaxon. "I see you remember," Jaxon said, making Hunter pull his lips back in a sneer.

"I remember," he said. "I remember traveling and stopping along side this little cemetery to take a walk and just stroll through the old headstones. You know, stretch my legs for a bit. I really didn't have anywhere in mind, just driving until I felt the need to stop. I was walking along when all of a sudden this lake appeared and I was confused as to where it came from. I didn't remember seeing any water when I started to walk, but there it was. Then, a man came up to me and asked me if I was okay. Said I was looking kind of pale and stuff. I asked him where the lake came from and he backed away from me like I had a disease or something."

"I didn't understand then, not then. But the next day, when I was leaving the hotel, a car ran me down. I remember lying on my back looking up and darkness covered the sun. I saw a dark form coming towards me and it was laughing this watery horrible laugh. I thought I was going to hell, but Saul here showed up and drove that thing away."

"He brought me here and told me what was happening. That I was taken before my time, and that the Dark had used the Omen Lake to do it. I know that the people buried me in that same cemetery and that the Lake there is bad news."

"You understand why I want you to protect my daughter then?" Jaxon asked, looking deep into Hunter's eyes.

Hunter didn't want to protect anyone associated with the lake. "I'm afraid I must decline your offer," he said, snapping his wings open as he prepared to leave.

"Hold on, Hunter," Saul said, breaking any further movement or further silence. "I think Jaxon's plan is a good one. If you will give me a moment to fill in a few details, maybe you will see our need and change your mind."

It actually took Saul and, eventually Jaxon, two hours of talking and arguing before Hunter finally caved and agreed to help.

"Excellent," Saul said, grasping Hunter's hand and sealing the bargain. "You will go back in human form and it will be up to you to figure out a way to stay close to Dee and protect her."

"Do not let down your guard," Saul warned. "The Dark will be able to see you for what you are and they will come after you both. Can you handle this?"

"Yes," Hunter said. "I know how to fight the Dark and I will not forget my 'mission' as you called it." He directed that promise to Jaxon. "I am far from soft and can take care of myself and my charges."

"As of right now, you only have one charge," Jaxon said. "Don't forget what you are up against."

Hunter arched a brow at Jaxon and only swallowed his retort by reminding himself that he was dealing with a father first and an Immortal Hunter second.

"Good," Saul said, rubbing his hands together. "Now let's do something about your clothes."

Jaxon laughed.

Hunter did not.

Chapter 23

Hunter had forgotten that humans did not wear robes as a norm, as he had never given a second thought to his own appearance. It took Jaxon laughing at him to make him willing to change to once again fit in with the mortals. "What would you have me wear?" Hunter asked.

"What would you like to wear?" Jaxon countered. "What look do you like that your charges are wearing now?"

"Hmmmm," Hunter said, trying to picture something modern that he would like.

Hunter looked at what Saul was wearing and rejected the idea for himself. Not that a polo shirt and jeans was a bad look, but just not his style. He looked at Jaxon and liked what he saw better. The black shirt, black jeans and shoes were more to his liking, but he did not want to copy the Immortal Hunter's look. He needed something he could call his own.

"Close your eyes," Saul instructed, "and think of what you would like to be wearing."

Hunter followed Saul's instructions, letting his mind run wild.

Saul and Jaxon waited and waited and waited until finally Hunter opened his eyes and looked at his creation. Jaxon frowned and Saul shrugged his shoulders.

"You look pretty normal," Jaxon said. "You took longer than a woman to make up your mind. I was kind of expecting something, well, more," he said, pausing and tapping his finger on his cheek as he walked a full circle around his chosen protector.

"I thought about my choices," Hunter snorted at Jaxon. "I figured I should probably kind of blend in and be comfortable at the same time."

Saul too looked the Immortal over and nodded his head in agreement with Hunter. He would blend in, be comfortable, and look good all at the same time. "I approve," he said out loud.

"Cool," Hunter said, looking down at his humanly clad form again. He had settled on a pair of faded blue jeans that looked worn but not ratty, a light blue work shirt that had the long sleeves rolled up to his elbows, revealing strong forearms, and a pair of medium brown work boots that laced up the front. His dark brown hair hung over his collar and brushed his eyebrows. The feathery style let it lay perfectly mussed and gorgeous at the same time. His green eyes were rimmed with thick, long lashes that were as black as jet. His cheeks and chin were lightly covered with a dark stubble of a beard, giving him a slightly dangerous air.

In life he was considered more than slightly dangerous by anyone who had gotten on his bad side, and as an Immortal Guardian he carried over that image and lived up to it. He knew how to fight and his muscles gave proof to the strength. Those muscles rippled just beneath the surface, waiting to be unleashed for those in need. He had been fiercely protective of his friends in life and gave his all to his charges as a Guardian.

Jaxon had chosen well for his daughter. "I will leave it up to you to come up with a story as to why you are there when you meet Dee, and about a past, if you so chose to tell her about yourself," Jaxon said, moving on now that the clothing had been chosen.

Hunter nodded in agreement. "Don't worry," he assured them. "I'll come up with something believable."

"What name are you going to use?" Saul asked.

Hunter shrugged his shoulders. "What's wrong with my own?" he asked.

"Nothing," Saul said, "except it's on a head stone in the cemetery."

"If memory serves me correctly," Hunter said, "it's not even close to the rest of the headstones. I was a stranger, so they buried me way off to the side and to the back. I remember a tree also, so I think there is not much of a chance that Dee will be finding the named stone any time soon."

"If she does the mission is over. You do realize that, don't you?" Jaxon asked.

Jaxon was not sure how much more Dee could take before she broke. She had had to deal with so much in her lifetime, and telling her what Hunter really was would put a strain on any mind, even one as strong as his daughter's. He didn't want to take the chance of her overloading and shutting down.

"I'm still going to use my own name," Hunter said, steel riding his tone. "I will be with her most of the time, and I will keep her from finding out anything she shouldn't. You chose me to take care of your daughter, so I will be making the decisions. If you want to interfere then you can find yourselves another Guardian."

Silence followed Hunter's ultimatum, until both Jaxon and Saul nodded their heads in consent.

"Very well," Saul spoke for them both. "We will trust your judgment. But if you should have need of us, either one or both, you have only to call and we will come to your aid."

Hunter took them at their word and relaxed his tight muscles. "I have to leave for a little while, but when I return I will be ready for you to show me your daughter and begin her protection."

"Thank you." Jaxon was feeling relief that all the kinks seemed to have been worked out. "Don't be long."

Hunter arched a handsome brow at Jaxon before snapping his golden wings wide and leaping into the air. In seconds, he was out of sight but far from being out of Jaxon's mind. "I hope this works," he said quietly to Saul, not taking his eyes off the spot where Hunter had disappeared.

"I think your plan is a good one and, since you chose the protector yourself, you must have faith in his abilities. Let him be and do not interfere." Saul replied. He felt the need to reinforce Jaxon's decision and ease his mind.

"Easier said than done," Jaxon murmured. "I still wish it was me that was watching over Dee."

"I've felt that way many times when I've had to turn over the care of a charge to another, but it is for the best. You are too close to be as effective as Hunter will be. Relax. We have done all we can to give Dee a fighting chance, should the Dark come calling." Saul said then turned and walked away, destiny had been set in motion.

Jaxon was not reassured.

Chapter 24

"Are you ready, Mom?' Dee called, before she was fully past her mother's front door jam.

Hannah walked out of the bedroom, putting the strap of her purse over her shoulder and reaching for her keys. "Hello to you, too," Hannah said, as she gave her daughter a quick squeeze. "And, yes, I'm ready."

"Sorry," Dee said, as she took a step to the side to allow Hannah to move past her. "I didn't mean to rush you."

Hannah just smiled, as her unusual eyes smiled into Dee's, holding no rebuke in them. "To tell you the truth," Hannah said, as they moved down the stairs and out the door, "I'm dying to know what your surprise is."

Dee gave Hannah a huge smile and unlocked the doors to her car, never once giving any clue to her surprise.

"Are we going to stop for lunch first?" Hannah asked, as her stomach gave a deep rumble showing her reason for asking.

"I'll be feeding you in about half an hour," Dee said, as she started the car and was soon heading south.

Hannah was satisfied with the answer and settled back to let her eyes wander, taking in the scenery as they drove. It didn't take long before buildings gave way to rolling hills and green pastures. Hannah was not too concerned and her curiosity not too deep as she snuggled down into the soft seat and let Dee take her where she wanted.

It was not until they were pulling into an almost hidden drive that she sat up a little straighter and a frown settled on her brow. The archway they passed under declared they had arrived at a cemetery. Hannah read the name of 'Omen Lake Cemetery' before they passed through it and into a small parking lot. Instead of stopping, they continued on until Dee pulled the car up to a weather-beaten house surrounded by tall old trees where she put her car in park and killed the engine. The silence beat at their ears with no sound to break it.

Hannah did not know why but her hands turned white as one gripped the console and the other the door handle.

"We're here," Dee said, excitement ringing in her voice. She turned her head to face Hannah, but the words of explanation froze in her throat, as she saw the expression on her mother's face.

"Mom?" Dee asked. "Mom, what's wrong? Are you ok?"

Hannah heard her dimly under the buzzing in her head. She had no reason to be alarmed but she was. "Why are we here?" she asked Dee. Her voice was thin and reedy. "Are you sick? Is that why you brought me here? To tell me something bad?"

Dee's heart jumped into her throat as she realized she had scared her mother without meaning to. "No, Mom," she hurried to assure her. "I just wanted you to see the place where I live and work now."

"What?" Hannah asked, in disbelief. "You what?"

"I took a job here a couple of days ago and it came with this house to live in. I got all moved in before I told you because I wanted to surprise you."

"What kind of job?" Hannah asked, getting herself under control.

"Let's go inside so I can show you around while we talk," Dee said, opening her door so she could hurry around and be standing there when her mother got out.

It took Hannah a full thirty seconds to loosen her hands and let the death grip go before she could exit the car. Dee stood aside as she got out and led the way to the front door, opening it in invitation for Hannah to enter. Hannah didn't want to enter this place. She wanted to pull Dee back out, get in the car, lock the doors and head back into town. She had no reason to feel the dread she was feeling, nor could she explain why she felt this place held danger for Dee, but she did.

"Come in, Mom," Dee said, still waiting for her mother to step over the threshhold.

Against everything inside her, Hannah moved one foot until it was inside the door and then the other. She deliberately took more steps until Dee could follow her in and shut the door.

"Welcome to my new place," Dee said, rubbing her hands together. She was nervous that her mother would not like it. Yes, she was a grown woman, but Hannah's opinion had always been important to her and she wanted her approval.

"Tell me how this came about?" Hannah said, letting her eyes wander. What she could see was beautiful wood and warm colors making up the walls and the floors. Serviceable, yet pretty rugs were strategically placed, giving a homey appearance, and she could see small touches of her daughter in the few knick-knacks that were sprinkled around.

"I answered an ad in the paper for a caretaker," Dee began. Her explanation was given as they moved from room to room. "I got a call a few days ago and I was offered the job."

"And the job is?" Hannah left the question hanging.

"It's just mowing the grounds, pulling up weeds, planting flowers and watering everything," Dee said. "The last person who took care of the place got too old to keep up, so he retired." Dee sort of lied. "I think this is a great job for me," Dee said, as she and Hannah again stopped in the living room.

"How is that?" Hannah asked, doubt clouding her mind.

"I don't have to be around objects or people," Dee said. "I don't have to worry about what I touch. I really want you to say this is okay. Mom, please."

Hannah's heart hurt as she saw the pain her daughter fought so hard to hide from her. Her gift was bad, but Dee's was worse. Dee was at the mercy of anything and everything she came into contact with. So Hannah could see why this job would be so appealing to Dee. It offered her peace and quiet, nothing to fear, and no memories with which to deal. Hannah shut the hurt away until she could be alone to deal with it and faced her daughter. "I see the appeal," she said and forced her lips to curve into a smile. "The house is beautiful," she said, telling the truth, "and from the outside, I never would have guessed it to be so warm and comfortable. Why didn't you tell me about all of this before, Dee?"

"I wanted to be sure this was for me. With every little piece of me that I moved in and put away, it felt more right. I just knew it was where I was meant to be. Does that sound weird?" Dee asked.

"No," Hannah said, seeing the truth of what Dee said radiate from every part of her body. "No, I know just what you mean. I felt the same way when I saw the building I eventually bought and turned into the store that we have now. It was the same for me."

Dee gave a sigh of relief and relaxed with her mother's understanding.

"Come here, Mom," she said, leading the way into the kitchen where she had already set the table and prepared the meal, all in anticipation of her mother's visit.

"Have a seat," she said, pulling out a chair before she moved to the cupboard and began gathering their meal. She didn't stop until she had a cold, crisp lettuce salad assembled in bowls, thick B L T's on plates, and frosty glasses of soda poured and set on the table.

Hannah smiled to herself, thinking that two servings of lettuce was a little much when chips, pickles and carrots would have worked just as well. But she loved that Dee had worked hard on the house to make it ready for her visit, as well as preparing a meal for the two of them. There was nothing to criticize here.

"Thanks honey," she said, as Dee finally sat down to join her. Hannah raised her glass and waited until Dee did the same. "Here's to your future," Hannah said, surprising her daughter with the toast. "If you ever need me, I am just a phone call away. I am so proud of you. I love you, Dee." She finished by clinking her glass to her daughter's in a toast.

"I love you, too, Mom," Dee said. "I love you, too."

Roman gagged.

Chapter 25

Roman had watched Dee move her things into the small house in the cemetery. He bided his time until she was finished and waited until she brought her mother to her new home. He stayed in the shadows by the arch, and climbed aboard when they passed him by. It had been easy to kick Hannah's motherly fears into high gear, to give her feelings of dread about this new job and the place that Dee had told her nothing about until this very day. He would have liked those feelings to overtake Hannah, to cause a rift between the two humans. But the love they shared was strong, and the trust Hannah gave her daughter was more than he had bargained for. He watched as Dee made a meal for them and squirmed with failure when Hannah had accepted Dee's choice in jobs.

Listening to them tell each other of their love made him gag, and he wanted to hurt something. That is until he detected the doubts Hannah still harbored in her heart and in her gut. Her instincts were good, and she was right to fear for her child in this place of death.

Roman would be careful when dealing with one of Saul's charges and the loved ones of an Immortal Hunter. But he could not leave them alone. This family was like an addiction for him, always drawing him to their sides, just begging him to interfere. He was happy to feed his addiction when the opportunity presented itself. A cemetery was a playground for the Dark, and the chance to get Dee to live and work there was perfect. Humans had a fear of cemeteries because of the images and dreams planted in their heads. The fear of the dead rising and coming for them was a great trick of the Darks'. They played with this fear and fed it in the blackness of night. In the quiet of the night, in a lonely bed, they made every sound sinister and every shadow menacing.

What fun it was to make humans quake with fright. Such child's play for the Dark, and Roman was going to take full advantage of Dee living and working in a cemetery. He danced in the shadows as he planned on the nightmares he would give her, until she screamed in fear and her mind broke under the strain. He just had to be careful not to be detected by Saul until it was too late. Too late to save his pet from madness.

For now, Roman was happy to leave the humans to themselves. Until the sun went down. Until it was his time. His time to come out and play.

Until it was Dark.

Chapter 26

Dee and Hannah had finished their lunch, lingering over the strawberry shortcake that Dee had served for dessert. They talked about Dee's job and what it would entail. To Hannah, the tasks did not seem too hard and the peace of mind that her daughter would find more than made up for the isolation she was imposing on herself.

After the food was gone and the dishes washed, dried, and put away, mother and daughter decided to take a walk outside to check out the sights.

Hannah could see why Dee was so taken with the place. Aside from it being a cemetery, the land, trees, and even the wild tall grass were beautiful. The more time Hannah spent there, the more the peacefulness of the place soaked into her soul. She could picture Dee working here, and more and more of the misgivings that she had been feeling took leave. Listening to Dee talk about what she would do here, the plans she had for the landscape, was soothing to Hannah. She hoped that this place and this job would live up to all Dee's expectations, and over the years be somewhere Dee would grow old.

Dee was like a little kid as she danced around her mother, stopping often to point to a spot and tell Hannah her plans for it.

"I think you have wonderful ideas," Hannah praised Dee. "From the way you describe everything, I think it will be picture perfect when you get done."

"Thanks Mom, "Dee said, and gave her shoulders a lingering squeeze. "It means a lot to me that you are okay with my choice. I wasn't sure you would be."

"I want you to be happy," Hannah said. "That's all I have ever wanted for you."

"Let's go back to the house," Dee suggested, as she turned to retrace the route that had brought them there.

"I hate to be a party pooper, but I need to get going pretty soon. I have some book work to do for the store before tomorrow." Hannah said as they walked.

Dee nodded her head in understanding, sure that it was not just an excuse to just get out of the cemetery.

"I'll get my keys when we get back, and maybe I'll even stay and let you cook me supper when we get to your place."

"I think I can do that," Hannah laughed, always glad to have the company of her daughter.

They reached the house and made it to the front door before both jumped as a voice came up behind them. "I'm looking for Madison Priest," it said, dark and smoky.

Goose bumps rose on Dee's arms and a shiver racked her spine as she felt that voice in every pore of her body. She felt like a person dying of thirst and the words, the words, were the life-giving cool water she craved.

Dee and Hannah shared a look before both turned to face the stranger at their backs. Dee could not help it, as her mouth fell open and the spit dried up faster than a puddle in the July heat.

Standing at the bottom of her steps was one of the most gorgeous men she had ever seen. Her eyes ran from the top of his dark head all the way down to his boots, before making the same journey in reverse.

Dark, dark hair lay in thick feathery layers and lifted with the puffs of breeze that blew across the yard. A tanned face was lifted to her, letting her see the deep green eyes that held mild curiosity and were ringed with thick long black lashes. The same color eyebrows with dark slashes rested above them, one slightly cocked with his statement. A nose that was slightly flared, led her to a mouth that made her own lips buzz with the desire to taste it, become intimate with it. His cheeks and chin were covered with dark stubble of beard that did nothing to distract from his looks. Instead it gave him an air of mystery, and she wanted to bracket his face with her hands, to hold it still, as she took him all in.

His shoulders were wide and the shirt he wore stretched across his chest, letting her know that there were muscles and power beneath the light blue layer of cloth. His waist was flat and the jeans around it showed no excess flab. His legs were long and he wore his pants tight, not baggy and hanging off his ass.

Dee was like every other woman, preferring a man in a great fitting pair of jeans. Oh yeah, there was nothing like a man in a tight pair of jeans to make your heart speed up and your hands itch to slide into the back pockets as you snuggled close.

Damn but this man was yummy, Dee thought. Not that she had a lot of experience with the male species, but she had eyes that liked to look and definite opinions that told her what she found attractive. "I'm Dee." She finally got a greeting out, tipping her head back as the stranger mounted the steps to stand beside her. His six foot three inch frame seemed to tower over her, making her feel small and delicate in his shadow.

"Dee, then," he said, and held out a hand to shake hers in introduction.

"I'm Hunter," he said, as his fingers folded around hers. "Hunter Gunn."

Green eyes met and were held by some of the most unusual eyes he had ever seen. The deep brown irises were laced with fiery red streaks that began to glow like hot embers, making Hunter lean down and stare harder

He swallowed hard, as the human feelings that he had forgotten began to stir. His blood heated with feelings of want. His thoughts were interrupted as the human female at Dee's side cleared her throat, demanding attention.

"I'm Dee's mother," Hannah, the mortal said. "Hannah Priest."

Dropping the hand he still held in his, Hunter shifted his own to hold it out to the mother in greeting. "Ma'am," he said, waiting a few seconds until Hannah finally clasped his strong hand in hers.

"And you are?' she asked, suspicion riding her tone.

"Oh yes, sorry," he said, having forgotten to also introduce himself to Hannah, as he was so caught up in Dee. "Like I said, I'm Hunter, Hunter Gunn."

"What can we do for you, Mr. Gunn?" Hannah asked, stepping in as her daughter did not seem inclined to ask.

Hunter's eyes became dark and fierce as he locked gazes with blazing red orbs before answering. "I'm here for your daughter."

Chapter 27

Hannah did not hesitate before stepping between Dee and the stranger. "Maybe you would like to explain that statement," she said, ready to defend her child with her life.

Hunter drew back, as the threat from this mother was obvious. He had seen this type of maternal protection many different times while helping his charges. The protection a good mother felt for her child was a strong power. There was nothing a female would not do if her child were threatened. They fought to the death to keep them safe and thought nothing of their own safety while doing it. This female was a mystery to him, as Saul and Jaxon had told him nothing of her. Instead they had concentrated on the one he was sent to protect.

He knew he had to tread lightly and win this mother's trust, or his job would be a hundred times harder than it needed to be. These two were obviously close, and he did not want Dee to have to choose between his presence and Hannah's approval. He had come up with a plan of what to say when the question was asked of why he was there. Now seemed the time to air the tale out. "I was hired by David a few years back, when the work became too much for him. I took care of all the equipment, and I was told by David I was to continue to do the same for Miss Priest."

"What makes you think Dee needs any help taking care of the equipment here?" Hannah asked, still on the defensive.

"Well, if she can fix a mower when it breaks down, or repair the sprinkler system when it springs a leak, or any number of other things that need doing, then I guess I am out of a job." He replied with a reassuring tone.

The silence stretched out as Hannah thought about Hunter's explanation before coming to the conclusion that it made sense and maybe, just maybe, he was telling the truth.

"David didn't say anything about you," Dee spoke up, almost afraid to voice her thought. Her mother seemed to be on a rampage, and never having seen this side of her before, Dee was not sure what to make of it.

Hannah, with her arms crossed over her chest and her eyes narrowed, waited for Hunter to explain that one away.

"I think David figured he would have a few more meetings with Dee, and have a chance to introduce us before he turned over the reins completely. I'm sorry he can't." Hunter replied to Hannah's questions.

"Why not?" Dee and Hannah asked in unison.

"David died last night," Hunter told them. His voice was low and sorrowful.

Dee was chilled to the bone, as the first thing she thought of was Omen Lake. She was not going to say anything in front of her mother, but saw in Hunter's eyes the truth of the story. He believed it was all-true, and had no doubts the Lake was what got him.

"I was also the person the gravediggers came to when they were needed," Hunter said. "David showed me where he was to be buried the last time I talked to him."

"He showed me too," Dee said, remembering the way he had stood behind his wife and son's headstones, before showing her the one he had placed beside them for himself. "You will take care of all that for me?" Dee asked, very glad she did not have to deal with that unthought-of aspect.

"If I still have a job," Hunter said. "If you still need my help."

"I think I am going to say yes to your offer of help and keep you on," Dee confirmed.

Hunter relaxed as his reason for being near Dee had been accepted. "I just came by this afternoon to meet you and to let you know the workers will be here in the morning to get things ready for David. You will not have to do anything. The two guys have been doing this for a while now, so they will just go about their business, if that's okay with you?"

"Yes, yes, of course," Dee agreed, thinking that before they brought David out for the last time, she was going to make sure the grass was groomed and everything looked good. That was all she could do for him now.

"Well, I'll be going then," Hunter said, turning to leave.

"Do you live around here?" Dee asked, wondering if there was another house on the property that she had not been told of.

"Not far," Hunter said, flashing her a crooked smile, and he left it at that.

"I'm giving my mother a ride back to town," Dee said. "Can we give you a ride home?"

"No, that's okay," Hunter said, "I like to walk."

"Mr. Gunn," Hannah said, waiting for him to turn around before using her powers to see what kind of person he really was. She was not going to trust him just yet, until she saw for herself that he was not a monster underneath all those good looks and charm.

Hunter did as was expected and paused to turn back. Hannah's power hit him square in the chest. He was not sure what she would see, but he did not have to worry about his true self, an Immortal, being revealed to her.

All Hannah saw was a bright golden light where a man had stood just seconds before. She grunted and threw up a hand to shield her eyes, wondering what it meant.

When Hannah withdrew her power, she once again saw only a man standing tall and strong in her daughter's yard. She was confused by what she saw but had no grounds to think Hunter was evil.

"Nice to meet you, Mr. Gunn," she said. "But I think it's time for me to be going."

"Hunter, please," he said, and raised a hand in farewell. "Nice to meet you too ma'am. And Dee, I'll see you in the morning, say about eight or so?"

"See you then," she agreed. She waited until he disappeared down the drive before turning to her mother asking, "Mom, did you use your powers on him?"

"Yup," Hannah said, entering the house to gather her purse and Dee's keys.

"Well, what did you see?" Dee asked.

"Nothing except for a big ball of bright light." Hannah replied.

"What does that mean?" Dee asked, as she pulled her front door shut behind her.

"I've never seen anything like it before. But I don't think he's dangerous." Hannah said to reassure herself as well as her daughter.

Dee gave a sigh of relief as she started the car and headed back into town. She was glad her mother had not seen a monster. She was drawn to Hunter and would have hated to go against her mother. But she knew without a doubt that she would have done just that.

That and more.

Chapter 28

Dee woke up the next morning to the soothing sounds of rustling leaves and waking birds. No beeping horns and loud voices, no smells of car exhaust, and no under lying twinges of trash cans waiting to be emptied. She stretched under the sheets and smiled, before opening her eyes to greet the day. It was her first day on her new job and she felt excitement begin to build. First times for anything were something to be treasured, and Dee never forgot that. Trying something new, meeting someone new, and seeing something new all were treasures that made memories worth savoring. Dee hoped that she would never run out of firsts, and with that thought in her head she flipped the covers back and headed to the bathroom and a warm shower.

After her shower was complete, Dee stood before her closet, trying to decide what to wear. She pulled a pair of her favorite old jeans from their hanger and wiggled into them, liking the way the fabric felt soft and comfortable. A dark blue tee shirt followed, and lastly, a light long-sleeved flannel shirt completed her choice for the day.

She stopped in front of a full-length mirror to check out the results, not that it mattered, of course, she tried to convince herself. Not that she was trying to impress anyone. Not that she was giving any thought to the fact that Hunter was gong to be showing up in... ten minutes. Ten minutes!

Dee gave a yelp of shock and made a beeline for the kitchen for a quick breakfast. She had managed to get a smoothie mixed up and in a glass before she heard a knock on her front door. Gulping and walking at the same time kept Dee from leaving Hunter on her doorstep for long.

She reached the door at the same time the brain freeze hit her between the eyes. Pinching the bridge of her nose and bowing her head to the pain, Dee managed to pull the front door open and motion Hunter to come inside. Neither one of them said a word until Dee raised her head to see Hunter watching her with an alarmed look on his face.

"Is something wrong?" Hunter asked. "Are you hurt? Has someone hurt you?" he demanded, his eyes making a swift tour of the house.

"No, no," Dee said, as the pain finally began to subside. "I just drank a smoothie too fast and I got a brain freeze. Come on in, while I get a few things together before we start."

Hunter followed her deeper into her home and stood by while she gathered a pair of gloves, a Husker baseball cap, and a jug of water with ice in it. "Would you like a glass, or can you drink straight from the jug?" she asked.

Hunter shrugged his shoulders, as he was confused by the question. Did *it really matter?* "I really don't need a glass and if you can stand drinking from the same container as me. Then we will have less to carry. I promise that I have no germs and will not make you sick," he said with a solemn face as he made a cross over his heart and a reassuring smile came to his handsome face.

Dee licked her dry lips, imagining ways to pick up germs from Hunter. Each idea made her heart beat just a little faster, until she had to shut her imagination down or faint because of it. "Let's go then," she said, and led the way out the door.

What was wrong with her, she wondered. It wasn't like she had never seen a good-looking man before. But something about Hunter was different. He seemed to attract her like a fly to flypaper, and if she were not careful she would be just as stuck on him as the helpless flies to the sticky paper. Or some other similar comparison, she thought, smiling inside.

"What would you like to do first?" Hunter asked, as they paused on the steps.

Dee was silent for a moment as she took deep breaths of the fresh air and allowed her eyes to scan the outdoors. It was so beautiful and peaceful here, and she marveled at her good fortune at having this job practically fall into her lap. Yes, she was one lucky lady. "I would like to get the mower out and take care of the spot where David will be, before anything else," she replied. "It needs to be pretty for him."

Hunter nodded his head in agreement and headed for the shed. It took him about an hour to teach Dee how to run the big mowing machine. He planned to follow behind her in the old pickup with a trailer and the tools. She would drive through the wild grass with the mower, until they reached their destination.

Once there, Dee was careful and cautious as she mowed the long grass around the three headstones. When the grass catcher was full, Hunter helped her dump it and stood back until she was satisfied with her efforts. He pulled out the trimmer and finished the job, giving Dee time to study the hard muscles that bunched and coiled as he moved the trimmer back and forth, side to side. Dee followed behind him raking the fallen grass into a pile and gathering it up to add it to the heap on the trailer.

"What next?" he asked, joining Dee as she stood looking at their combined efforts.

"I think we need some flowers or something pretty," she said, trying to picture what would look nice.

"They will bring those out with David," he said quietly. "I think we have done all we can for now. The diggers will be here soon, so I think we should move to another area."

Dee's shoulders slumped a little before she agreed and climbed back on the mower to leave.

"Let's start at the beginning," she said, answering his earlier question, as she put the mower in gear. She bumped along, pausing only once to look back. The spot they had cleared looked bare and lonely. She didn't feel a sense of accomplishment with her work, only sad.

Hunter could feel her sadness and his hands gripped the steering wheel just a little tighter. There was nothing he could do, as she learned a lesson in life. Sometimes all you could do was your best, even though it didn't seem like enough.

Hunter let out a sigh as he was reminded again that being human was hard. He did the only thing he could do. He kept driving.

Chapter 29

Dee and Hunter spent the rest of the morning working side by side, doing just as Dee wanted, starting at the beginning. The entrance to the cemetery was given attention and they did not stop until the archway to the grounds was cleared of weeds and the air was filled with the scent of newly mowed grass.

When they did stop for lunch, Dee went to the house to fix thick ham and cheese sandwiches, piled high with lettuce, tomatoes and mayo. A bag of chips, along with tall glasses of pop completed the simple meal which they enjoyed picnic style under one of the old trees in the yard. Dee figured this was what the chairs and small table were meant for, finding it a perfect place to relax and rest.

Once the cemetery was groomed and pretty, Dee was making plans for what she would do to her yard to bring it back to beautiful. A few beds of flowers, a natural rock garden and maybe even a fresh coat of paint for the house would do the trick.

"What are you thinking about?' Hunter asked, as Dee fell silent and seemed deep in thought. Not that they had been burning up the air with conversation, but she seemed miles away, and Hunter was curious as to why.

"Oh, I was just thinking about what to do with the yard once I got caught up with things," Dee supplied, coming out of her thoughts. "It's so pretty here that I would like to make the house and yard pretty, too.

Hunter looked at the house with fresh eyes, picturing it as Dee described her plans. "It sounds like it will be nice when you get done," he said, giving her encouragement to try.

Dee smiled and dusted a few crumbs from her fingers before rising to gather the trash from their meal and take it into the house. She took time to visit the bathroom and rinse the grime from her face, before joining Hunter once again.

"Well, I'm ready," she said, pulling on her gloves and turning to walk back to the entrance. She still had some finishing touches to get done before calling it a day. Dee liked the idea that she did not have to punch a time clock to tell her when to work and when to stop. She knew it would not be dark when she stopped, but once the project was finished maybe Hunter would stay and they could get to know each other better.

"I have something to do this afternoon," Hunter said, making no move to follow her. "I used to stop out here every two or three days with David. It worked out pretty well, so I think I will just stay on that schedule, if that's okay with you?"

Dee had stopped walking and turned in surprise. It never occurred to her that Hunter would not be here all the time, and she was a little disappointed that she would be left on her own without him. "How will I get ahold of you if something breaks down or I need you?" she asked, before he could walk away.

Hunter walked to her side and smiled down at her. "If things break down, just leave them until I get here. I think you will find plenty to keep yourself occupied. Or you could try thinking of me. If you need me, just think of me and I will come." He winked at her and moved off down the driveway. He turned to raise a hand in farewell before rounding a corner and was gone.

Dee stood where he had left her, wondering why he had not given her his phone number. Maybe he was married and didn't want his wife getting the wrong idea if a strange woman called. Maybe he was a criminal and was on the run, so he didn't want to leave any tracks for someone to follow. Or maybe he just didn't like phones, so he didn't have one.

No, Dee thought, that can't be it. None of the excuses she had come up with felt right to her. Thinking back over the morning, Dee realized that what conversations they had had while they worked and ate had come mostly from her. She knew no more about Hunter Gunn now than she had this morning before he had arrived.

"He's hiding something from you," a suspicious voice in her head said. "You knew deep down that he was just too good to be true, didn't you?" The little voice continued to poke at her. "You should have taken off your glove and touched him," the nagging voice said. "He can't hide things from you, if you touch him."

Dee had never had to touch someone to find out things she wanted to know. Most people liked to talk about themselves, and all she had to do was listen.

I can't do that she thought in answer to the voice's suggestion. *It would not be right. If he wants me to know things, then he will tell me.*

He didn't talk about himself because we were talking about work and how to run things. That was it, Dee decided with a sigh of relief. She was letting her imagination get the best of her and creating problems where there were none. Feeling a weight lift from her shoulders, she headed back out to the entrance and spent the rest of the afternoon making sure everything was just right.

When the sun began to set, Dee gathered up her tools and stood back to look at her efforts. It looked wonderful she decided, and felt pride rise up in her. She had worked hard and it seemed to have paid off.

No longer was there knee high grass cloaking the bottom of the archway, and the weeds that grew along the fence on either side had been pulled out and the fresh earth raked until it was even and smooth. She had gone hunting for rocks the size of softballs to edge the area with, and had found some that shone with mica. The whole effect was fresh and inviting, leaving the entrance looking proud with the makeover.

Dee cleaned the hoe, shovel, rake and wheelbarrow like Hunter had told her, before putting them back in their assigned spots. Hunter had made it a point to tell her that all the tools should be kept free of rust and put where they belonged so they would be easy to find when needed. It made sense to Dee and she had no problems following his instructions.

Now that her first day was over, she went into her home and closed the door for the night. She did not think about keeping the bad things out, only of securing things before turning in. Habit.

But that is what she had done. Shut the bad things out. She had no way of knowing that the shadows that had grown long with the setting of the sun held things that had been waiting for just this time of day to come out.

Come out and play.

Play in the dark.

Chapter 30

Roman had not even waited for the sun to set before he had come slinking through the shadows to watch Dee. Normally he shunned the daylight, but when it came to his addiction, he found he had no control. And this job Dee had taken was like a present being dropped into his lap. Spooky, scary, and creepy, it was all he could ask for and more. His plan to give Dee nightmares and to see the walking dead was going to be a treat he would not deny himself. Oh sure, he could have asked one of his followers to do what he had planned, but he could not make himself assign or trust the task to another.

Roman had left Dee alone while she moved her earthly belongings from one home to another, biding his time until she was settled in and alone. All alone. Roman knew that Dee would not be able to run to her mother if she was scared or needed her help. She was too far away to be of immediate assistance, and he giggled with his good fortune. No interference from Hannah was a plus in his favor.

How to begin? he pondered. The question was of utmost importance to him. Should he start with images of people standing in the graveyard, dead people that only Dee could see? Or should he start off more slowly with say making her feel sad and alone? Maybe even depressed as the solitude of her situation sunk in slowly, creeping up on her, before she was aware of what was happening. Whatever he decided was going to have to be done slowly, as to not alert Saul and the Guardian he'd sent to watch over this human.

They really didn't think sending an Immortal to protect her was going to be lost on him, did they? He smirked. He had been able to detect him right off the first time he saw him. The light he generated had made Roman shrink back into the meager shadows, and he had wanted to moan out his rage at the obstacle that was thrown in his path. However, his luck had changed when the Guardian had left Dee alone for the afternoon, and more importantly for the night.

Roman followed Dee into the house and dogged her every step as she made a light supper, ate it alone, and then cleaned up the few dishes. He stayed with her as she turned on the television. It was then that he decided it was time to begin his torment. Reaching into her mind, he tricked it, causing her to reach for a blanket to wrap around herself as she attempted to ward off the sudden chill she was feeling.

The shadows seemed to be deeper, darker, and Roman made sure she felt the cold darkness of his presence. A few goose bumps rose on her arms and he smiled when she turned the set off and made her way to her bed. Hiding under the covers would do her no good. She was about to learn that the Dark could reach you no matter how much you cocooned yourself in warmth and comfort. Roman stayed until the dawn began to chase the dark away and claim the time of day for its own.

He had no regrets leaving and danced one final time as his work for now was done. He had made sure Dee's rest was fitful and her dreams filled with sadness of being alone, all because she'd made this move. A move that took her so far away from her mother and the people who cared about her.

Not a bad start, he decided. And for now, he would retreat.

Retreat and plan.

Chapter 31

Hunter walked away from Dee, waiting until he was out of sight before he faded away to join Saul and Jaxon. "I suppose you were watching?" he asked, facing the two with arms crossed over his muscled chest.

"Of course we were," Jaxon said before Saul could open his mouth. "I have concerns," he said.

"Excuse me," Hunter said, bristling with what he perceived was going to be criticism.

Saul stepped forward placing himself between the Guardian and the Hunter before things got out of hand. "We just want to go over your day and get your feelings on how it went," he supplied, taking a much softer approach.

Hunter relaxed and stopped bristling with Saul's words. "Sure." he said. "How about if we go somewhere we can talk?" With that said, he moved off with Saul and Jaxon following, not stopping until he plopped down on a boulder on the side of a mountain.

"Why here?" Jaxon asked, not bothering to sit, but standing on the same boulder, towering over the Guardian at his feet.

Hunter shrugged his shoulders looking up at Dee's father. "I like it here," he said, not feeling an ounce of intimidation at the position of power Jaxon had assumed. "I've always liked the mountains."

Saul sat beside Hunter looking out over the valleys and trees. The place was peaceful and he approved of the quiet. It was a good place to think. "So what have you found out?" he asked after a moment of silence.

"I met Dee's mother, Hannah," Hunter started. "You failed to fill me in on the strong bond the two shared. She was very protective of her daughter meeting a stranger, and she used her powers on me."

Jaxon smiled as he remembered the jolt Hunter had gotten when Hannah had tried to see his inner self. "She's something, isn't she?" he asked, with pride in his voice.

"She's a mother," Saul chimed in, "and she will protect her daughter from any threat, with whatever resources she has. I expected no less."

"I agree," Hunter nodded, "but you still could have given me a heads up on what I would encounter."

"Yes," Saul said, "I should have filled you in on all aspects of Dee's life. Is there anything else you think you should know before you go back?"

"Not right off the top of my head, but as things come up I may be asking for direction." Hunter replied.

"Help will be given," Saul assured him. "Let's get back to your day. What else did you find out? Did you detect any Dark beings?" he asked, getting down to the meat of his concerns.

"Nothing I could see," Hunter said. But a frown creased his brow.

"Why did you leave so soon" Jaxon butted in, wanting his question answered.

Saul rolled his eyes at the father's bluntness. Jaxon was new at this and his technique left much to be desired. "We were concerned that you left after only half a day with Dee," Saul said, using a calm even tone once again.

"Why didn't you stay?' Jaxon again voiced his question. "I asked you to protect my daughter from the Dark. You can't do that if you're not there."

"You chose me, remember?" Hunter said. "I would think you would trust your own choice."

Jaxon backed down, having to agree with the Immortal. He had chosen him and, as such, he should give him room to prove himself. "You're right," he conceded. "I have no excuse."

"You're a father," Hunter said, easing the tension between the two. "You want your flesh and blood protected. I get that. I've seen it many times. I won't let you down," he said, squinting up at the still standing Jaxon.

Jaxon finally came down off his high horse and lowered himself to sit, forming a group. "I need her to be safe," he said, directing his comment out into the mountain air. "I can't protect her myself and it eats at me not to be there for her."

"Yes," Hunter said. "I remember those feelings of protection from when I was a human."

"Okay," Saul said. "Tell us what your plan is." He hoped hearing the plan would give them a point from which to begin, and to understand. To be of one mind.

"I spent only half a day with Dee because at first everything seemed fine. But later, I detected a Dark force in the area. I couldn't see it but I felt it." Hunter replied.

He stopped when a deep growl rumbled in Jaxon's chest before escaping his mouth. The air burned with his anger and his fingers left grooves in the boulder as he clenched his fists.

"Be calm," the protector said to Jaxon. "I only gave them this one chance so they would move in and I could find out who the Dark has sent to attack Dee. If they think they have a clear shot at her, they will let down their guard and make my job a lot easier. No surprises are what I'm after." Hunter concluded.

"If one fails there will be another," Saul said wisely.

Power sang through Hunter's veins as he anticipated the coming fights he would be asked to win. *Just me and the Dark* he thought as a cold smile bloomed on his face. He had never liked to lose and he was not going to get used to it now. "Trust me," he said. His eyes going flat and still. "I'm not afraid of the Dark."

Turning his eyes, he locked the orbs on Jaxon, letting him see the green fire that was banked behind an iron will. Held in check for now, curling in his belly, waiting for the time when the wall would come down and it would be let loose to do what it was meant for.

Burning the Dark.

Burning them to ash.

Chapter 32

Dee woke up more tired than when she had gone to bed. Her dreams, what she could remember, were filled with people who walked the cemetery. She remembered working and catching movement just out of the corner of her eye. Every time she turned to look, there was no one there. Not until she focused on her work again. All night long she had tried and failed to get the people to talk to her, but no one would. They stayed hidden, taunting her to find them. She ran around in circles getting nowhere, finding nothing, but frustration and the beginning of fear. As Dee lay in her bed, she found herself wishing she had someone else there to put their arms around her and tell her everything was just a dream. Dreams that could not hurt her.

But the house was quiet except for the ticking of a clock somewhere in another room. It was a lonely sound, one that brought to the forefront the fact that she had no one to call except her mother. She had no one special in her life to call her partner, her friend, or her lover.

Dee dragged herself out of bed and headed straight into a hot shower, trying to wash her troubled thoughts down the drain with the soapy bubbles. But some of them lingered, to ride with her as she started her morning.

Dee dressed in clean clothes before pulling her long dark hair over her shoulder, working it until she had a fat braid in place. She heaved a deep sigh. Breakfast. Not that she was very hungry, but she knew she would need some energy to get her through her morning work.

Cold cereal and a cup of coffee was all she had the oomph to fix and consume, before she headed to the hallway closet that held her work gloves and her favorite Husker baseball cap for her head.

When she finally closed the front door at her back, she was as ready for her day, or as ready as she could get. The early morning air was cool but felt wonderful to Dee, and proved to have a positive effect on her. She drank in the clean air and felt the lingering cobwebs being cleared away. Feeling more energy seep into her, she headed to the shed to check out the tools and kill some time until the dew dried up and she could pick a spot to start mowing.

She decided to start with the front row and work her way back, clearing the grass and weeds away until the grounds looked groomed and pristine. There were beautiful benches placed along walkways that sat waiting for her attention. She couldn't wait to uncover them and bring them out to be enjoyed by the visitors that came here to be with their family.

She had just pulled the mower out and was loading her water jug when she heard a droning sound that throbbed in the otherwise still morning. She stopped moving, trying to place the sound, until she finally left the mower where it was and began walking towards the sound. She didn't figure it out until she saw the machine heaping bucketfuls of dirt onto a neat pile that grew taller with every dump, right beside David's headstone. Her stomach clenched and her heart hurt when she realized what was going on. They were here to dig David's grave.

She did not know him well, but she felt his loss and would attend his burial, taking the place of his family. No one should be buried unattended, and she hoped that others, along with her, would show up to pay their final respects. She watched until she could stand the loneliness no longer. It was then she turned back to her work, to fill her mind with something other than death.

"That's going to be you," a knowing voice taunted in her head. "You have no friends to speak of, and when it's your time to die there will be no one to come to see you put in the ground. No one to say nice things over your coffin and no one will shed a tear that you no longer walk this earth."

Dee felt a cold sweat break out on her skin, as she tried to deny the truth of the words in her head. But they held a truth she could not ignore. Because of her gift she had kept to herself, never letting anyone get too close. She would always have to explain her strangeness, and then see the shock and disbelief in their faces as they turned away from her. Been there, done that. She finally gave up trying to build a circle of friends.

She was the odd one out in school. No boys had ever been brave enough to ask her out, even though her beauty had been tempting. Instead they laughed at the girl who wore gloves and never joined in. They laughed and told stories behind her back, and the whispers she heard had cut deep. Everyday she came home to her mother, and every day she lied, telling her mother her day had been good. Her mother had her hands full with her own gift, and she would never willingly add to her burden.

When she finally graduated from high school, Dee entered college. There it was easy to go unnoticed in the sea of students moving from class to class, each having their own problems. The few jobs she had taken were an ordeal that she felt she needed to cope with so her mother would not have to support her. She learned to live with her isolation and be content with her life.

"You lie even to yourself," the voice said. It was relentless and would not let her hide behind the wall that she had built over the years. It would not let her live in the land of denial any longer. Dee clamped her jaws tight and shut the voice down in her head, getting back to work. She started the mower and began to cut the grass, trying to focus on the work at hand. A sheen of moisture dampened her dark eyes and the veins of red dulled to almost black.

The seeds of loneliness had been planted, and Roman made sure they went deep. Step one was in the books, and Roman laughed.

Chapter 33

Saul trusted Hunter to keep an eye on Dee, so there was no reason he had come to check on her. He just needed to see for himself that she was adjusting to her new life and that all was well. What he found was Dee riding her mower with tears in her eyes and sadness in her soul. He never once considered calling her protector to handle the situation. Instead he gently placed his hands upon her shoulders and took her sadness into himself. In doing so, he was able to see the cause of her distress, and his heart hurt along with hers. What should he do? He wondered this, after lifting her burden and leaving her to continue her day in a much happier mood.

He tasted bitterness on his tongue, knowing the Dark had been there and was responsible for the state in which he had found Dee. He needed to find someone to be there for Dee, to give her comfort when she was alone without tampering with her destiny. Saul walked the cemetery unseen by human eyes as he pondered the problem before him. He walked up and down the straight rows, weaving in and out of the headstones, looking for inspiration. Suddenly he stopped and stared at the answer, as it huddled in the tall grass, hungry and alone.

Saul bent down and gently lifted the small bundle of calico fur, cradling it against his chest. Its tiny mews were weak, and he knew its time was short if a human did not come to its aid. Saul had no fear that someone would see a kitten floating in the air, as he extended to this small creature his ability to travel unseen, undetected.

"I have a plan for you, my little one," Saul whispered into the oh-so-small ear. "I am going to place a human into your care, and I trust you to give her love and warmth. She is alone like you, and needs you to give her a forever home in your heart. Are you willing to do this for me?" he asked. The kitten looked into Saul's dark eyes, snuggled her head under Saul's chin, and began to purr in acceptance.

"Thank you, my friend," the mighty Guardian said. "Watch over her well and be her friend. Should you sense danger, you have only to call and I will come."

He moved until he was a few headstones ahead of Dee. Then, he gently placed the kitten on top of one and stood back to see if his plan would work.

Dee was paying close attention to her work until she pulled along side a stone and happened to look up. She killed the engine and sat for a full five seconds, staring at the small kitten that perched on top. It looked at her with such hope in its eyes that Dee could do nothing less than scoop it up in her hands and cradle it to her heart. It was nothing but skin and bones and Dee's heart picked up speed as she wondered what to do.

"Come on, baby," she said, as she began to walk back home. "We're going to get you warm and fed." She walked quickly, never breaking stride until her feet hit the first step of her porch.

Opening the door, she headed straight for the kitchen and the milk in the fridge. After pouring a small amount in a saucer, she put it in the microwave for a few seconds to warm it up, then set it on the counter and gently placed the kitten before it. It clung to her with tiny claws and mewed in protest at being pulled from the warmth and comfort of her beating heart. Dee kept her hand on its back and directed its nose towards the milk, hoping it would be able to drink. She had never had a pet before, so had no idea if the tiny creature was weaned from its mother or not.

She didn't have long to worry, as it got a whiff of the warm liquid and dove in headfirst. It ate as if it was starved, and Dee smiled as she crooned encouragement to it. She let it drink all it wanted, before picking it up again and gently stroking the soft fur. Her heart melted when it cuddled under her chin and the first soft purrs vibrated into her chest, warming her soul.

"Oh baby," she said into the tiny ear. "You are so sweet, aren't you? Yes, you are such a pretty thing." Dee continued to whisper to the small kitten in a low soothing tone until the tiny body relaxed in her arms and, giving her its trust, fell asleep. Putting all of its faith in her to keep it safe and warm, the kitten was able, in a few seconds, to wipe away the lingering emptiness from Dee and fill her with joy and purpose. Dee had found something that needed her. She was sure this baby had been sent to share her life, needing her as much as she needed it. "What should I call you?" Dee whispered, as she walked with her sleeping ball of fur. "First you're going to have to tell me if you are a girl or a boy you know," she said, stopping in front of the bathroom mirror so she could look at her new friend without waking it up.

The fur was deep black with spots of yellow gold and a streak of snowy white mixed together, and was as soft as anything Dee had ever felt. "You look like a girl to me," she said, smiling at the sleeping bit of fluff. "I can always change your name if we figure out you are a boy," she said, making up her mind to think of her new friend as a female for now. "How about we call you Callie, Callie Co?" Dee liked it, and gently rubbed her chin over the back of her new responsibility.

"Now for the hard part," she thought. "I'm going to have to get some supplies." She made a list in her head as she fetched her keys, grabbed her purse, and headed out the door. She got in the car, shut the door, and grabbed a sweatshirt she always carried in the back seat before buckling her seatbelt. Arranging it in her lap in soft folds, she ever so gently snuggled the kitten in the make shift bed before heading her car north and back into the city.

Dee drove to a pet store not far from her mother's shop. One that she knew would let you bring your pets in with you. She gathered up Callie, and went in to buy out the store.

First came a litter pan and the litter to go with it, then a scoop for cleaning up. She then chose some kitten food, wet and dry. Next came a few toys and a brush for grooming. And oh yes, she couldn't forget a bed to sleep in and a tree thingy to climb on and scratch up. She looked at collars, but the tiny neck was too small for any on the shelf so that could wait until later. So, satisfied with her choices, Dee took her purchases to the counter, she swiped her card, grabbed her bags, and headed back to her car.

Before heading home, Dee made one more stop, unable to resist showing her mom what she had found today. "Hey, Mom," Dee called out, as she mounted the stairs. "Where are you?"

Hannah met her at the door and smiled with pleasure in seeing her. "This is a surprise," she said, closing the door when Dee was in. "What's up?"

"I have a surprise," Dee said, with her back still to her mother.

"Umm," Hannah paused. "Is it anything like the last one?"

"No, Mom," Dee said, turning so Hannah could see what was in her arms. "I had to stop and show you what I found today. Or maybe she found me, I'm not sure."

Hannah moved closer until she was able to see the small bundle nestled in Dee's sweatshirt with its big eyes looking up at her.

She smiled.

Chapter 34

It was two hours later when Dee and Callie left to head home. Hannah had fed both, petting and showering attention on the newest member of the family, until there was no question that the Priest family had grown in numbers from two to three. As Dee and her bundle were getting ready to leave, Hannah made a wise statement, one that Dee had not considered.

"Don't forget to get her checked out by the vet before too long," Hannah suggested.

"Okay, Mom," Dee said, realizing she might have missed that one if Hannah had not brought it up. "I think I will wait about a month or so and get her fixed at the same time."

"You're going to make a great pet owner," Hannah said. "Drive carefully and call me if you need anything." She waved, calling, "I love you" as Dee pulled out onto the street.

"Love you, too," Dee said, waving at her mother as she drove away.

The trip home seemed just that, a trip home. Dee had someone to share her home with, someone to come home to when she was away.

Dee kept her new friend in her lap, her hand busy brushing the soft fur as she drove south. In no time at all they pulled to a stop in front of their house. All was quiet as Dee turned off the engine, except for the motor running full bore in her lap. Dee cuddled Callie in one hand and grabbed her treasures in the other, before making her way inside and closing the door.

It didn't take long for her to set up the house and place all the new items to her and Callie's satisfaction. Litter box by the back door, toys and cat tree in the living room, and her bed right beside Dee's. Dee filled the litter box right off and placed the kitten in it, hoping it was not going to be too difficult to housetrain her. She didn't have to worry as Callie stepped right in and did her business without blinking an eye.

"What a good girl you are," Dee praised, as she scooped her up and reinforced her actions with positive feedback. "Such a smart baby you are."

Callie again purred and snuggled down in the arms that protected her. If she could have spoken words, she would have thanked Dee for taking her in and for loving her, because that is what she was feeling from her human, love. Instead she did the only thing she could, snuggle and purr.

Dee took her to the kitchen and was forced to let her down as she cleaned up the dishes and found a place in her cupboard for the canned cat food. She opened a can and placed a good-sized teaspoonful in Callie's new bowl before bending over and setting it on the floor. She was pretty sure that she would be hungry, after drinking only milk at Hannah's.

Callie walked over and gave the food a sniff before digging in with gusto. Dee smiled and stood up, leaving her to finish at her leisure. Dry food and water were next on the list, and by the time they were set in their permanent spot, Callie had licked her plate clean and decided exploring was the next order of business.

Dee waited until Callie wound down before showing her her new bed. She watched until the kitten curled up and went to sleep, before exiting the house and bringing the mower back to the shed. She still had lots of daylight left, but she opted for spending Callie's first day in her new home with her.

Putting everything back in its place, Dee shut the shed and headed for home. She walked with a spring in her step, feeling better than she had in a long time. She had a new job, new home, and now a new friend. Well, to be honest, Callie was the second new being to come into her life in the last few days. Maybe Hunter would show up tomorrow and she could introduce him to her new companion.

Dee smiled to herself as she stepped onto her porch and opened the door, eager to be home. Strange sounds greeted her as she stepped inside, and it took a couple of seconds for her to figure out what she was hearing. It was a guttural growl coming from Callie.

Dee rushed the few steps it took to reach the living room and stopped to stare at her new bundle of fur.

Callie was crouched down with her fur ruffled and her ears back, growling at the shadows in the far corner. Her eyes were nearly black, and the sounds coming from her small throat were deep and mean.

"Callie, baby, what's wrong?" Dee asked, trying to calm the kitten with her words. Callie gave an evil hiss before backing up to where Dee stood.

Dee bent over with care and lifted the tiny creature into her arms. She stroked her fur and kissed her tiny head, but was having no success in calming the angry kitten. Her body stayed rigid, no matter what Dee tried to do.

A few minutes later, without reason, Callie suddenly relaxed and crawled up under Dee's chin.

'Well, that was weird', Dee thought, as she calmed herself, the event obviously over. Little did she know, or suspect, that Callie had stayed on guard until Saul came to the rescue. With Saul's coming, he sent the Dark being that had been spying in the corner fleeing back into darkness.

Saul folded his great expanse of wings back into place only after he had made sure there were no more threats lurking in the shadows. He stood before Dee as she held and stroked Callie, and looked into the big eyes that stared up at him.

"I heard your call," he said softy to the kitten, before reaching out a hand and stroking the small head. "You have done well and I am thankful for your warning. You were right in guessing the thing in the house meant to harm Dee." Callie responded by purring and blinking her great green eyes.

Saul smiled and stepped back. "I have sent a protector for your human and you will know him when you see him. You will not be alone. When he is not here, I will rely on you to warn us of danger and to keep this mortal safe." The great green eyes blinked in understanding, and Saul could see the might of a lioness contained in this small body. With one final stroke on the head, Saul too, disappeared, leaving Callie to watch and guard Dee.

He went to find Hunter, but would return if Callie called. The Dark just didn't learn and he was more than willing to dole out a few new lessons. But first he needed Hunter. The Guardian had better have a good reason to be absent from Dee's side.

Good indeed.

Chapter 35

Saul did not call out to the Guardian Hunter Gunn, but instead searched until he found him sitting on the same rock he had taken Jaxon and himself to not long ago. Hunter was there, but he was not alone. Two other Guardians and a new spirit were there also. Rather than interrupt, Saul hung back and listened to the conversation, smiling to himself when the group joined together in laughter. It was good to hear Hunter laugh along with the Guardians, Sam Barnhart and Ashton Rider. Saul finally recognized the spirit that had yet to be introduced to the legion of Guardians as David Tower.

It seemed David was telling them some of the funnier things that had happened to him in his mortal life. The tales made the Guardians laugh as the group bonded. It was the way of things. It was how the transition was made easier for those who came to join the protectors of mankind.

Saul looked at David. Instead of the old man he had been on earth, he now was young, strong, and appeared the way he had been in the prime of his human life.

"I see you have decided to join us," Saul said, as he made his presence known.

All three turned to look at the mightiest of the Immortal Guardians as he joined them.

"I am Saul," he said, looking at David, waiting for him to give his name.

"So I've been told," David said, holding out his hand for a shake.

Saul smiled at the mortal gesture, but complied as expected by firmly gripping the hand in greeting. "Welcome," he said. "I hope Hunter, Sam, and Ashton have been making you feel welcome before you are given to another for training.

"Yes, they have," David replied, his voice as strong as his grip. "I met this one before, well, before...you know." he said, a nodding gesture to acknowledge Hunter.

"Before he died?" Saul provided.

"Yes," David said, feeling uncomfortable as yet talking about death, not knowing if it was acceptable or not.

"First things first," Saul said, as he looked at Sam and Ashton standing side by side. "I see you both have adopted the more casual look started by Jaxon."

Ashton looked down at her body and then at Sam, liking their new looks better than the robes they had originally worn. "I like it," she said, totally comfortable with the blue jeans and deep red long-sleeved tee shirt she had chosen. The deep red of her shirt could not compare to the rich red of the wings that graced her back. Her dark hair flowed back from her beautiful face, and she fairly glowed with happiness and contentment.

Saul smiled at her and nodded his head in agreement. "Yes," he said, "you look very nice."

"Nice?" she asked. "I think I look better than nice."

Sam laughed at her banter and hugged her close to his side. Since Ashton had come for him, they had become inseparable. Having been soul mates in life and now as Immortals, made them a good team for their charges.

"How have you been, Sam?" Saul asked. "It's been a while since we last met."

Sam nodded his head. "Yes," he said, "it has. I've been well, thank you."

Saul liked the way Sam looked, his choice of attire being black slacks and a dark grey dress shirt, with the sleeves rolled up to his elbows. His choice in clothing was not as casual as the rest, but it fit his personality to a tee. Business-like and professional, just the way he had been as a human. Only here he did not kill. He had chosen to be a Guardian to stay with Ashton, instead of a Hunter like Jaxon. Saul had understood his decision and was happy for the two.

The grey and black of his clothing matched the wings that he sported on his strong, muscled back, black on top, growing lighter until the tips ended in a pale, pale grey. His dark hair ruffled with the breeze, and Ashton brought her hand up to brush it from his face.

"It's good that you are here," Saul said to the couple. "You have been assigned the training of our newest member, David. I am curious though." he said to David, "Why didn't you choose to pass on and be with your wife and son?"

"I got to see them," David said. His eyes looked at something the others could not see. "I got to tell them how much I missed and loved them."

"But?" Saul asked, as David paused

"But they understood that I still had more to do. They will be waiting for me when my work here is done." David finished, a look of love in his eyes for his family.

"How will you know when your work, as you say, is done?" Saul questioned

"I'll know," David said, "I'll know."

"So be it," Saul said. "I will leave you to begin."

"Well, if you don't mind," David said, "I would like to change my clothes, too. I don't really see myself in a dress."

Sam stepped forward and told him what to do. Before long he stood before them in the clothes he had been most comfortable in. He looked down at the soft, worn jeans and a blue and grey plaid shirt and he sighed in pleasure. "I feel better," he said, "except for this itching in my back. Is this supposed to happen?" he asked, as the itch grew a hundred fold in intensity.

The four Immortals stood back and waited for what was to happen next. It didn't take long before a pair of wings grew and spread wide. Their color was the smoky blue of a sunset after the sun had dropped below the horizon.

"Well, I think I can live with this," David said, flexing his new wings.

Sam and Ashton bracketed him, as they made ready to give him the knowledge he would need to be a powerful Immortal Guardian.

"See you later," Sam said, bidding Hunter and Saul good bye, before disappearing with David and Ashton.

"Later," Hunter said before turning to Saul. "I assume you came to find me for a reason?" he asked.

"Dee needs you." Saul replied. "Now!"

Hunter frowned.

Chapter 36

"Why do I get the feeling you are reluctant to return to protecting Dee?" Saul asked, sensing Hunter's hesitation.

"Are you sure, you and Jaxon I mean, that I am the best choice for this assignment?" Hunter asked, turning his back to look out over the mountain scenery.

"Jaxon did not consult with me when he chose you to protect his daughter," Saul said, giving Hunter the time he obviously needed before he could face him again. "That being said though, I think he chose wisely. Why?"

Hunter took a deep breath and let out a long sigh before turning back to Saul. He stuck his hands in his pockets and clenched his fists before continuing. "I had forgotten the feelings that humans have," he said. "I'd forgotten even though I've watched mortals deal with emotions every day since I became a Guardian."

"And what feelings are you having trouble dealing with?" Saul asked, ready to help.

"Feelings of attraction," Hunter gulped out. "I felt something the first time I met Madison Priest, Dee if you will. I got kind of shaky and my mouth got all dry and sticky. I wanted to touch her, hold her hand, and feel her against me. It made me pull back and leave her alone, when I should have been by her side to ward off the Dark. What's wrong with me, Saul?" he asked, almost dreading the answer.

Saul had a feeling this was what Hunter was going to say even before he began to speak. "You said it yourself, you are attracted to her. There is nothing to fear here," he continued. "Why does this make you want to leave her alone?"

"I'm not sure what will happen if I spend the time I need to with her to keep her safe, as Jaxon wants," Hunter ground out. He hated the weakness he was feeling, so he clamped his mouth shut, until a tick began pulsing along the stubble-covered jaw.

"Would you rather I go to Jaxon and ask him to pick another? Someone that will spend the time with Dee that you don't want to?" Saul goaded.

Hunter's green eyes shot fire, as he thought of another with Dee, just as Saul knew he would. All he could force passed his stiff lips was the word," No!"

"Very well," Saul returned. "Then you must go back and find a way to tolerate being the shield this mortal needs between her and the Dark. Since you left her alone, I have placed another creature by her side to warn her of danger," Saul said.

"Who?" Hunter demanded, bristling with anger at the interference.

"Not who, but what," Saul calmly replied. "I have given her a feline that will keep her company and hold back the feelings of loneliness the Dark has tried to instill in her.

The kitten needed a human to love and to take care of her and Dee needed something to keep her company. I've seen in this kitten the fierceness of a lion. I have spoken to her, asking for her to be the warning bell when we are not there. I have given her the power to hold off a Dark Being until help arrives, but the cost may be her life. This creature will not be enough to save your human on her own, but she will be an aide to you, should you not be by Dee's side when they attack."

Hunter ran his hands through his thick hair in a totally human gesture of frustration. Saul stayed quiet, letting him work this out on his own. "I'm scared, Saul," he finally admitted, getting to the heart of the matter. "I'm scared of feelings that may grow. Feelings I never even had when I was human. Why now?"

"Maybe it is your destiny that is finally being fulfilled," Saul supplied. "I can not say."

"Can not or will not?" Hunter shot back.

"Does it matter?" Saul asked, having no intention of giving the Guardian the answer that he wanted.

"Make your decision now," Saul said, forcing Hunter to act. "Do you return or do I call Jaxon and tell him to find another? The Dark will not wait for you to find the courage to decide. It wants to use her to get revenge for Jaxon not choosing to join their dark forces. It will do everything it can to make her life a hell on earth, unless we stand against them. Choose."

Hunter felt torn in two. He knew if he went back he would end up wanting something that could never be, something he already desired. But if he did not return, Dee would be given to another. Could he live with that? With his heart on fire and his blood boiling, Hunter coiled his muscles, threw back his head, and let loose a roar that shook the tree-lined earth. His heart broke open and bled for the sacrifice he was being asked to make. The sacrifice being that this heart that was breaking now would be ripped to shreds when he had to leave Dee behind. Could he do it? Could he do it and still want to exist afterwards?

Could he?

Chapter 37

Dee awakened the next morning as the sound of a train invaded her sleep. She frowned without opening her eyes, trying to figure out how she could hear a train when there was none within miles of her home. Giving up trying to sleep, she opened her eyes and realized the sound was not a train but a fuzz ball of fur that was perched on her pillow, watching her sleep with sparkling green eyes.

"Good morning, Miss Callie," Dee said, reaching her hand from under the covers so she would be able to stroke the kitten in greeting. "Are you hungry?" she asked, when Callie mewed loud and long. Callie seemed to know what she had been asked, as she jumped from the bed and headed towards the kitchen.

Dee, sporting a huge grin, swung her legs over the bedside and rose to follow. When she entered the kitchen, Callie was sitting in front of the cupboard looking up in anticipation of breakfast. Dee got the food and again put a healthy spoonful in Callie's dish before setting it on the floor in front of her friend. Callie gave her a grateful look before digging in, appearing to be just as hungry this morning as she had been last night.

Dee left her to eat while she went into the bathroom and readied herself for the day. Making it quick, she went back to check on Callie's progress, finding her licking the bowl as she finished. "What shall I do with you today?" Dee asked, as Callie tried to crawl up her pants leg. "Shall I bring you with me while I work, or would you rather stay here in your new home?"

As if in answer, the kitten bounded to the front door and looked back at Dee in anticipation.

"Okay," Dee said, grabbing her things together. "We'll give it a try." She scooped the kitten up and went outside. The morning was clear and bright, perfect for spending the day outside. Getting the mower out and loading it on the trailer was accomplished, without Callie running away in fright. She seemed to know that the noise came with her need to be by her human's side.

Dee drove to where she had left off the day before and in no time, with Callie sitting on her lap, Dee picked up where she had left off. The grass was dry and the mower made short work of the tall weeds, until the catcher was full and needed to be dumped. Dee was careful and dumping went off without a hitch.

The day continued uneventfully as Dee systematically mowed until the first two rows of the cemetery were now visible for what they were, headstones. The trimmer was a little more difficult to maneuver, but Dee took her time cutting around each stone, picking up the piles she made until it was time to stop for lunch.

Shutting everything down, she reached into the pickup and grabbed a lunch pail filled with both their food. Before heading over to a big tree and sitting down under it, she pulled out a dish and took the lid off, exposing Callie's food which she set down in front of her.

While Callie ate, Dee unwrapped a sandwich for herself and popped the top on a pop, taking a long cool drink before digging in. The two ate in silence, enjoying each other's company. When they had eaten their fill and sat relaxed in the grass, Callie crawled onto Dee's lap, curled up, and fell asleep while purring.

Dee closed her eyes for a few seconds, listening to the breeze as it rustled the green leaves over her head. She must have dozed off, because she did not hear the foot steps approaching until Callie stirred in her lap, digging her tiny claws into Dee's leg for a second, bringing her painfully awake. "Ouch, honey," she said, trying to release the claws from her jeans.

"Aw, the joys of owning a cat," a deep voice said, carrying a smile that reflected onto his handsome face.

Dee jumped and a small squeak escaped her mouth as Hunter announced his presence. "I didn't hear you come up," she said, trying to wet her dry mouth as she swallowed.

Hunter crouched down on his heels and reached out a hand to pet the animal who was looking up at him from her lap. He enjoyed the soft warmth of the kitten, having forgotten how nice it was to feel life. "Who's your new friend?" he asked, lifting his eyes to gaze into the pair from which he had tried to stay away. Tried and failed. His need for self-preservation paled compared to the need he felt to be with Dee.

"Umm, this is Callie," Dee said, lifting the kitten and handing it to Hunter, glad to have a distraction for her hands so they would not reach out and touch the face next to hers. She licked her lips when their hands met, as the little body was transferred from human to Guardian.

It did not occur to her, and would not until later, that when their hands touched she had felt nothing. Nor had she seen anything! Nothing at all! For the first time in her life, all the while possessing her gift, she had not been able to see the past of the person she was touching.

What did it mean?

Chapter 38

Dee woke up the next morning tired, but happy. She had spent most of the night thinking of Hunter, replaying the day over and over in her head. In her dreams. As she was lying in the dark with Callie curled up at her side, it hit her. She realized that she had not been able to see Hunter's past when their hands met. The confusion she felt was short-lived though, as thoughts of the way he made her feel when they were together crowded all else from her mind. She had no idea that Hunter had come to her and took those thoughts away before they could cause a problem and raise questions that he had no intentions of answering.

Hunter had spent the afternoon with Dee, working alongside her until the sun began to set and it was time to put their work away.

"Would you like to stay for dinner?" she had asked, as they stood in front of the shed, neither one wanting to be the first to say good night.

"Yes," Hunter said, clearing his throat, when his deep voice cracked. "Yes, I think I would like that."

Dee smiled as their eyes met. It wasn't far to the house so Dee turned and led the way with Callie cradled in her arms. Hunter followed her up the steps and reached around her with his taut muscled arm to hold the door for her. Dee smiled to herself and stepped under his arm and moved to the safety inside the cozy house and Hunter followed her, closing the door behind them.

Dee turned to put her gloves on the shelf but stopped short not realizing he was so close behind her. Just turning around had brought her within a hand's breath of his wide chest, and it filled her vision until she could see nothing else. They stood that way until Callie broke the spell, letting them know that it was her suppertime and she was ready to get to it.

Dee cleared her throat, there seemed to be a lot of that going around, before stepping back and heading towards the kitchen. "The bathroom is down the hall," she threw over her shoulder, "if you would like to wash up while I feed Callie."

Hunter smiled as he detected the nerves in the warm voice, and relaxed knowing he was not the only one on unfamiliar ground here. "Thanks," he said, changing directions. "I think I will clean up a little."

"Check in the cabinet for clean towels and whatever you need," Dee said, from the kitchen. She fed the cat and noticed her hands were not quite steady dipping out the food and putting down fresh water. She had never had a man alone with her in her house before, so she was nervous and unsure what to do next. Should she change her clothes or make them some drinks? What should she make for them to eat? Definitely not sandwiches as that was all she had fed him since they had met.

'*Take a breath,*' she told herself, '*just breathe and relax*'. With a handsome man in her house she doubted relaxing was going to be easy.

"Your turn," Hunter said, coming up behind her on silent feet.

Dee whirled and her hand made a grab for her heart, before it could jump out of her chest. "You have to stop doing that," she panted.

"Doing what?" Hunter asked, confused as to what he had done.

"Sneaking up on me," she replied, hoping he hadn't noticed her trembling hand.

"Sorry, I'll try to stomp harder from now on," Hunter said, giving her a smile that turned her bones to jelly.

"I'll be right back," she said, backing up towards the door. "You can make yourself a drink, or there are other things to drink in the fridge."

Hunter just continued to smile until she turned her back and fled into the bathroom.

"How did things go today?" Saul asked, appearing where Dee had been standing.

"Good," Hunter said. "Are you going to be checking up on me all the time?" he wanted to know.

"No," Saul said, glancing down the hall to make sure Dee did not come back while they were talking. "I just wanted you to know that there was a Dark being here the night before last and you should be on your guard."

"How do you know the Dark was here?" Hunter asked, standing up straighter, more alert.

"Callie warned me," Saul said.

Hunter glanced down at the kitten sitting by his feet watching them. "She did, huh?" he asked.

"Yes, she did," Saul said. "I asked her to watch over Dee when she was alone and to send a warning should she find trouble. She did and I came."

"Well, I'm here now," Hunter said, reaching down and picking up the kitten in his arms. "You can take the night off from guard duty," he said looking into the big green eyes, which stared back at him. "We'll make a good team, won't we?" he asked, as Callie began to purr, giving him her approval.

"If you should need me, just call," Saul said, cocking his head as he heard Dee open the bathroom door. "I will stay close." With that, he disappeared before he was seen.

"What are you hungry for?" Dee asked, as she entered the kitchen.

"This," Hunter said, as he gathered her in his arms, took the plunge, and kissed her.

Saul smiled.

Roman burned.

Chapter 39

Dee's world did more than spin when Hunter pressed his lips to hers. It turned upside down and inside out all at once. 'Where had that come from?' she wondered for an instant, before her world was reduced to a pair of warm lips, strong arms and a hard body.

'I should stop this,' she thought. She knew nothing of the man she was letting kiss her, and warning bells began to tinkle the deeper the kiss became.

"What if he is a serial killer?" a tiny voice in her head asked. *"What if he is involved with someone else and was just playing with you?"* it whispered slyly. *"What do you really know about this man?"* The voice finished up, successfully putting her on guard and destroying her pleasure in the moment.

Hunter knew the instant a Dark being had begun to whisper to Dee. Her kiss had tasted sweeter than anything he could ever remember, and she had melted into his arms, into his body, and into his soul. That is until the bitterness that came with the Dark almost burned his tongue and stole his enjoyment of the first mortal kiss he had had in decades.

Hunter felt Dee stiffen against him, and when she would have pulled back, he tightened his arms and tucked her head under his chin as he bent his body to hers in protection.

While doing this Hunter slipped inside Dee's mind, to look for the Dark that he knew was hiding there. He found it, too. Found it hiding in a corner, hiding until it discovered a Guardian was on its tail and tried to flee. Hunter was never going to allow it to escape, as he reached out hands that closed around its throat, like the death grip that it was meant to be.

The Dark little weasel squirmed and wiggled in a futile attempt to escape with its life, but Hunter was having none of it. He added power behind his grip and smiled in satisfaction as the wisp of evil burst into flames, its screams echoing until it was no more. Hunter dusted the ash from his hands and, satisfied there had been only one threat, withdrew from Dee's mind.

He was alarmed when he came back to find Dee holding her head in pain. Her muffled low moans hit Hunter hard, as he realized he was the cause of her pain, having destroyed the Dark menace in her mind, leaving behind pain in the aftermath. Hunter wanted to kick himself for not considering this aspect before he engaged the enemy.

"Shhh," he crooned softly to Dee. Putting his lips to her head, he closed his eyes and took her pain into himself. It's what Guardians did. They helped their charges by taking their pain and fears away. It's what Hunter did for Dee, and he would do more when needed.. "Are you okay?" he asked, his lips still touching her soft hair.

"Yes," Dee said softly." I don't know what came over me. I'm sorry." Her voice sounded weak and vulnerable.

"You're better now though, right?" he asked again, wanting to make sure she was okay and would say the words he needed to hear.

"Yes, really," she said, finally stepping back and brushing the hair from her eyes.

"Let's go make something to eat." She was hoping to change the subject as she led the way into the kitchen.

Hunter followed close behind, spending the next hour helping where he could and following directions as the meal came together.

Fried chicken breasts, mashed potatoes, gravy, and corn were set on the table, before they sat down and began to eat. Hunter tasted the first bite, closing his eyes in forgotten pleasure as the tastes swirled around his mouth and were swallowed.

'This is great," he said, smiling into dark eyes, watching the rivers of red deepen and glow, exposing her feelings to him. She was happy with his compliment. They carried on small talk between bites, and smiles were flowing freely by the time the meal ended. Hunter declined the offer to go into the living room while Dee cleaned up, preferring to stay close. Every time their hands touched or their bodies brushed against each other, Hunter remembered the kiss. The way it tasted, the way it felt, the way she felt in his arms, and he wanted to kiss her again.

"Would you like anything for dessert?" Dee asked, drying off her hands for the final time.

"May I kiss you again?" he asked, his voice deep with want. "I kind of took the last one without giving you a chance to say if it was okay with you. This time I'm asking," he said, as he reached out a hand and gently took her smaller one in his to pull her closer to him.

Dee's voice died in her throat, and her heart began to gallop out of control with this handsome man's sweet question.

"Yes, please," Dee said, low and husky as she stepped closer to him, waiting for him, wanting him to draw her closer again. Hunter did not disappoint.

He wrapped his arms around the human body he so wanted, pulling her flush against him.

Dee raised her arms to wrap them around his neck, as he lowered his wanting lips to the ones raised and waiting for him. Soft, sweet, and warm kisses were shared, until two pairs of legs threatened to buckle with the weight of desire each supported.

Hunter had raised one hand while he kissed Dee's lips, burying it in her thick dark hair. His hand tingled with the warmth it detected and he tightened his hold, wanting to hold her to him for all time.

"I'm not very good at this," Dee said, pulling back a hair's breath, trying to regain her balance and right her world as she felt it spin out of control. "What are you doing? Why me? I don't understand what's happening."

"Truth?" Hunter asked.

"Please," Dee begged more than asked, floundering in the unknown.

"I'm not sure," Hunter said, telling her the truth or as much as he could. "All I know is that I can't get you out of my head. From the first moment we met, you seem to be all I can think about. All I want to think about. I tried to stay away from you but I failed. I don't mean to scare you, but I need you, Dee. I need you so badly, and I am praying that you will feel the same way."

Dee let out the breath that she had been holding. And, against her feelings of self- preservation and protection, she took a leap of faith, closed her eyes, and fell in love.

Chapter 40

It was an hour later when Hunter found himself standing on Dee's porch, his thoughts his only company. His lips could still feel the softness of Dee's mouth as she pressed it to his. He could still taste the lingering sweetness of her tongue, as he invited it into his mouth and claimed it as his own. Long dead senses had been awakened, and he wanted more. He called on every ounce of his willpower not to reach out with his immortal hands and rid himself of the only barrier that stood between himself and Dee. A mere splinter of wood, in truth, but it might as well have been made of the strongest of metals, so effective was it in keeping Hunter from what he craved.

"Tisk, tisk," a voice sounded from the night's deep shadows that lay like a thick blanket over all. "Poor Guardian denied your human pet, I see. Did you forget how to be a human man when it counted?" the oily voice snickered. "Maybe you should step aside and let me show you what it takes to please a woman. Doors don't get shut in my face, ever. Who would have thought that an Immortal Guardian was so weak as to let a human control what is to be?"

Hunter's muscles bunched as he slowly turned to face the darkness at his back. Seconds before, he had been fighting his urges to stay in control, but now he smiled, cold and cruel, as he found a new target for his energies. Golden wings unfurled and green eyes blazed, as Hunter prepared for a fight with the Dark worm that crawled from shadow to shadow, unaware of the sleeping giant with which it was playing. "Mighty words," he taunted, "from a parasite that hides in the dark. Afraid to come out and face me?" he snorted in challenge.

"I fear no Guardian," the Dark shrieked, as it twisted and squirmed, showing itself as Hunter had planned. "I, Luther, hide from no one and nothing. Especially a weak Guardian such as you, that lets a human run it around by the nose. You are weak. It will be my pleasure to end your existence."

Hunter waited until Luther twisted in the moonlight before he descended the steps, heading away from the house and into the silent graveyard in anticipation of the upcoming battle.

Luther crowed in victory as he took the Guardian's departure as a sign of retreat. "You run from me?" he laughed, even as he pursued his prey. "I will turn you to ash. And when I finish with you, I will toy with the mind of your precious Dee until she screams in agony and her fragile will is broken by my power. Stop running! Stop running and meet your fate! Stand and fight me!" he commanded.

Hunter stopped when he was good and ready, but not before. He turned with wings spread wide and his hands clenched into fists. "Do you really think you were chosen because your master thinks you could win in a fight with me?" he sneered. "Are you really that stupid?"

Luther burned with the insult as he moaned out his rage. "It is you who is ignorant," he hissed. "If you think it will be anyone but me who leaves this place tonight, you are sorely mistaken. Take a last look around, because it will be your final memory. This place and my face will be the last thing you will see before I end your pathetic life. But before I do, I would like to know the name you go by, so I can brag to my fellow Dark brothers about the measly Guardian who died at my feet so easily."

Hunter allowed a slight smile to curve his handsome mouth, as he savored what he knew was to come. "By all means," he said, bowing slightly at the waist. "Let me introduce myself to you. I am known to my kind as Hunter. But I believe you may know me by another name."

"Really?" Luther said moving closer, as he prepared to strike. "What would that be?"

With a voice that dripped death, Hunter smiled and replied, "The Butcher."

Luther screamed.

Chapter 41

"Ahh, I see you've heard of me," Hunter said, watching Luther's mouth drip black drool in his shock and confusion. "Isn't this the part where you wet yourself and run, trying to save your own life?" he taunted.

Luther's fear at hearing who his foe was almost rendered him helpless. Almost. But Roman too had known what he was doing when he chose this particular minion to face the Guardian known to their ranks as 'The Butcher.' Luther was cold and knew no mercy when it came to dispatching his enemy, human or immortal alike. He took extreme pleasure in killing his victims in painful and bloody ways, bathing in their spilled blood and bragging on high about each victory.

To his credit, Luther pulled himself together and did not retreat. Instead he swallowed the fear still pulsing in his black heart and stood as tall as his smoky, wispy form would allow. "If you're waiting for me to cower down to you, then you have sadly underestimated with whom you are dealing. I've no doubt that you think you are something special, but it will only make it that much sweeter when you die by my hands."

Hunter merely stood his ground and smiled at his enemy. He had no doubt that he would come out the victor in this confrontation, but was not above playing with his target. "How unlucky for you to have been chosen to interfere with my human," he said, crossing his arms over his chest and shaking his head in mock concern. "Or was it just that you drew the short straw and this is your punishment in some kind of a bet?"

Luther pulled back black lips to smile at the Guardian and his pointed grey teeth shone in the moon light with slime and ooze. His rotting tongue flicked in and out, catching and flicking fat droplets of spit that burned the ground like acid where they fell.

To a lesser being his appearance would have been that of nightmares, but to Hunter it was nothing more than run of the mill, everyday bull crap.

"As much as I am enjoying this witty conversation, I really am bored now, so why don't we get on with it?" The human he had become was gone now, and in its place stood an Immortal Guardian. He had no need to play any parlor tricks, but as he pulled his powers deep inside, his body began to glow until the light that was his essence burned white hot and left no shadows for the Dark to hide in.

"As you wish," Luther said, and flew towards Hunter's chest with the speed of an arrow. A black arrow with sharp claws and gnashing teeth, hell bent on the Guardian's destruction and a deep hunger to taste the dead blood of Hunter when he killed him.

Hunter watched the Dark being come at him and refused to move until he could see the foam of insanity ringing the black hole of a mouth. With perfect timing, Hunter crouched and turned until his wings were in line with the black flash coming for him. He jumped with speed and grace straight into the air, drawing his wing across Luther's body, hovering with ease as his foe staggered to a stop where he had been but seconds before.

Luther looked down and brought a bony hand up, staring in wonder and disbelief as the black tar that passed for his blood ran from his fingers to pool on the ground. He didn't feel any pain and was almost in denial as to what had just happened.

But Hunter was not. He had known exactly what he was doing when he used the razor sharp edge of his wing to slice a deep cut from the Dark's hip all the way to his opposite shoulder. Normally he would have continued to cut until his foe was nothing but chunks piled high on the ground at his feet. But tonight he just wanted the confrontation over.

"Consider yourself lucky!" Hunter boomed from behind him where he had come back to earth. "I have no desire tonight to fight, so I have chosen to end this quickly. I almost wish I could leave you alive so you could take a message back to Roman to leave this alone, but I can't. You understand, don't you?" he sneered. "You threaten something I hold dear and I will die protecting her."

Instead of slicing his enemy to pieces per his reputation, he reached out death- giving hands and roared out his rage until fire leapt from them, sending Luther screaming into oblivion.

"Is that all you've got?" he questioned the shadows in the graveyard. "Is that all you've got?"

When he heard no answer, he gave a mighty leap into the air and went to find Saul. Had he stayed he would have come face to face with the leader of the Dark, as Roman appeared on the spot where Luther had just met his death.

Roman stood quietly for a moment before bending down and touching the black blood that stained the now dead grass. When he rose, he burned with anger so great that the light from the moon and all other light were sucked into his form, leaving behind only pitch black and ugliness to cover the graveyard. He wanted revenge on Saul and his hoards of Immortal Guardians for getting in the way. The Guardians were always getting in the way, and he was going to get them! Get them and make sure the punishment he dealt out would make the skies shake with cries of the dying. And Hunter was going to be first. Roman twisted with his need for wrath, moaning as he disappeared.

In the house, Callie heard the unearthly moan as it rolled from Roman's throat.

She growled.

Chapter 42

Dee woke the next morning none the wiser as to what had happened right outside her home in the dark of the night. Her dreams had been full of the sweet, hot kisses she had shared with Hunter. They had been the last things she thought of before sleep had taken her, and were now the first thing she thought of as the sun announced a new day. She smiled as she lay in bed remembering the way he tasted, the way he smelled, and the way he felt against her.

She had surprised herself by using will power she had no idea she possessed. *'Damn will power,'* she thought now. If she had only pulled him closer instead of pushing him out the door, she might have woken up to a warm male body instead of a furry one that was now making her presence known. She reached out her hands and gathered her purring friend to her chest, stroking the soft fur as she kissed the small head. Sensing the kitten's need for food, Dee pulled herself up and made her way to the kitchen to get Callie her much begged for breakfast.

It did not take long for her small companion to fill her belly and for Dee to follow suit. When both were satisfied, Dee gathered up her friend and a few bottles of water and headed out to start her day.

She mowed and trimmed, never really stopping except to give her little one some water and food for lunch. Her own appetite, it seemed, was meager so when Callie was finished Dee put her in the pickup on a soft blanket to rest and went back to work. As the afternoon waned, Dee tried to keep her mind on her work, but flashes of Hunter intruded and she could not help but feel disappointed that he had not come to join her.

The sun had traveled far into the west before Dee stopped and took stock of what she had done this day. She was surprised at the work she had accomplished. The grass that had once been untamed, thick, and wild now looked more like a lawn, the rolling green uninterrupted except for the headstones that were now visible as far as her eyes could see. She had been careful when cutting over and around the final resting places of the residents that lived here, and felt pride at the work she had done.

Hunter had set the timers for the sprinklers to water during the cool of the evenings. Dee sighed as she realized she would not be finished with the tall grass before it would be time to cut the new growth down. It dawned on her that while the weather was good she would be working from sun up till sun down to keep ahead of nature.

Dee was taking off her gloves and getting ready to call it a day when a hum invaded the peace. She stopped and looked around until she found the source of the sound. Her shoulders slumped a little with her discovery. A dark hearse was making its way up the road and, as she watched its progress, she figured out where it was going.

She was right. It came to a stop beside the spot David had chosen to be laid to rest, beside his wife and son.

Leaving her work behind, she gathered up Callie and went to join the four men as they stepped out of the car. As she neared, one of them came to meet her and held out his hand in greeting. "You must be the new caretaker?" he asked. Dee nodded her head in agreement.

"Yes," she said. "My name is Dee, Dee Priest. And you are?"

No answer came as the man stared at Dee. He stared into her unusual eyes, and before Dee could take his hand to shake it, he withdrew it crossing himself as he stepped back. Dee dropped her hand but not her eyes as she stood her ground, refusing to feel shame for what made her unusual. "And you are?" she asked again. No smile for him this time, just the question.

"Uh, oh, yes," he stuttered. "I'm Mr. Berry."

"I assume you are here with David?" Dee asked, as the now uncomfortable Mr. Berry just stood in front of her in silence.

"Oh, yes," he said, finally coming around. "I didn't have a number to call so I just went ahead with the arrangements that David had requested."

"That's fine," Dee said, holding Callie a little closer to her for support. "I will just wait here until you're finished."

"Of course," he said, and backed up to rejoin the others in lifting out the casket.

Dee watched as the plain brown coffin was taken out of the back and set over the grave. There were no mourners to sit and see the process, so without any fan fare, David was lowered into the ground. Then, with a nod of his head, Mr. Berry and his staff got back into the hearse and drove away.

Dee walked over to the grave and looked down with sadness in her heart. It was sad that no one was here, except for her and Callie, to say good-bye to David and wish him safe travels in his next life. She thought she was alone, but she was not, as David himself, Saul and Hunter stood by her side, unseen but still there.

"Well this is weird," David said, looking down at the box that held his human body.

"Weird how?" Saul asked.

"Well, I just never thought I'd be standing here at my graveside seeing the final period being put to my life." David replied quietly.

"It's not the end," Saul said, resting his hand on the new Guardian's shoulder.

"I guess you're right," David agreed. "Can she see or hear us?" he asked, nodding his head toward Dee.

"No," Hunter said, joining the conversation. "Humans can only see us if we want them to. And now is definitely not that time or place."

David smiled, as he had to agree with Hunter. When he was the caretaker of the cemetery he would have run screaming if Saul, or one of his kind, had showed up at a burial. There had been a few times when he could have sworn that he was not alone out here, but he had never been able to find another living soul.

"Are you ready to go?" Sam asked, as he and Ashton appeared. "We still have much to teach you before you are ready to be on your own."

"Yeah, I guess so," David said, stepping back from his grave to join the other Guardians.

"Take care of her," he said to Hunter, as he prepared to leave. "This place is lonely, and I know you said she's in danger. I can feel it."

"That's the plan," Hunter said, as he unfolded his wings and wrapped them around Dee and Callie, taking her feelings of sadness into him and leaving her with the knowledge that David was happy and in a better place.

Saul watched as Sam and Ashton disappeared with David and prepared to depart himself. "I'll be here if you need me," he assured Hunter. "Call if I'm needed." He said and disappeared, leaving Hunter alone with Dee and her pet.

Hunter dipped his head to rest it on the mortal he held in his embrace. He knew he had all he needed right here in his arms.

He was home.

Chapter 43

The sun had set behind the mountains before Dee moved from her vigil at David's graveside. She had felt safe and warm standing there saying her good byes to a man she had only known for a few weeks. She didn't know how, but she knew that he was happy and safe where he was. He had no regrets and was at peace.

Callie's mews had finally roused her and made her walk back to her truck to pack up her things for the day. She did not feel sad as she drove the short distance home, but a kind of loneliness seemed to be her companion as she put her tools away and headed for her home.

She held the door open wide, allowing Callie to run in before her. She pulled only the screen door closed behind her, allowing the night air to cool and freshen the air in the house after being closed up all day.

Her nights had become routine. First she fed Callie then she jumped in the shower before eating herself. Tonight as she walked into her bathroom she did not turn on any light, but instead lit candles to give the room a warm glow. The flames flickered with the cooling breeze, bathing her in their soft intimate light, surrounding her with a dark musky scent that calmed her senses and soothed her soul.

Dee left her clothes in the hamper and piled her long, dark hair on the top of her head before stepping into the shower and pulling the curtain closed behind her. The water she turned on was not hot but instead only warm enough to relax her tired body. She stood under the spray, not moving for long minutes, allowing the water to do its job as it washed away the day's tensions. Knowing she should rouse herself and wash up was pushed aside as she thought to herself, '*just a few more minutes. Just a few more.*'

Dee's hand was just reaching for the bar of soap when it froze and her heart began to beat wildly in her chest as she heard a voice speak softly to her from the other side of the thin curtain. "May I join you?" It whispered quiet and deep. Her knees turned to jelly and her breathing stopped with the knowledge of who was asking permission to join her. She swallowed hard and put a hand on the wall to steady herself before standing tall and making her decision.

Slowly she reached out, and just as slowly she pulled the curtain aside. Stepping out, she stood before Hunter, feeling small and beautiful as his green eyes blazed, almost burning her with his need for her. Without saying a word, Dee lifted her wet hands and began the slow process of unbuttoning his shirt, allowing her finger tips to follow its path as it slid from his shoulders, down his arms, falling forgotten to the floor.

She paused a brief moment to trace the chest before her and curl her fingers in the dark hair that lightly covered the hard muscles and male skin. She traced that same hair as it tapered down, following it until her seeking hands were barred from going further by soft denim. Slipping her fingertips inside the band, she let them drift lightly around to his sides before returning to the center and the button waiting there. By its presence alone, it invited her to release it, to discover the pleasures it was hiding.

She accepted the invitation.

In what seemed like slow motion, she undid the button and lowered the zipper one tooth at a time, drawing out the moment when she would push the jeans from the body she so badly wanted to know. When the last scrap of clothing lay on the floor and the only thing that separated the two bodies was the flickering shadows, only then did Dee once again raise her eyes to meet the green ones above her.

Had she done anything wrong? She was not experienced enough to feel confidence in taking what she wanted. The fire in those green eyes allowed her one indrawn breath before it was snatched away from her.

Moving back, she raised one small foot and then the other as she stepped back under the spray that now felt cool on her hot skin. Turning back, she lifted her hand in invitation, and in a voice low and sweet said the two words Hunter needed to hear to set him free.

"Yes, please." she whispered.

Chapter 44

Hunter had stayed that day with Dee and Callie, until Dee had finally moved from the grave and headed for home. He had done all he could to take her sadness and make her feel that all was well with her fallen friend. He knew the pain death caused the ones left behind, and it weighed heavy upon him every time he witnessed this mortal emotion. As much as he could relieve the pain, a sense of loss always remained and was beyond any Immortal's ability to totally take away.

He walked beside Dee as she entered the house, and stood by her as she put food down for her companion. He stayed in the kitchen when she went to take her nightly shower, not following her as he so desperately wanted.

Callie stopped her attack on her food for a moment to look up at him, and he smiled as he saw the look on her face. It seemed to say, *'well, what are you waiting for?'*

He moved down the hall. As he approached the open bathroom door, he heard the water start and the sigh that escaped Dee as she stood beneath its healing spray. He stood rooted to the spot as human emotions swirled through his body, making him feel on fire with desires he had until lately forgotten existed. '*Leave,*' his voice of reason spoke to him. '*She is not for you. You are here to protect her and nothing more.*' Hunter clenched his jaw until it ached as he fought with himself. There was no denying what was right and what he should do, but it paled in comparison to what he wanted. And he wanted Dee!!

Hunter felt what it was to be human as the battle was lost and he moved to stand outside the flimsy shower curtain, the only thing standing between himself and Dee. He bent down and took off his boots, preparing to fling his clothing aside and step into the shower. He stopped before any more clothing could be removed and swallowed hard, deciding to leave the choice up to her. The choice of whether they would spend this night together. If they did, Hunter knew he would not be easily parted from her side. He hoped she would know it too.

While he stood there, he detected a movement behind the curtain, and taking a chance asked to join her. Her hesitation seemed to last an eternity, but in reality only seconds passed before the curtain was pulled back and he saw her for the first time. Saw only her.

Her skin was wet with droplets of water that sparkled like diamonds in the candlelight, clinging to her in places that his hands wanted to be.

Hunter stood as still as a statue, waiting for her to give him her answer. But instead, she stepped out and stood before him. His human heart beat hard in his chest as he felt her small hands reach out to him, and with slow deliberation, began to unwrap his body, layer by layer. He wanted to reach out his hands and feel her flesh beneath them as she opened his buttons, but held still, reminding himself that she had not said the words he needed to hear so he would be sure it was him she wanted.

When his shirt had fallen to the floor, he almost broke, as her hands traveled on his body where his wanted to travel on hers. Her touch seared his skin and his muscles quivered wherever they were touched. He was taller than she, and the only thing he could see was the top of her head as she explored him for the first time. He was reduced to nerve endings, as her hands traveled down to his pants. He waited until finally the last barrier was removed. But still she said nothing.

When he felt he would explode with her delay, she stepped back into the shower, held out a hand to him, and finally released him from the chains that kept him from her by saying only, "Yes, please."

He took her hand in his and moved to enclose them under the warm wetness of the running water. "Thank you," he whispered in her ear, as he bent his knees so he could wrap his arms around her. "I'm so in love with you," he whispered, before his lips took hers and speech no longer was possible.

Or necessary.

Chapter 45

Dee heard the words Hunter had whispered into her ear, but from far away, as if it were a dream, not real. The only reality she knew was Hunter himself and the journey he was taking her on.

He bent his head to capture her lips in a kiss that made her rise up on her toes to better fit herself to him. His strong arms came around her to hold her to him tightly, as if she would try to escape and he could not bear for this to happen. Hunter kissed her, nipping at her lips with his teeth, tasting her mouth with his tongue, only tearing his lips from hers when his hunger to know more of her grew beyond his control. He let his mouth wander her neck and down her shoulders, sucking the water from her skin, taking her taste into his mouth and making it a part of his being. He let his fingers travel her back, going from nape to the cheeks that fit in his hands, as if made for them. He cupped them and lifted until she was on his level and above.

He groaned when she placed her hands on his shoulders and leaned back, giving him access to the pink tipped mounds, bringing them to his waiting mouth.

Dee wrapped her legs around the waist of the man who was her world, and gave herself over to the lips that seemed to burn her skin. He took her nipples, one at a time, between their softness, pulling them inside his mouth with gentle suction.

With each tug of his mouth, her body tightened and she craved more of him. She wanted him inside her, but was unable to ask for what she wanted, what her whole body needed. She had no voice. All she could do was press herself harder to him asking without words, until he rested at her moist opening. "Please," she finally got out. "Please."

Hunter heard her soft breathless plea and his whole body caught fire. He loosened his grip, only enough to allow her to slide down inch by inch until he could feel himself being taken into the depths of her body. He turned with her until her back was to the wall and his hands were holding her in place, allowing him to begin moving slowly in and out.

Dee felt him enter her and she moaned in pleasure as he filled her to bursting. She could do little more than hold on, as he entered and withdrew over and over until her flesh felt him grow even larger inside her, until her pleasures matched his. Dee felt herself come apart, and she dug her nails into Hunter's back to keep herself on earth. Even in her pleasure, she felt Hunter explode inside her and heard his moan of fulfillment, as he too reached the pinnacle of pleasure.

Both panted from their dance of love, resting in each other's arms until Hunter slipped from her body, allowing her to slowly lower her legs. He held her to him and chuckled softly as her legs refused to hold her, lending his support until she could stand on her own.

Smiling into her eyes that were only now returning to normal after the streaks of red had turned to streams of molten lava, Hunter reached for the forgotten bar of soap and bathed Dee with hands that both cleansed and aroused.

Before she could again fall under Hunter's spell, Dee took the soap from his hands and returned the favor, cleaning his body until he groaned with pleasure. Turning him to stand under the water, she lathered his hair and rinsed him one final time before shutting the water off and reaching for the thick towels hanging outside the curtain.

"Here," she said, giggling as she handed one to Hunter. She began to dry herself off and succeeded, for the most part, in removing the moisture, before Hunter lifted her into his strong arms and carried her to her bed, joining her there.

Hunter looked into her eyes and reaching up, removed the pins still holding her hair up. It fell and pooled around her head in deep dark waves, framing her face with soft beauty. He had never seen such beauty and his eyes gleamed with love.

"Was it true?" she asked, touching his face, his lips.

"What?" he asked, turning his head to taste her hand with his mouth.

"What you said before you made love to me," she said, lowering her eyes in case he denied knowledge of what she was talking about.

"Yes," Hunter said, pulling her chin up until she had to look at him. "Yes, it is true. I love you, Madison Riley Priest. Until the end of time, I will love you."

She cried.

Chapter 46

As an Immortal Guardian, Hunter had had no need to sleep but, in his human form, he fought the need, wanting to stay awake and watch Dee as she slept. No such luck was his, as he finally closed his eyes and fell asleep with Dee wrapped in his arms. He slept like the dead, not waking until the sun shone softly through the curtained window.

Hunter knew before his eyes opened that he was alone in the bed and he came fully awake in a split second, searching the room for signs of his human.

He found Dee standing before the window, the sunlight outside leaving her in shadow. Her arms were wrapped around her waist and her head was bent, her chin hidden in the collar of the shirt he had worn the night before. Her legs were bare beneath the shirttail and he felt powerful, realizing how big his body was compared to her slight frame. The shirt proved that as it covered her from knee to throat.

Hunter wanted to peak into her mind to see what her thoughts were on this, the morning after their first encounter, but he found himself feeling scared. What if she was regretting what they had shared a few hours ago?

He continued to watch her, until he decided it would be all right to simply ask her what she was thinking. So he did. Pulling himself up to a sitting position, he gathered the sheets over his lap and called out to her. "Dee?" he asked quietly. "What are you doing?"

Dee had been deep in thought and had not heard Hunter stir until his deep voice called to her, sending shivers racing up and down her spine. Taking a deep breath, Dee turned back to the bed and was held transfixed by the sight of this wonderful, beautiful man in her bed. A shy smile curved her lips and a slight blush warmed her cheeks at being caught wearing his shirt.

"I hope you don't mind," she said, waving her hands down the shirt in explanation.

"No," Hunter said, smiling in pleasure at the sight she presented. "In fact, I think I am quite jealous of my shirt at the moment."

Dee brought a hand that was hidden by the long sleeves up to her mouth and giggled into the material.

"Come here," Hunter entreated, holding out a hand that itched to touch her. "Please?"

Dee did not have to be asked twice before walking to the bed and climbing up to sit on her knees facing Hunter.

A slight frown marred Hunter's brow as Dee sat facing him, instead of climbing under the covers to lie next to him. "What is it?" he asked, taking her hand in his and raising it to his hungry lips. "Please don't say nothing, because I can see that you have something on your mind," he said, when her face betrayed her wanting to deny anything was amiss.

"I have something to tell you and I'm scared," Dee said, gripping his hand that still held hers to his mouth.

"Tell me," Hunter said, sitting up fully with his back to the headboard. "It can't be that bad."

Dee pulled her hand from his and tucked a fat strand of her hair behind her ear, trying to delay the moment when she would run the risk of chasing off the man she loved with what she had to say.

"Dee, tell me," Hunter said again, beginning to feel anxious himself at her delay.

"My family," she began, "my family is different. You've seen my mother, right?' she prompted.

"Yeah," Hunter said, seeing in his mind the beautiful woman he had met. The woman who would protect her daughter at all costs. The woman with the blood red eyes that could see inside a human and tell the true nature of that person. The one that, until Saul had recruited Jaxon as her protector, had been on the Dark's radar for extermination. He knew her well. "What about her?" he asked, as expected.

"Mom has well, for a lack of a better explanation, powers." Dee said with hesitation.

"Such as?" Hunter asked, not letting on he already knew what she was going to say.

"She can look at a person and see what their true nature is," Dee said, swallowing when she finished. "If they are good people, they don't change much, but if they are bad then their faces turn into gruesome masks. She got her abilities when she was young and has learned to live with it and what she can see. People think because of her eyes she is a freak or something, but she's not. She is a good, kind person and a great mom."

"Okay," Hunter said. "I'm with you so far. I even think I know what you're talking about. When I first met her, I felt something from her, a kind of wave of energy, I guess you could say. I take it she was what, reading me, right?"

Dee smiled as she remembered the incident well and remembered also how she could not believe her mother had done that to a man that had seemed harmless to her.

"Is that all?" he asked, as Dee had fallen silent.

"No, not exactly," she said, fidgeting with the sleeves of his shirt that had once again fallen over her hands. They hid the fists she now clenched, as the tale she was telling was about to get personal. "I kind of have abilities, too," she blurted out, spitting it out before the secret could choke her.

"Okay," Hunter said again. "Tell me."

Dee looked at Hunter and tried to see if he thought she was crazy, or if he was considering bolting from her life and labeling her as delusional. But he was sitting calmly with his hands folded quietly in his lap, waiting for her to trust him with everything she needed to reveal.

"I can't see what my mother can, but when I touch things or people, I can see what has happened to them in their lives. Good and bad. Lately, I've been able to focus my powers to just my left hand, so I can pretty much live like everyone else." A rather far away look came into her eyes as she looked at something Hunter could not see. "I used to touch my father's things and see him when he was alive. I loved to touch everything of his that my mother had. I missed him because of this, and even though he died before I was born, I always wished he could be here with us. Anyway, I just thought you should know what you might be getting into if we get involved."

Hunter reached out his hands and peeled back the cuffs of his shirt until he could enfold Dee's hands in his large, warm ones. "Nothing you've told me would make me leave you," he said, staring into her dark marbled eyes.

"I'm not finished actually," Dee said, wanting to get it all out now that she had begun. Hunter hid his surprise at this, because he was not aware of anything else that Dee could tell him.

"I'm listening," he said, with sincere interest.

"When I touch you," Dee began, "well, I don't see anything. It's almost like you have no past, like nothing has ever happened to you. That's never happened to me before and I'm kind of wondering what it means. To tell you the truth I've been trying to figure it out and I just can't find an answer. Even when my mother looked inside you, she couldn't see anything but a bright golden glow surrounding you. She said that had never happened to her either." With her secret out, Dee slumped down and released a sigh of relief. But her relief was short-lived as it dawned on her that Hunter was sitting in her bed and was not saying a word.

"Hunter?" she asked. "Are you okay?"

Hunter was indeed quiet.

He was thinking fast.

Chapter 47

Hunter had known this question might come up, but he had hoped that he had blocked it from her mind enough to keep it buried. Evidently not. 'Now what?' he wondered. Everything inside him rebelled against lying to Dee, but he really had no choice in the matter. Should he reveal to her the true nature of his existence, he didn't know what would happen. All he knew for sure was he could not tell her he was an Immortal Guardian, sent to her in human form by her dead father to keep her safe from the Dark Beings that chose to meddle in her life until she went insane.

That, obviously, would never do. The human mind was not made to understand too many things of a supernatural nature. Sure they knew of ghosts, spirits, angels and things of this sort, but when it came to Immortal Guardians, they had no clue that they even existed, and for the greater part it had to stay that way. Only a very few were chosen at birth to have the ability to see what was hidden from the average mortal being. Dee and Hannah had been two of these special ones. But even they were not allowed to see all that there was, all that was kept secret.

'Damn it all!' Hunter fumed to himself. He loved Dee, and it had taken him more than a lifetime to find her. Really, why couldn't he trust her to know what he was and to share with her everything he knew?

"Be careful," Saul's voice warned in his ear. "Should you tell her all, then this mission is over. You must remember why you are here and what you are here for."

Hunter's eyes darkened and his lips grew thin with the interference of Saul.

"Go away," he thought, so only Saul could hear. "You don't have any business coming here and spying on me."

"On the contrary, it seems that I am needed here," Saul said with certainty. "I do not come here to spy, but to give you aid when you need it. I could feel you were troubled, so I came to assist you. Nothing more."

"Really, now," a dark sly voice jumped in. "What harm would it do for him to reveal himself to her?" It was not often a member of the Dark could enter a Guardian's mind without being detected immediately, if at all, so Roman could not resist the opportunity, as he had been listening to Hunter and Saul's exchange. His stay would not be long, so he was hoping that his comment would take root and have Hunter defying Saul.

Both Saul and Hunter reacted the instant the voice spoke, each switching into fight mode and preparing to attack.

"Don't bother," Roman said, laughing at his victory. "I'm not staying. I just stopped by to give you my opinion and a fresh point of view. Haven't you discovered yet," he addressed Hunter, "that life is too short to hold back? Didn't I teach you that when I ended your life before?" With that, he withdrew from Hunter, trailing a laugh that set Hunter's teeth on edge.

"This is what happens when you let down your guard," Saul admonished Hunter. "You leave yourself open to the Dark and the seeds of doubt they plant."

Hunter burned with the rookie mistake he had made, leaving himself open and vulnerable to Roman's invasion.

"I assume you now know what needs to be done?" Saul asked, his tone meaning to sting and accomplish its goal.

"Yes," Hunter replied. "My guard will not fail again. Now get out of my head!"

Saul did not wait for a second invitation to be issued and did as asked.

He left.

Chapter 48

The exchange had taken only seconds, but Hunter could tell that, for Dee, his hesitation had seemed like an eternity. She sat tense after spilling her secret to Hunter, and his lack of response made her cringe with regret. She should have waited until later to say anything, and maybe never saying anything was what she should have done.

Hunter cleared his face of the grim look and leaned forward to take her clenched hands in his. Holding them tightly, he drew her uncertainty into himself and spoke to give her some peace. "Thank you for trusting me," he began, "with something as important as this. I knew you were special the moment I laid eyes on you, and now you have shown me that you think I too am special. You have given me a gift, the gift of your trust, and I swear I will not make you regret it."

He waited for Dee to raise her eyes to his, before he continued. "I think when you become close to a person it may blind you to faults they may have. This may be a way to protect yourself." he said in a reassuring tone.

"From what?" Dee asked, listening hard to what Hunter was saying. She wanted so badly to put her doubts to rest and be able to just be with Hunter.

"From learning everything there is to know about me and robbing you of the chance to trust me. Trust me to answer any questions you may have and trust the answers I give you. I think to know everything about me would take away the mystery that comes with beginning a relationship and having it grow. And maybe it's a sign to show you that I am meant to be someone important in your life. Can you see things when you touch your mother?" He asked this out of curiosity.

"No," Dee said, trying to examine what he had said from every angle.

"Then I think I have hit on the right explanation. It's a way of shielding yourself from knowing too much and not having a chance to get to know me by just talking to me, and I hope falling in love with me."

"It's all happening so fast," she said, swallowing a lump in her throat that had appeared when he mentioned the "L" word.

"Not fast," Hunter said, gripping her hands tightly. "None of us knows what the next moment will bring. I could walk out the door and get hit by a car and never have the chance to be with you," he said, telling her, without her knowing, what had happened to him. How he had died before.

The thought of never getting to see Hunter again made Dee's heart speed up in fear, and gave her the courage to lay down her questions and close the door on the voice that nagged at her in her head.

Nodding in agreement, Dee leaned forward until she could wrap her arms around Hunter's strong neck, and gave no resistance when he lay back and pulled her on top of his body. She melted when his hands tunneled into her thick hair and he pulled her lips down to his for a kiss that's beginning was sweet and soft. In the beginning, maybe, but Hunter deepened it until both lost all thoughts except for each other, as his lips demanded and received the taste he would surely die without.

She grew hot when his hands wandered down her back and pressed her to him, letting her feel how much he wanted her. Letting her know what she did to him. Dee felt an unfamiliar strength, knowing she held power over his body the same way he did hers. She spread her legs until her thighs bracketed his hips, and let herself rest against his desire, slowly moving back and forth until he groaned in agony, wanting to be inside her.

Dee wanted, as much as Hunter.

Neither one noticed the particularly deep shadow in the closet, so focused were they on each other, but it did not stop the form from twisting in distaste and disgust as it watched their joining. Abe had been working on Dee for days, making her doubt Hunter and her new feelings for him. Even though they had lain together last night, he had felt he was making progress in seeing that it never happened again by becoming the nagging voice in her head. Telling her something was not right with them and he, Abe, had been sure the Guardian would not be able to explain it away.

Slobbering from the black hole he called a mouth, the Dark minion could stand to watch the pair no longer and faded away to report back to Roman. His report was obviously going to be one of failure.

But he did not give up hope that his plan would still work, as he had been able to go undetected by the Guardian this once and was sure he could do it again.

"I'll be back," he giggled and gagged, as he left the closet and returned to the dark below.

"Next time," he whispered.

"There's always a next time."

Chapter 49

The sun was well up in the sky before Hunter and Dee left the comfort of her bed. After stopping for many kisses and touches, they finally made it out the door to work together as a team. Actually, a trio, as Callie refused to be left behind. Hunter stayed close to Dee, not only because he wanted to keep her safe but also mainly because he could not bear to be farther away from her than he could reach.

The smell of the freshly mowed grass scented the air and the light breeze swirled it around with bits of chaff that glinted in the sunlight. Hunter paused often to let his eyes follow Dee as she rode the powerful mower through the tall grass, leaving a lush carpet in her wake. He followed with the trimmer and cleared the last of the stragglers away so each headstone could be seen without obstructions. And, finally, he turned the sprinklers on to give the green a drink of much needed water

Before calling it a day, Dee had put the mower in gear and cleared the walking path of tall weeds. As she did, she could see where gravel had been spread so the ones who came to visit their loved ones could walk easily on their journey.

Calling to Hunter she pointed this out, and giving him a sweet smile asked, "Do you think you could somehow bring in more of the rock to make the path beautiful again?"

"I'll tell you what," Hunter said, traveling the path's length with his eyes, "I'll do that and I'll even clean up and paint all the benches you've uncovered. How does that sound?"

Dee smiled wide with pleasure at his offer and nodded her head enthusiastically. "You know between the two of us this place is going to be beautiful," she said.

At that moment, Callie decided she had had enough for one day and, becoming quite vocal, she let Dee and Hunter know too. "Come on baby," Dee soothed, as she lifted the kitten in her arms. "Let's call it a day."

Tools and equipment were retrieved and loaded, until all three were in the pick up and headed for home. Turning her head to glance out the back window, Dee was proud at what she could see. No longer were there oceans of run away grass and weeds to clog the cemetery and hide its beauty. Instead, because of her efforts and Hunter's too, there was a velvety carpet of lush green to greet the eye and welcome any visitors who came to call.

Her sense of accomplishment was huge. When the path was clothed in fresh stones and the benches painted, her work would only consist of upkeep and maintenance. Sure there were a few places where she wanted to plant some flowers and other pretties, but the hardest work was behind her. Mowing the expanse would now seem like a breeze, compared to the long hours she had put in to get it looking the way it did now.

Before she turned around the sprinklers came on and, in the fine mist they emitted, she saw a beautiful rainbow. It made her smile because she was the only one to see it, so that made it just for her, right?

A warm hand coming to rest on her thigh brought her back from her musing. Smiling up at the man behind the wheel, Dee brought her hand to rest on top of his. A furry nose and a soft paw let her know that her companion wanted some attention also. Her smile grew wide as the ones she loved occupied both hands. 'Yes life was good,' she thought, as they all three bounced along the road towards home.

"But for how long," a voice questioned in her head. *"How long will it last before one or both leave you?"'* Without knowing she did it, Dee tightened her grip on Callie and Hunter, trying to hold on to her happiness and deny the questions in her mind.

"What's wrong, baby?" Hunter asked, feeling the pressure increase on his hand.

"Nothing," Dee lied, "nothing at all. I'm just happy is all."

Hunter knew she did not tell the truth, but short of an interrogation, he also knew he would not get the truth from her. He held back from peeking into her mind. He had decided that for him and Dee to work out as a human couple, he had to treat this as a totally human relationship. He squeezed her hand a little tighter and continued on to the home they had shared the night before.

Both were quiet while tools were put away and the doors closed on another day of work. "Would you like to stay?" Dee finally asked, not willing to assume he would.

Hunter gathered her into his arms and bringing her chin up, he lowered his head and kissed her until her knees turned to water and her breath came in gasps. "Yes," he said. "I would love to stay here tonight."

Dee relaxed her shoulders that she had been holding tight since issuing her invitation. "Let's go in and make some supper then," she said and, grabbing his hand, led the way inside.

Two people walked through the door, but Callie did not. She paused on the steps and turned back to gaze out over the yard. Her green eyes grew black as she sniffed the air and stared into every shadow. Something was out there and Callie knew it. Her eyes could not find the intruder, but she sensed one just the same.

"Stay away," she hissed, as her hair began to rise and her back arched. *"You have no place here."* Her hissing turned into a growl that was deep and powerful for such a small harmless looking fur ball, but it carried the warning and its intent for all within range to hear. She licked her lips, looking back one more time before entering the house. *"Stay away,"* she thought, hissing one more warning as she flicked her tail and disappeared inside.

Abe watched as the little beast hissed and spat on the steps of the house. He sneered, as he listened to the warning it issued. His long bony fingers itched to tighten around the upstart's neck, until he had silenced her voice forever.

"You think you can stand against me?" he whispered deep and dark. "Don't bet on it!" he challenged. "I've got a plan and it doesn't include you." He, too, issued a growl, before he faded to nothing.

"I'll be back," he promised.

"I'm coming back. And when I do, we'll see if you can stop me!"

Chapter 50

Hunter awakened to find Saul sitting in the only chair in Dee's bedroom.

"Don't you knock?" he asked, finding the Immortal Guardian's presence to be not what he expected upon opening his eyes.

Saul chuckled as he stood and walked to the bed. "I have need of your assistance with one of your charges," he said, looking down at Hunter as he sat up and stretched.

"I thought you had given my assignments to another," Hunter said. He was alert now, all signs of sleep gone.

"Yes, I did," Saul confirmed, "but the Dark has made a move on one of them and I think you need to lend a hand in dispelling the threat."

"Very well," Hunter said, swinging his long legs over the side of the rumpled bed. "I'll get dressed and tell Dee I am going into town to pick up the rock for the path. I was planning on doing it anyway, so she will suspect nothing when I tell her I need to be gone for a short time."

"I will be waiting," the Guardian said, as he faded from sight.

Hunter did as he said he would. He dressed and, after taking care of his very human needs, went in search of Dee to tell her his plan. He found her on the porch with a cup of coffee in her hands and a colorful feline at her feet. "Hey, sweetie," he greeted her, as he came up behind her and wrapped his arms around her narrow waist. He bent his head and buried his lips in her hair, until he found the soft skin of her neck. The taste of her skin was all the nourishment he needed to begin his day, leaving him anticipating more.

Dee tipped her head to the side, giving him better access and leaned back against the strong body she had been daydreaming about. "Good morning to you," she said, as she turned in his arms and connected their lips. "Did you sleep well?"

Her question brought delicious images to Hunter's mind of the night just spent and he smiled. "Mmmmm," he growled, as he pulled her body snug against his. "Did I happen to thank you last night for coming into my life?"

"Not with words," Dee purred, as she could think of no better place to be than in his arms. "What would you say to taking a day off and just taking a drive, with a picnic lunch for two?" she suggested.

Hunter wanted more than anything to say yes and spend the day with her, but Saul's words echoed in his mind and he could do nothing but respond to the call for his help. "Actually I have to leave for a little while," he said, feeling her stiffen slightly in his arms. "I thought I would go pick up that rock you wanted and get the paint for the benches. I shouldn't be long and it won't take long to get the rock spread out and the benches completed when I get back. Could we do the day off tomorrow?" he asked. The half-truth that he gave as an explanation was really not setting well with him.

"You'd rather work than spend the day with me?" she teased...sort of.

"No," he said, "but I kind of figured if all the work was done, we might be able to make the day trip into an overnight stay in a hotel and stretch it out to a two or three day break. I was going to suggest it tonight, but you beat me to it," he lied.

He hated to lie. But the thought of taking her away for a mini-vacation had its appeal, and he could make it up to her, even if she did not know he was doing so.

Dee had only a second of disappointment, before it disappeared and she was able to smile up at Hunter. "I think I can live with that plan," she said with a kiss.

"I need to borrow the pick up to haul the rock," Hunter said, stepping back as he was anxious to be off. "Or at least to make arrangements to have it delivered, do you mind?"

"Nope," she said, giving her consent. "I will just do some cosmetic work on the grounds while you're gone. I have a few ideas about some flower beds and I can get them ready to plant."

"Thank you for understanding," Hunter said, gathering her close before he left. "I shouldn't be too long."

"Drive safely," she said, kissing his lips before stepping back.

Hunter walked down the steps, turning to meet the great green eyes when he reached the bottom. Reaching out a hand, he stroked the soft head and relayed a message to the look out. "Keep an eye on her while I'm away," he said quietly. This was meant for Callie's ears alone. "If you need me, just call." As he straightened up, Hunter received a wink in confirmation, and he nodded his head. Message received.

Hunter jumped in the pick up and shut the door while cranking over the motor. Putting it in gear, he headed down the driveway He waved his hand in farewell as he rounded a curve and was hidden from human sight.

The facade of his humanity fell away, and in its place a warrior Guardian, emerged. The vehicle vanished as Hunter spread his wings and headed off to find Saul. He almost pitied the Dark Being that he was about to confront, because someone was going to pay for pulling him away from Dee. And it just happened to draw the short straw.

'Bad move,' he thought as he raced away.

Bad and stupid!

Chapter 51

Roman paced back and forth as he listened to the plan his follower was presenting to him. He did not see it working for long but, for the short time that it did, he would have the satisfaction of seeing a Guardian in pain. Definitely a bonus! "Very well," he told Abe. "You may try this idea of yours out and see what happens. I caution you though to be careful and watch your back. These Immortals are smart and sneaky. If they find you out, you will most likely die. You do understand this, don't you?" he asked.

Abe kept his black eyes downcast, as he nodded to his Master. "Yes, I do," he confirmed. "But I think this plan will see not only the Guardian perish, but his human as well."

"Very sure of yourself, aren't you?" Roman asked, not being fooled for a moment. He knew Abe envied him in his position and sought favor to rise in the ranks by his deeds. And maybe even take his place someday. '*I don't think so,*' Roman thought to himself, as his eyes began to emit small tendrils of smoke and his sticks, which passed as fingers, curled into claws.

Abe would have done well to heed the warming signs, but he did not. If he had he would not have puffed himself up, and would have given pause to wonder what Roman was thinking. He should have also taken the time to see why he had displeased his Master.

"I will report back soon," Abe said, giving but a small bow before disappearing from sight.

"Will you really?" Roman questioned. He would do nothing to help his minion. Instead, he would let the Guardians do what they do best and rid him of the upstart. He had no doubt that Abe's days were numbered and his death would come at the hands of the Guardian posing as a human. But, then again, if Abe were to succeed he, himself, would have to step in and put him in his place. And that place would be a dark pit of endless night. That thought brought what passed as a smile to Roman's face and an itch to his hands to begin the deed.

'*We shall see*,' he thought, and began to laugh in anticipation of a future filled with death. Only time would tell whom it would be that fell.

Delicious!

Chapter 52

Dee kept busy making ready the places she had picked out for the flowers, for the ferns, and for the other plants. The smell of the freshly turned earth relaxed her, and she was filled with anticipation to see the final results of her labor. Her focus was on her work, so when a voice sounded at her back her response was a scream of fright. She jumped to her feet and backed away with a hand to her thumping chest. "Can I help you?" she asked the man she was now facing.

"I didn't mean to sneak up on you," he said. "I thought you heard me approach. I'm very sorry."

"No, no, that's okay," Dee replied, tipping her head to look into eyes far above her own. "Can I help you?" she asked again, taking in the complete man before her.

He was tall, well over six feet, and the sun glinted off his blonde hair, forming a golden halo about his handsome face. His skin was tan, which only allowed his bright blue eyes to appear that much more brilliant as they returned her stare, before letting them wander as hers were doing. Muscles bulged under a tight lime green polo shirt, and tan slacks covered long legs that, though covered, showed muscles to rival those in his arms.

Dee was slightly dazzled when he smiled and held out a hand for her to shake.

"My name is Abe," he said, waiting for her to shake his hand. "Abe Black."

"Yes, of course," Dee said, unable to do anything but smile back. "I'm Dee Priest," she supplied, "the caretaker here." She reached out her right hand and stared at it as it disappeared inside the clasp of the very masculine grip offered. "What are you doing here?" she inquired.

"I was told an aunt of mine was buried here, and this is the first time I've been able to visit her. I've been away." Abe replied.

"I see," Dee said, pulling her hand from his and taking a step back. "I am fairly new here, so I'm afraid I won't be much help in locating your aunt if you don't already know where she is."

"That's okay," Abe said. "I have directions."

"Well, it was nice to meet you," Dee said, wanting to end the meeting but not knowing why. "I'll leave you to your visit." Even though the sun was warm, she felt a chill race up and down her back while she stood in the strange man's presence. He was handsome and seemed nice, but she just couldn't shake the feeling that she needed to be gone, somewhere safe. Without thinking, she reached out with her left hand and came within a hair's breadth of touching him, before he too, stepped back and made a move around her.

"I'm sure we will meet again," Abe said, pinning her with his intense blue eyes. He smiled and walked away.

Dee wrapped her arms around her chest, trying to warm up and calm the instinct to retreat. Succeeding only a little, she began to gather her tools, having every intention of getting in her house and locking the door behind her.

With the shovel, hoe, and her bucket of tools she was ready to head home, pausing only long enough to call Callie to her. But her furry friend was nowhere to be found.

"Come on, Callie," she called. "Let's go, baby." Callie had always responded to Dee's voice before so when she failed to come Dee began to panic. First this strange man showed up, and now Callie was a no show. Take a breath, she told herself, don't be a fool. Callie was probably just napping under a nearby tree. Putting her tools back down, Dee went in search of her friend, calling as she went.

Callie had heard her human call to her, but she was busy doing what she did best as a cat. She was stalking prey. She followed silently, keeping low to the ground as the being walked away from Dee. She did not call this thing a human because she could smell the foul odor coming from every part of him, and she knew he was not good.

She followed until he stopped and crouched down before a headstone, brushing imaginary dirt from the name. Callie silently leapt on top of the stone and issued a low growl of dislike.

Abe raised his eyes until they were level with the cat and smiled. Not a nice smile, but one filled with ice and disdain. He would let this flea of an animal glimpse a small portion of his true self, knowing it would flee in terror. But he had underestimated his power to scare, as Callie rose up and with the speed of lightning, reached out razor sharp claws, and left deep furrows in the flesh before her.

The cheek was not so pretty now, as black blood flowed down that same cheek and fell in fat blobs, marring the headstone of a stranger. Eyes, that had been so blue before, now turned flat black, and the pearly white teeth that Abe had flashed at Dee now turned grey and jagged. Foul breath leaked from the mouth, filling the air with the smell of rotten flesh.

"I'll kill you," the Dark hissed, reaching for its attacker.

But Callie proved again her worth, as she used both paws to scratch the hands that meant her harm.

When Abe jerked back, Callie jumped down and ran for her human. She needed to get her to safety until the Guardian came back.

Dee finally found Callie, as the fur ball bounded towards her. When they met Callie jumped into waiting arms, purring in encouragement as Dee went back to gather her tools and made the trip home as quickly as possible.

Only when they were both inside, with the door locked, did Callie calm down and wait for Dee to lead the way into the kitchen and her empty bowl.

Before she followed, she sat down and sent out a call as directed.

"Danger!" she warned.

"Danger has come!"

"Danger has come, and it smells like death!"

Chapter 53

Saul and Hunter had eliminated the threat to one of Hunter's humans and were talking it over, trying to figure out why it had been so easy to defeat the Dark Being, when Saul stiffened and cocked his head to listen. Listen to something only he could hear. Hunter too became alert; as he knew something important was going on.

"What is it, Saul?" he asked, preparing to go into battle once again with his friend.

"We have to go," Saul said, spreading his wings with one powerful twitch of his shoulders.

"Tell me," Hunter demanded, as he too, followed Saul's lead and unfurled his wings.

"Callie calls," Saul said, leaping into the air and taking off like an arrow.

It took Hunter only a few seconds to catch up, allowing the two Guardians to shoot across the sky as one. His Immortal heart beat hard and heavy in his chest as he processed what Saul had just said.

"Dee is in trouble?" he asked, wanting information about his lover. "What kind? What happened? From who? Is it the Dark?" His questions burned the air, just as his wings lit up the sky with their power and speed.

"Callie said there was danger," Saul supplied. "That's all I got from her. But I am assuming it's the Dark that brings danger to her. Yes, I'm sure it is," he said, his voice coming from between gritted teeth. "I also think this answers our question about why our recent battle was so easy to win. It must have been a ploy to get us away from her side."

Hunter agreed with Saul's assessment of the situation and he growled in anger at having fallen into the trap so easily. The Guardians' wings dug deep, as they reached for the speed that would bring them to Dee's side before harm could be done to her.

The ground shook as first Saul and then Hunter came to rest, where Hunter had disappeared earlier.

"Don't forget to bring back the rock and paint you promised," Saul said, as the missing pick-up appeared and Hunter climbed in.

"I can handle this," Hunter said. "You don't need to come."

"I'm coming," Saul said, leaving no room for argument.

Hunter opened his mouth to argue, but one look at the forest fire that burned in the dark eyes made him rethink his objections. Having the most powerful Guardian at his side was nothing but an ace in the hole for him and for Dee.

"Meet you there," he said and spewed dust from tires that spun hard as he took off.

Hunter chafed at the speed of the truck, knowing he could have gotten to his destination in an instant if he did not have to take this mortal means of transportation.

He had no choice, and gritted his teeth until he pulled to a sliding stop before the front door.

"Be careful," Saul cautioned, coming to his side. "Remember you have no idea what has happened until she tells you."

"Yes, of course," Hunter said, not having thought of this before Saul brought it up. "Damn it." Taking a deep breath, Hunter exited the vehicle and closed the door in what he hoped was a normal fashion. He climbed the steps and opened the door or tried to, having found it locked. "Dee," he called, knocking on the wooden obstruction as he did. "Are you in there?" He heard the lock click and it swung open revealing Dee to his hungry eyes. "Why was the door locked?" he asked, when she moved into his arms and clung to him.

"I'm glad you're back," she said, her voice muffled in his shoulder. "Come inside," she urged, stepping back, but retaining her contact with him by gripping his hand and not letting go.

"How was your day?" he casually asked, when they were both inside with the door closed behind them.

"Good, good," Dee said, daring to relax for the first time since meeting the strange man in the cemetery. "I got the plots ready for the flowers and stuff," she babbled, walking ahead of Hunter until she reached the kitchen. "Are you hungry? Can I fix you something? I was just about to make something for myself."

The last thing Hunter wanted was to eat, but he could see she needed something to do, something normal to calm down. "That sounds good," he said convincingly. "Can I help?"

"No, I got this," Dee chirped, moving to the fridge to pull out some cube steaks and tater tots for a quick meal.

"You quit work early today," Hunter said, as she put the tots on a cookie sheet and popped them into the oven to bake. He leaned forward on his elbows, watching her flour the thin steaks and put them in a pan to fry. "Are you tired?" he asked trying to get her to open up.

"How about we eat first and then we can talk about our days?" she suggested, finding that making the meal and having Hunter by her side allowed her to finally relax and breath again.

Hunter looked over at Saul as he stood in the corner and frowned in frustration.

"Give her a minute," Saul said, for his ears alone. "She will tell you when she is ready. I will have a look outside while you have your food, but I will be back to hear what happened when you are finished." With that, he faded from the room.

"I can wait," Hunter said to Dee, as she brought the golden brown steaks to the table and turned back for the potatoes. He retrieved the dishes and set the table for two, before joining her and taking his first bite of the fare. "Yummmm," he said, as the flavors hit his tongue and ignited his human hunger. "This hits the spot," he said, letting her know that her efforts were appreciated. "Thank you."

"You're welcome," she said, as she too took a bite and found she was hungry after all.

Hunter swallowed the bite in his mouth and found he could not wait for his dessert. Reaching over, he captured her lips in a sweet kiss before licking the taste of her from his lips and returning to his meal.

Dee's cheeks turned pink and the rivers of red in her eyes glowed with Hunter's gesture.

"I'm glad you're here," she said, before dropping her eyes and toying with the food on her plate.

"I'm glad I'm here, too," Hunter said, wondering if she would still feel the same if she knew about him, all about him.

But he swallowed his confession before temptation could overcome him, and it was bitter.

The lie of omission was bitter indeed.

Chapter 54

Saul walked the cemetery, looking for any clues as to the danger that Callie had called out her warnings about. He moved as a gentle breeze, barely rustling the grass as he passed. He left nothing of himself for any human to detect, moving his eyes, missing nothing. It was not long before he found what he was looking for. The dark blood Callie's attack had shed was dry now and remained as black, ugly streaks, marring the face of the headstone where Abe had stopped. Saul could smell the rot of the Dark Being's blood, and wondered what had happened.

"I'll tell you what happened," the spirit form of Jessie Cooper said.

Saul raised his eyes and smiled at the spunky young teen now sitting on top of, instead of lying beneath, the befouled headstone. "Hello, Jessie," Saul said, giving the spirit the respect the dead deserved. "My name is Saul," he supplied. "It's nice to meet you."

"Oh, bull," Jessie scoffed. "How nice could it be to talk to me? I'm dead, remember?"

"Yes, I remember," Saul said, feeling the pain of the ghost before him. "I still consider it a pleasure to meet you though. Why are you still here?" He asked, lifting his arm to indicate the cemetery

Jessie hopped down from her perch and walked a few steps away, scuffing the toes of her sneakers through the grass before turning to look up at the Immortal.

"I'm waiting," she said, shrugging her shoulders, and placing her hands in the back pockets of her favorite jeans. Thank God her parents had had the sense to bury her in her favorite clothes, instead of some foo-foo dress or such.

"For...?" Saul asked, even though he knew the answer.

Jessie didn't want to tell this stranger, but she had not talked to another soul for a long time. So she hunched her shoulders and told him the truth. "I'm waiting for someone else I know to die and join me. Someone I know needs to get dead."

"Why?" Saul asked, when she offered no more.

"I didn't want to go to wherever by myself," she finally admitted.

"There is nothing to be afraid of," Saul said, coming to stand before her and resting his hand on her shoulder.

"Are you dead?" the young girl asked, hoping to find another like her. If he were, then she would not have to be alone anymore. She had always considered herself an interesting person, at least when she had been alive. But talking to only herself for a few years had become boring. Jessie wondered if she would be considered crazy, like the living who talked to themselves were.

"Not dead," Saul explained. "I've never been alive as you know it. I'm a Guardian, an Immortal Guardian," he supplied at her puzzled look. "It is my job and those like me to protect humans and help them fulfill their destinies."

"Well, someone didn't do a very good job protecting me," she said, as the air around her crackled with her anger.

"What happened to you to bring you here?" Saul asked, giving her the chance she needed to voice her anger about her death

"I was just minding my own business," she said, the words gushing from her as she finally had a chance to get some answers. "Just walking around, you know, and I came upon this cemetery. I decided to take a look at some of the headstones, just to kill a little time. While I was looking around, a lake appeared out of nowhere and scared the crap out of me. I mean, it wasn't there before and all of a sudden it was. Totally freaked me out! So I left! I didn't tell anyone about it, you know, about the lake I mean. Less than a week later, I was in a gas station getting some munchies, and a guy comes in and robs the place. I was just in there because I was hungry, and the next thing I know I get shot. And now, here I am. So, can you tell me what happened?" she demanded of Saul. "Why me? Why am I here? And, while you're at it, explain that damn lake to me."

Saul smiled a gentle smile and held out his hand to the young girl. "I can have all your questions answered," he promised. "But I need you to trust me and go with Ashton."

"Who's Ashton?" Jessie asked, thinking to herself how great it was that the only person she'd been able to talk to might just be a nut job.

"I am," a sweet voice spoke up right behind Jessie.

Jessie twirled around to find a beautiful woman with wings the color of blood standing at her back.

"I'm here to take you to where you need to be," Ashton said, nodding her head to Saul in acknowledgement of the assistance he had requested.

"Ashton's going to help you," Saul assured the skeptical spirit. "But before you go, I would like to hear what happened here," he said, pointing to the dried blood streaking her headstone.

Jessie stared at Ashton with hungry eyes. After all of this time Jessie wanted so badly to have a friend and a mentor, but she was afraid to trust and believe. "There was a big blonde guy here," Jessie started to explain, talking to Saul but not taking her eyes off Ashton. "He was talking to the pretty lady who takes care of the cemetery before walking over here. Then he started acting like he knew me or something."

"Do you know him?' Saul asked. His attention was fully on her story.

"No," Jessie said, shaking her head.

"Do you know what this man and the woman were talking about? Could you hear their conversation?" Saul probed for more information.

"No," Jessie responded again. "But whatever he said to her, it seemed to scare her."

"How's that?" Saul questioned, moving closer to the girl.

"Well, at first she smiled at him, but as they talked she backed up and got all stiff like. Her cat was the one that made the blood here," Jessie said, pointing to the dark lines. "It jumped up and scratched his face and hands, before running back to the lady. Then, the lady quickly picked up the cat and they rushed away."

"Did he see you?" Saul asked, mulling over what he had just heard.

"Not," Jessie said, standing up as straight as she could. "He was bad. I could feel that he was bad, so I hid."

"You were very wise to do that," Saul praised her, as he now looked to Ashton to jump in.

"It's time," Ashton said, coming to stand beside the girl and take her hand.

"Time for what?" Jessie questioned. Jessie was afraid that now the time was here for her to go somewhere where she would be even lonelier.

"I will take care of you," Ashton said, as she spread her wings and prepared to take flight.

Jessie looked to Saul, and only after he had nodded his head in reassurance did she curl her fingers around those that held hers. "Saul," she said, "take care of the lady that works here. I think she's in trouble. And I think the man that was here means to hurt her. I sort of feel it. He's deep down bad."

"I will," Saul promised her." I will."

Jessie nodded her head, accepting his promise before turning back to Ashton. "Don't let go," she whispered to her Guardian, gripping the hand that held hers with all the strength she had. "Just don't let go."

"I won't," Ashton said, letting the warmth in her voice and the touches of her hand give Jessie the courage to begin the next step of her journey.

Ashton spread her beautiful wings and slowly rose into the air, lifting the spirit of Jessie with her.

In the blink of an eye they were gone and Saul knew it was time for him to leave as well. He needed to get back to Hunter and warn him of the danger that had come.

Come in the form of a man.

A man that needed killing.

And he planned on unleashing Hunter "The Butcher" to do just that.

Kill.

Chapter 55

Hunter waited until the food was eaten, the dishes were done and Dee was wrapped in his arms, safe and sound, before pressing her gently for information about her day. Squeezing her tight and placing a kiss on the top of her head, as it rested on his chest, he jostled her and asked, "So babe, how was your day?"

"What did you find out about the rock for the path?" she deflected, but not before Hunter felt her tighten up in his arms. "I noticed there wasn't any rock in the truck. Did you get the paint for the benches?"

"Me first then," he allowed, and answered her questions. "They will deliver the rock tomorrow and the paint is in the cab of the pick up."

"What color?" she asked, stalling with whatever she could think of.

"The rock is a really pretty white and I got a dark green for the benches. I figured we could take care of everything tomorrow. I'll help with the rock and you can work on the benches until I'm finished, and then

I can pitch in there. Does that sound like a plan?" he asked.

Dee could picture how the grounds would look when the path was completed and the benches had a fresh coat of paint. "That sounds good to me," she said, and snuggled deeper into the arms around her.

"Now, your turn," Hunter said, not letting up until she dished the dirt on what had happened.

Callie walked over and jumped on Dee's lap, giving her comfort as she purred her love for her human. "We got all the spots ready for planting, didn't we, Callie?" Dee asked, petting her friend. Callie mewed her answer and both Dee and Hunter chuckled, as it appeared she had understood the question and answered in reply.

Hunter prodded when Dee would say no more. "Dee, what else happened today?"

"I met a man today," Dee started, picking at some imaginary fuzz on her jeans.

"Really?" Hunter asked, knowing this was what had had Dee so on edge since he had gotten home.

"I was just finishing up when he came up behind me and scared me," Dee said, still not looking into Hunter's eyes.

"Did he touch you?" Hunter asked, his green eyes catching fire as his protective side reared its head.

"No, nothing like that," Dee assured him. "He just started talking and I hadn't heard him come up behind me, so it scared me for a few seconds."

"What did he want?" Hunter pried.

"He just said he was here to visit the grave of an aunt is all. He shook my hand and told me his name."

"Which was?" Hunter butted in.

"He said it was Abe, Abe Black. After that, he left to go do his visiting and Callie and I came home," she explained.

"Why was the door locked when I got here?" Hunter asked, knowing there was more to her story.

"You're going to think me silly," Dee said, trying to get up, but finding the arms around her held against her efforts.

"Try me," Hunter encouraged her.

"I got the feeling from him that he was trouble," Dee mumbled. "I just couldn't shake it and I needed to get home and lock us in, so I did. He was just creepy. I don't know how else to explain it. I mean he looked normal and everything, but he made me cold. I tried to touch him and see if I could see some of his past, but he backed up and left before I could. That's all. That's all that happened before you got home." Dee took a deep breath.

Hunter glanced into the corner, and saw Saul standing there, listening as Dee had talked.

"We need to talk," he said to Hunter. "Now."

"I'm going to go get us something to drink," he told Dee, as anxious to hear what Saul had to say, as Saul was to tell it.

Hunter left Dee on the couch and made it to the kitchen, before he turned to confront the Guardian.

"What did you find out?" He asked, without making a sound.

"There was a man here today," Saul confirmed. "Dee told you the truth."

"How did you find this out?" Hunter asked. Not that he doubted Saul, but he wanted to know the source of his information.

"I talked to a Jessie Cooper," Saul said, waiting for the next question to come.

"And she is?" Hunter did not disappoint.

"A spirit who was afraid of the next step," Saul explained. "It was her headstone that this Abe stopped before, and it turns out Callie had a bit of a tussle with him before she and Dee made it to the house."

Hunter looked down at the floor, finding Dee's small protector sitting by his feet, listening to the Immortals. "Good job," he said, giving Callie the praise her actions deserved. "I am in your debt."

Callie yawned, as if to say no big deal, and began her nightly bathing, giving her permission for the story to continue.

"Jessie seems to think the being is bad news, too," Saul continued. "I think the Dark has either taken over a human body or have done as we have and come back in human form to insert this person into Dee's life. I am also certain the reason is to do harm and or death."

Hunter agreed with Saul's assessment and said so. "We need to make a plan," he said to Saul.

"About the only thing we can do is to stay vigilant until the Dark makes a move. Then we can find out what their end game is," Saul said.

Hunter didn't like this plan and shifted on his feet with irritation. "There has to be something we can do to draw this Abe out," he hissed in frustration.

"If we do the Dark will be aware we are on to them, and they may just postpone what they have in mind. We cannot afford for them to rethink what they are doing. We must wait."

Hunter wanted to curse and go hunting for Abe. "I'm not good at waiting," he said, not telling Saul anything he did not already know.

"When we are sure, we will talk again," Saul said. "You should be getting back to Dee." Before he left Hunter for the night, he paused and laid a hand on his shoulder.

"We will know when the time is right. And when that time comes, the reins of your restraint will be cut and you will hunt this being down."

"I'll do more than hunt," Hunter said, smiling. The handsome human standing before Saul disappeared, and in its place was a Guardian ready to do battle.

The Protector would be put away, and a killer would come out to play.

Hunter was ready.

Chapter 56

The night passed without incident. When Dee and Hunter woke the next morning, it seemed that Dee's fears had been laid to rest. This morning her smile had been bright and, unable to resist the beacon, Hunter kissed her until her lips turned cherry red and her eyes overflowed with stars.

Kissing Dee might have been enough to start Hunter's day off to perfection but Dee had other ideas. She wrapped her arms around his strong neck and when Hunter could have gently pulled away, she held on until the last thing on his mind was escaping.

She took the lead in their lovemaking, using her hands and her mouth on his body until finally, taking pity on him, she ended both their agony, leaving them sated and fulfilled as only true lovers could be.

Hunter reluctantly rose from the bed and took a shower, while Dee, wrapped in a soft robe, began fixing a breakfast that would fill their bellies the same as their lovemaking had filled their souls. A tall order. She hummed along with the radio and harmonized with

Hunter as, he too, sang along from the shower. Her life was good.

Licking jam from her finger, Dee answered her phone when it began to ring. She smiled when she heard the familiar voice on the other end. "Hey, Mom," she said. "How are you?"

Hannah could hear the smile in her daughter's voice and had a good idea the cause of it. "Hi, sweetie," Hannah said, setting down her morning cup of coffee. "I'm good. How about you?"

Dee smiled remembering how her day had just started, but refrained from sharing with her mother just how good she really was. "I'm fine," she responded. "What's up?"

"Well," Hannah said. "I was just wondering if you would like to grab some lunch with me today and maybe catch up a little. I haven't had a chance to talk to you since you first took the job at the cemetery. So I thought today would be a good day for a chat. What do you think?"

"I think you read my mind," Dee said, happiness in her voice. "But would it be okay to have lunch here?" she asked, thinking of the rock that was to come today and the benches that needed to be painted.

"Sure," Hannah agreed. "Should I wear old clothes?" she asked, knowing her daughter well.

Dee laughed and explained what she had going on that made her suggest they spend the day together at her home.

"It sounds like fun," Hannah said. "How about I come out, say around ten?"

Dee did a little happy dance in the kitchen, while telling her mother to drive safely and that she would see her soon.

"Who was that?" Hunter asked, coming into the kitchen just as Dee was hanging up.

"My mom," Dee supplied, and told him the plans they had made for the day.

"Does she know I'm here?" he asked, wanting to know what kind of reception to expect from Hannah.

"I haven't had a chance to tell her, but she's already met you and I think she's going to love you," Dee said with conviction.

"Love me, huh?' Hunter asked, still wondering what the day held in store for him.

"Yes, love you," Dee repeated. "I love you, so she will too."

Hunter hoped she was right, but would wait and see what happened when the fierce mother got her next look at him. Patting Dee on her sweet little butt, he sent her on her way to take a turn in the shower, while he finished up breakfast and set the table so they could eat.

Raising his cup of coffee, in a silent salute, Hunter toasted Hannah before blowing on the hot liquid and taking a sip. "Here's to getting along," he thought. "We both have Dee's best interest at heart, so allies we will be."

He just had to make sure Hannah agreed.

Chapter 57

Hannah arrived at Dee's exactly at ten o'clock as promised. Stepping out of her car, she paused to breathe in the clean air before brushing the creases from her tee shirt and hitching her work jeans up a hair. Satisfied, she reached in, retrieved her purse and closed the door with a snap.

"Hey, Mom," Dee trilled, as she bounced down the steps to hug her close.

"How was the drive out?" she asked, turning to lead the way, then stopping to look back when Hannah did not follow.

"Traffic was hell, just like usual," Hannah said, as she moved around to the passenger side door and opened it up.

"Did you bring me something?' Dee asked, unable to see into the car with the sun reflecting off the windshield

The largest man Dee had ever seen unfolded himself from the car and the smile on his face rivaled the sun as he beamed and held his arms wide.

"Hi, sweetie," his voice boomed with glee. "Come here!"

Dee squealed with joy and took off running before she gave a leap and was caught in midair by strong, powerful arms. Arms that gathered her close and almost crushed her.

"Oh, Brandon," she said, unable to wipe the huge smile from her face, "Mom didn't tell me you were here." Squeezing his neck again, she filled her lungs with the woodsy scent of her mother's friend and one of her father's men from Special Forces. He had been protecting her mother when her father had been killed. It was Brandon who had stayed with Hannah and gotten her through the worst after she was left alone and found out she was pregnant. It was Brandon who brought mother and daughter home from the hospital, and it was Brandon that had moved heaven and hell to be by their sides when something important was happening or when he was needed. Dee couldn't remember a time when this wonderful giant of a man was not in their lives and she loved him with all her heart, giving him the love she would have given Jaxon if he had been alive. "I've missed you," Dee said, as she clasped his handsome face in her hands and planted a loud smack on his lips.

"Missed you too, little one," Brandon said, accepting the kiss and giving one more mighty squeeze before setting Dee down so he could get a good look at her. "Looks like this new job your mother told me about is agreeing with you," he said, finding her healthy and happy.

"It does," Dee said smiling up, up and up into the blue eyes that missed nothing as they gave her the once over. "Come inside and I'll show you around before we have to get to work. How have you been? How long can you stay? Why haven't you called?" Dee fired question after question over her shoulder as she led the way into the house.

Brandon looked at Hannah before laughing and wondering what to answer as these questions were excitedly asked. No time really to worry about it, as he was led away by the excited young lady who he thought of as his own. When Jaxon had entrusted the care of Hannah to him, he had promised on his life that he would take care of her and let no harm come to her. He had kept his word all these years by watching over her and Dee. Even when he was in Wyoming, he had trusted men that reported back to him. Neither Hannah nor Dee knew this, but he did what he had to in order to keep them safe and well. When the news of Jaxon's death had reached Hannah and him, he had cried right along with her. In fact, not a day went by that he did not think of his friend, and continued to wish he were with them.

Through the years Brandon's feelings for Hannah had grown into a love he kept hidden. Somehow it felt like a betrayal to his friend that he had fallen in love with her, and not once had Hannah shown him anything differently than warm friendship. So he was careful to never rock that boat, no matter how much he longed for more.

He thought he was the only one that knew of his feelings, but he was wrong. Every time Dee touched him, she was able to see how he would stare for hours at Hannah's picture, and how he hungered for more than friendship from her mother. She never told Brandon or her mother the images revealed to her, but she wished that they would just air out their feelings and get it over with.

Over the years she had watched how Hannah would light up when she talked about Brandon. Even if she were blind she would have been able to tell that her mother had a love for Brandon, also. She never pushed the issue, but every time all three were together it seemed like family to her, and Dee held hope that some day it would come true.

Reaching the steps, Dee bounded up and stopped beside the man she loved, turning to make the introductions. "Brandon, this is Hunter and Hunter this is Brandon. I'm sure you remember my mother," she continued, slipping her hand into the warm large one with a familiarity that was not lost on Hannah or Brandon.

"Hunter," Hannah acknowledged with a nod of her head.

"Ms. Priest," Hunter returned, "nice to see you again."

"Just Hannah," she responded and turned to Brandon to see his reaction to the man in her daughter's life.

Bright blue eyes became hooded as the giant took stock of the man Hannah had warned him about. The soldier surfaced as Brandon's instincts told him there was more here than meets the eye. "Hunter," Brandon said, as he finally offered his hand to see what kind of handshake the new boyfriend had.

"Brandon," Hunter said and took the offered hand.

The handshake appeared to be just that to Hannah and Dee, but the two men knew better. Hunter let the man taste a little of his power when he squeezed the human flesh until the blood left the fingers. A weaker man's hand would have folded like paper.

But Brandon was not an ordinary man. He arched a brow at Hunter and smirked as he too let the younger man feel his strength. 'You got nothing on me,' his handshake said, and both appeared satisfied with the silent exchange.

"Well, let's not just stand here on the porch," Dee said, holding the door open wide. "Come inside and we can talk for a few minutes before I put you all to work."

Hannah accepted the invitation as she scooped up Callie and carried her inside.

"We brought some stuff to eat," Brandon said. "How about giving me a hand with it?" he asked Hunter.

Hunter was not fooled for a second, knowing Brandon had something to say to him that was for his ears alone. "Sure," Hunter said. "Lead the way."

Dee joined her mother inside and the door swung shut behind them, leaving the men to walk back to the car alone.

Brandon opened the car door and, reaching in, hauled out the bags that he would have been able to handle by himself. He passed half to Hunter before closing the door. He did not make a move towards the house.

"You know what I'm going to say, don't you?" he said to Hunter.

"You're going to tell me to treat Dee right or you'll hurt me, right? "Hunter said, without malice.

"Nope," Brandon said. "Close but you missed the target. I'm going to tell you that I've known Dee all her life and I love her like she is my own daughter. So I'm going to promise you that if you hurt her, I'm not going to hurt you. Nope, I won't hurt you, I'll kill you."

Hunter looked into blue eyes that had turned to steel and read the truth.

They held the promise of death. Bone crushing, bloody, painful death.

His.

Chapter 58

After an hour of touring the house and nonstop conversation, Dee herded everyone out the door and into the pick up, just in time for them to meet the truck bringing out the rock for the planned paths.

Hunter and Brandon took charge of that project while Dee, Hannah, and Callie began to dress the benches with new coats of paint. Well, actually Dee and Hannah wielded the brushes while Callie laid in the shade and appeared to supervise, purring her approval as they finished one bench before moving on to another.

It was well into the afternoon before they all stopped and dug into the fried chicken and sides that Hannah and Brandon had provided for lunch. Callie was given small bites by all four, as she was not above begging for people food that smelled so good to her.

With warm weather and full bellies, if it had been a different day, an afternoon nap would have been in order. But as it were, everyone got back to work making the best of the daylight left to them. Sunset was still an hour away when Hunter and Brandon finally stopped and looked back on their efforts. Shirts off, both leaned on shovels and wiped the sweat from their brows. It was finally done. The pathways were finally completed.

The white stone was the perfect contrast to the lush green of the lawn and gave a polished look to the cemetery. Dee and Hannah walked over to stand, each by their man, and made all the hard work worthwhile as they complimented the results over and over again until two male chests puffed up with pride at a job well done.

Of course they returned the favor and walked as a group to admire the benches as they gleamed with their fresh coats of paint. Dee was more than happy with the way the grounds were taking shape. Before the day was over the flowers and ferns were placed in their beds and, with the last scoop of dirt finding its home, the landscaping was complete.

"It looks wonderful," Hannah whispered in Dee's ear, as she hugged her tired daughter. "Let's go back to the house, shall we?" And they did.

When they reached the house, Dee and Hannah left the clean up to the men and went inside to clean themselves up and start supper.

It was a tired but happy group that sat down to a thrown together meal of ham steaks, baked potatoes, corn, and fresh baked rolls with soft butter. It took a lot less time to plow through the meal than it did to prepare it and no one left the table wanting more. Dee and Hunter opted to do the dishes while their guests retired to the porch and enjoyed the quiet of the early evening.

"What do you think?" Hannah asked Brandon, as they relaxed and rocked on the glider swing built for two.

"You mean about Hunter?" Brandon asked, his eyes half closed.

"Him, Dee's new job, the cemetery, everything." Hannah answered.

"Well," he said, sitting up a little straighter," I think the job is perfect for Dee and she seems to take pride in how well the place looks, so I'd say thumbs up to that part."

"And the other?" Hannah asked, moving a little closer to the warm male body beside her and resting her head on the strong shoulder.

"Hunter seems okay," Brandon replied, with reservation in his tone. "I think he loves her," he finally said, and without thinking, put his arm around Hannah and drew her close.

"Yea, I got that feeling too," she agreed, thinking nothing of the muscles that surrounded her, giving her a sense of security.

"You know there will be hell to pay if he hurts her," Brandon said, giving Hannah a watered down version of his talk with Hunter.

"Thank you," Hannah said. "You are so good to Dee, to both of us, you know," she continued, raising her hand to let it rest on the hard chest she was using as a pillow.

"Hey, Hannah," Brandon started, and then stopped, as his mouth went dry and his heart started to gallop.

Hannah felt and heard his heart pick up speed and her eyes opened wide as she wondered what was wrong. "What Brandon?" she asked, dreading what he had to say. Maybe he was going to tell her that Hunter needed to go and she wondered how Dee would respond to their meddling.

"We've known each other for what, twenty plus years now, right?" he got out.

"Yes," she agreed, wondering what was coming next.

"Well, for about eighteen of those years, I've had something to say to you but never had the nerve to do it."

Hannah pulled herself up to a sitting position and turned to face her friend. It was dark out and the sliver of moon was no help in letting her see what was written on Brandon's face.

"You know you can tell me anything, don't you?" she asked, trying to ease his mind and let him say what he wanted. Silence drug out until Hannah opened her mouth to fill the void but she never got the chance.

"Even if I was to tell you that I love you?" His voice was a mere whisper in the night. "Even if I told you I want to spend the rest of my life with you by my side? I've waited a lifetime, scared to tell you how I felt because you seemed so in love with Jaxon that I figured you could never love me. But I have to tell you," he said, taking her face in his warm hands, caressing the still smooth cheeks and looking deep into the eyes that had haunted his dreams, since the day he had met her. "I guess it's pretty simple what I have to tell you. I love you, Hannah Priest," Brandon said, with so much feeling in his voice that Hannah couldn't breath. "I'm planning on moving here to Colorado and I have to tell you that you're the main reason for me doing that. I want us to be a family and I want to spend the rest of my life showing you how much I love you. Please say something," he begged, as she remained silent.

Hannah had bowed her head as Brandon confessed his love to her. When she did not respond, a large warm hand lifted her chin to his seeking eyes.

Brandon did not need more light to see her reaction to his declaration, as tears of blood dripped from her eyes and stained her cheeks. He remembered few times when he had seen her cry, and his heart hurt that he was the cause of these now. "Don't cry, baby," he said, sliding his hands into her rich dark hair and pulling her head to his chest. "If you don't feel the same way, I can live with that. I don't want to, but I will," he said, trying to swallow his disappointment with her unspoken reaction.

Hannah took a deep breath and in her mind spoke to Jaxon. "*I will always love you,*" she said, as a picture of his handsome face floated before her mind's eye. "*Brandon's a good man and I think we could be happy together. But my feelings for you will never go away. It's just, I think, maybe time to put the past away and see if I could be happy with another. Please understand,*" she said to her lost love, "*and if I could, I would ask for your blessing. I will assume you wish me happiness for the decision I am about to make.*" One last time she told Jaxon of her love for him, before with a sniff and a swiping of her wet cheeks, she raised her head and changed their lives forever.

"I love you, too," she told the big man at her side." I love you, too."

Saul turned his head to look at his companion and the earth trembled, as Jaxon fell to his knees and died all over again.

Chapter 59

Brandon's hand shook as he lifted Hannah's beautiful face to his and did what he had only dreamt of. He kissed her, resting his lips lightly on hers, letting her decide when to deepen the touch. When she did, his heart grew a hundred times in size, until he thought it would explode from his chest. "Say it again," he begged, breaking the contact before he grabbed her to him and things got out of hand.

"I love you, Brandon," Hannah complied. The smile that bloomed on her face shone like a beacon in the night, drawing him to her, binding his heart to her forever.

"Shall we tell Dee?" she asked, not knowing what to do next.

"Maybe we should start by telling her that I'm moving here and kind of ease her into it from there." he replied quickly, since he had thought of this often.

Hannah nodded her head, knowing that the first time Dee touched Brandon she would get the whole story first hand. She wondered what Dee was going to say.

"Let's go inside and tell them, and then I think we should start for home," Hannah suggested.

"Okay," Brandon agreed, and stood to help Hannah to her feet. His hand did not let go of hers until he reached for the door to let her go in before him.

Jaxon watched until the door closed behind the pair before he got slowly to his feet, his body feeling like it belonged to another and not him.

"It's for the best," Saul reasoned. "This is why humans are not allowed to guide those they have left behind when they come to join us as Guardians. The love you feel for those left behind stays with you, and the pain you feel is almost one of betrayal."

"I still love her," Jaxon said, that pain rolling through him like a tsunami. "What am I going to do without her?"

"You will never be without her," Saul said, trying to give Jaxon some advice that would let him see that Hannah needed someone in her life to love and to give her love in return. The love she had felt for Jaxon, and still had for Jaxon, would never be gone, only tucked away in a special place in her heart that only he would hold.

"Hannah will always love you," Saul said aloud, "until the day she dies she will love you. And on that day, she will come looking for you to once again feel your arms around her and she will rejoice in your reunion. Until then, you have to let her go to find happiness and companionship as a mortal."

"I have to go," Jaxon said, as he spread his wings and leapt into the air. Saul watched him fly away and knew he would try and outrun his pain with speed and distance. He had seen it before and knew he would not succeed.

"I'll be waiting for you, my friend," Saul said to the night, before he too disappeared.

The only one left was Roman who had been watching from a distance. At first, he had laughed at the pain the Guardian Jaxon was drowning in. But it didn't take long before he realized Jaxon had now become more dangerous to him and his hoards than ever before. He was going to take the pain he felt and heap it upon any Dark Being that crossed his path. Roman shivered and retreated to the safety of his dark lair, not wanting to be caught in the open by Jaxon. He was fierce in his hunting on any given day, but that would pale in comparison to what he would be capable of now.

Roman shivered again and hid like a coward. And because of this, His hatred for the Guardian, Jaxon, grew until he clawed at his face in suppressed rage.

Plans had to be made to handle this new threat and Roman would make sure it included pain and death.

The more the merrier!

Chapter 60

Dee and Hunter stood on the porch and waved in unison as Hannah and Brandon, after saying their good-byes, drove out of sight. Dee's world still tilted from the information told to her and the information that was not told to her tonight.

Hannah and Brandon had entered the house and walked to the kitchen just as Dee and Hunter were putting the last of the cleaned dishes into the cupboards. It didn't take long for Brandon to break the news that he was moving to Colorado, probably in the next week. He had sold his house and the packing would be completed by the time he returned home in two days. After that, he would lead the way to his new home that he had just purchased in Golden. He was excited, actually more than excited, to start this new chapter in his life.

Dee had not been surprised, as she had always wondered why Brandon had lived so far away from them as it would have made more sense for them to all live closer.

"It's about time," she said, moving to give the big man a bear hug of approval.

Hannah held her breath and watched closely as her daughter hugged her newfound love. She could tell the moment all was revealed to her. The slight stiffening of surprise and the few seconds of hesitation were obvious to her but no one else.

"I think this is a great idea," she said to Brandon, but looking at her mother. "I've always thought you should be closer, and now you will be," she said, giving the man a final hug of approval. "If you guys were not driving, I would say this calls for a drink in celebration, but it will have to wait. How about we all go out and celebrate when you get settled in?" Dee threw out, as a suggestion.

"I think that is a great idea," both Hannah and Brandon agreed. "We better get going now though," Hannah said, turning for the steps and a new start to her life.

Dee and Hunter walked with the pair to the front steps and Dee put her arms around her mother in farewell.

"You know, don't you?" Hannah asked, into her daughter's ear.

"I know," Dee confirmed, and she squeezed her mom harder.

"What do you think?" Hannah asked, wanting more than anything for her daughter to approve and make the transition from friends to family drama free.

"I think it's about time," Dee said just as quietly, as the happiness she felt and the happiness she hoped for, for her mother, was finally coming to pass. "I'm happy for you," she said, before stepping back.

Hunter and Brandon stood by slightly confused, as both women parted with tears in their eyes, wondering what they had missed.

"Take care of Dee," Hannah said, as she gave Hunter a slight hug before moving down the stairs and heading towards her car.

Hunter made no comment, preferring to let his actions speak for him. Words meant nothing without actions backing them up.

"Drive carefully," he said, turning to the mortal giant beside him. "I think both of our girls will be happy having you close to them," he said, not backing away from the hand Brandon extended.

"We will," Brandon said, and when Hunter gripped his hand in farewell, he drew him in closer so his words would be private. "Don't forget our conversation," he said a smile on his lips for Dee's benefit. "Treat her well, or you'll be answering to me."

"Same here," Hunter said, his voice hardening, as he looked Brandon straight in the eye. "Hurt Hannah and you hurt Dee. That I can't allow," the Immortal said, leaving no doubt in the man's mind that he was being put on notice. "Don't be a stranger," Hunter said louder, backing up and ending the conversation.

Brandon nodded his head before following Hannah's path to the car and home.

"I hope Mom knows what she's doing," Dee said, stepping into Hunter's arms.

"They're going to be happy," Hunter assured her, standing with her to stare out into the night. "Let's go in," he said, turning towards the door. "We've had a long day."

"Hmmm," Dee agreed, entering the house before Hunter closed the portal behind them. The change in her family was put aside for the moment as Hunter's arms, lips and body took her to a place that allowed room for only them.

Tomorrow was another day but tonight was for lovers. The two couples took full advantage of that promise, until the wee hours of the morning found them finally giving into sleep.

Saul left them to it. He had other things to attend to, his heart aching with the pain he knew his friend was fighting.

Sometimes being an Immortal sucked.

Chapter 61

Dee and Hunter showed up when Brandon arrived to move into his new home, lending their strength to the unloading. Of course, Hannah was there, giving advice as to where furniture should be placed and where boxes should be unloaded. Dee spotted her mom's and Brandon's discreet touches, but she just rolled her eyes and shook her head at their attempt to hide them.

"Really, Mom," Dee said, when they found themselves alone. "Both Hunter and I know you two are involved, so why are you hiding from us?"

Hannah blushed like a schoolgirl and stammered something about not going in for too much PDA, which made Dee laugh and drop the subject. She supposed they would let the world in on their relationship when they themselves became comfortable with it.

For their assistance with the move, Brandon took them all out to a mom and pop restaurant, suggested by Hannah, called The Griddle. They didn't have to dress up to walk in and enjoy the great home cooking, so it was perfect for the tired, hungry group.

Big burgers, fries, and shakes were ordered for all. The smells coming from the kitchen made Brandon and Hunter's mouths water in anticipation. The conversation was light. Even Hunter joined in, though he was a bit rusty in human company except for Dee's. When the food came, it was devoured with a speed and efficiency that even Dee's lawn mower would have been proud of. The plates had been removed and coffee poured before all felt the weight of the day.

"I think it's time we took off, Mom," Dee said, pushing back her chair and groaning when she stood, as her back was complaining from the unaccustomed activity she had put it through. Hunter followed her lead and lent his arms in support for her as good byes were said and promises given to visit soon.

This time it was Hannah and Brandon who were left waving as the young ones drove away. "She knows, doesn't she?" Brandon asked, as he openly took Hannah's hand to walk the few blocks to her shop and apartment.

"Yup," Hannah said, fitting her small frame against her lover's side.

"Well?" he asked, on pins and needles. "What does she think about us?"

Hannah giggled and looked him in the eye, as best she could. "She wondered why we were trying to hide it," she supplied, so his mind would be at ease. "Dee is happy for us. Did you ever doubt she wouldn't be?"

Brandon shrugged his muscled shoulders, but let out the breath he had been holding all day. "Good," he said, "that's good." He then let Hannah slip from his side as she led the way up the stairs to her apartment. "You know, tomorrow we are going to have to break in the new house," he said, before his lips were occupied and thoughts were not possible.

"Tomorrow," Hannah agreed catching her breath, as Brandon touched her in places she had forgotten.

Saul spared one more night, as he kept watch against the things that go bump in the night. He would give Hannah and Brandon one more night of happiness before his duties took him away from their sides. And he hoped, with all his heart, that one of the things that threatened the two humans would not be Jaxon. The Dark he could fight, but not his friend.

"Be at peace, Jaxon," he thought, hoping his friend would hear him. Otherwise, it was going to be a long night indeed!

Damn.

Chapter 62

For all intents and purposes, Hunter had basically moved into Dee's home. Each day found them working side by side to keep the grounds of the cemetery looking fresh and pristine, while the nights were spent in each other's arms, loving and laughing into the wee hours of the morning.

Dee's life was better than she could have ever wished. That a man such as Hunter should love her was still almost more than she could wrap her mind around. She shared her good fortune with her mother, and the two laughed like schoolgirls when they found the time to get together and the talk turned to the men in their lives. Yes, Dee was happy as every day found her good fortune holding true. And because of this, the weeks flew by as if on wings.

Today when she had opened her eyes, Hunter had taken her in his arms and, instead of making love to her, did nothing more than hold her and snuggle her close to his warm loving body. It was funny, but him doing that made her feel more loved and cherished than if he had made love to her. She wondered if that was normal. Of course she found their love making to be everything and more, but to just be held and loved was somehow just plain special.

"Hey, baby," Hunter said, walking into the kitchen, interrupting Dee's musing. "I have to run into town this morning and pick up a few parts for the sprinkler system. Do you need me to grab anything while I'm out and about?" he asked, as a piece of crispy bacon found its way into his waiting mouth.

Dee kissed his mouth and tasted the food he had snitched as she licked her lips. "Yum, you taste good," she said, her eyes lighting up with laughter.

"Me or the bacon?" Hunter asked, as his arms came up to pull her close.

"Both," Dee said, looping her arms around Hunter's neck so she could keep him close for a few more seconds. "And, no, I can't think of anything right off hand that I need."

"I'll be back by supper time," Hunter said, piling bacon and eggs on toast to make a sandwich to take with him. "What do you have planned for the day?" he asked, not out of idle curiosity. He did not forget his role as protector for a second, and if Saul had not called him to come he would not be leaving Dee's side.

Hunter listened carefully as Dee told him she planned on trimming up a few areas, and then she and Callie were going to take the rest of the day off.

"That sounds like a good day to me," he said, rubbing his whiskery chin on her neck, making her squeal and wiggle as he tickled her soft skin. Relenting after a few seconds, he replaced his chin with his lips and turned Dee's squeals into groans of pleasure before he reluctantly pulled away.

"I'll be back soon," he said, and gave her smiling lips one last kiss before heading out the door. Callie followed on silent feet and stopped just inside the door as Hunter, checking to make sure Dee was not following, bent down to pick up the cat and cuddle her in his arms.

"Watch over her," he whispered, for her ears alone. "Call if there is a need and we will come."

Callie purred her consent and rubbed her head against the hand stroking her. "Take care," Hunter said, before setting Callie back on her feet.

Hunter got inside the pickup and drove out of sight before he met Saul in the usual place.

"We have to go," Saul said, moving to Hunter's side as the pickup disappeared, leaving the two Guardians alone.

"Where are we going?" Hunter asked, leaping into the air and dipping his wings down hard to catch up with Saul.

"I need you to lend a hand with a situation," Saul said, giving Hunter no real clue as to what he was to expect.

"With what?" Hunter asked, not letting it go.

Saul turned his handsome face towards the Guardian he called on for help and locked their gazes, dark brown with brilliant green, before ending his curiosity. "We need to find Jaxon," he said, and flew faster.

"Why?" Hunter yelled, grinding his teeth as he reached for speed, not letting Saul get ahead of him.

"Since Hannah and Brandon declared their love for each other, Jaxon has been on a rampage, and we need to calm him down before he gets himself into a situation he can't get out of." Saul began to supply details to Hunter's question.

"How the hell did Jaxon find out about Hannah and Brandon?" Hunter asked.

"He was with me that night at Dee's," Saul filled him in, "and was right there to hear it all."

"What were you doing there in the first place?" Hunter demanded with anger in his tone.

"Jaxon wanted to stop by and see his friend and Hannah for a few moments," Saul said. "It was quite innocent until we were witnesses to Brandon telling Hannah he loved her. I think Jaxon was sure Hannah would not respond and when she did he was crushed. Ever since then he has been reckless, and now I need you to help me get Jaxon back on track and accept what has happened."

Hunter didn't want to help because he knew how he would feel if the tables were turned and he had had to stand by while Dee loved another. He couldn't blame Jaxon for feeling anger and pain.

"You understand, don't you?" Saul questioned as he watched Hunter's muscles bunch in anger.

"I understand what Jaxon is feeling," Hunter acknowledged, "so, yes, I will help." "*One day I may need him to do the same for me,*" he thought, his green eyes turning to hot flames.

"I'm coming," Hunter called to Jaxon, hoping he could hear him.

"I'm coming."

Chapter 63

Jaxon didn't need any help. He was doing just fine on his own. Every chance he got to find and engage the Dark in battle was taken and, to his way of thinking, the more Dark Minions that came after him the better.

Since the night his world had come crashing down, he had taken his anger and hurt out on any enemy within reach, and there had been endless numbers for him to dispatch. When he was fighting he did not have time to think, and he liked it that way.

Saul had called to him many times but Jaxon had ignored the Mighty Immortal, not wanting to have to talk about what had happened. "Leave me alone!" he had yelled back, as he cut and burned his way through the Dark that had come to kill him. "Just leave me alone!" That was the last thought he had sent to his friend and he was okay with that.

He was in no way foolish enough to think that Saul was going to do as he asked. But for as long as he could, he would hold off facing his pain and focus on the hunt and the kill.

It was daylight and Jaxon took his rest at that time, knowing the Dark would be hiding from the bright light, preferring to come out when the sun went down and the things that bumped in the night came out to play. Standing on a mountaintop, Jaxon looked out over his domain, missing the beauty before him as he looked with eyes that did not see. He felt the ground give, announcing the arrival of another, but he did not care, could not make himself care.

"Hello, my friend," Saul said, his voice matching the quiet of the place. "How are you?"

"Go away," Jaxon said, not bothering to turn his head in acknowledgement for his friend.

"I can't do that," Saul said, coming to stand beside his Guardian Hunter. "We need to talk."

"No, we don't," Jaxon ground out, his anger rising to match Saul's stubbornness.

"The pain you are feeling needs to be brought out into the open, and the wound you are bearing must be allowed to heal." Saul continued.

"Or what?" Jaxon spun to confront Saul, his wings unfurled and his stance defensive.

Saul did not flinch nor did he give up ground as he calmly watched his wounded friend. "I am not your enemy," he said, keeping his voice steady and even. "I have come to help whether you want my help or not."

"You can't help," Jaxon said. "You have no idea what I'm feeling!"

"Whether or not I have ever been in love is not the issue here," Saul stated. "What is, is that I can help you if you let me."

Jaxon pulled his wings back in and turned away to again face the vista laid out before him. "Just go away," he said, his voice low and tired.

Saul glanced over at Hunter and raised his eyebrows to let him know it was time to jump in.

Hunter stood where he had landed and looked at Jaxon with hooded eyes. He could almost see the pain rolling off him. He wanted to rage at him because Jaxon was the one that had gotten him into his current situation, and he knew it could very well be himself in Jaxon's shoes one day. "Not such a bad ass now, are we?" he sneered.

Jaxon turned to stare at the new intruder and his eyes shot daggers. "Who's watching my daughter?" he spat out. "If you're here, who's watching my daughter?"

"What do you care?" Hunter asked, his tone doing nothing to hide his disgust at the larger than life Guardian Hunter's behavior. "You're so wrapped up in your 'poor me' attitude that I'm surprised you have the energy to think of anyone but yourself. Nice of you to remember you have a daughter though, kudos to you."

Jaxon growled deep in his throat and his muscles bunched, as he was seconds from lashing out at another Immortal. But before he could move, Hunter advanced until he was nose to nose with Dee's father.

"Why don't you pull your head out of your ass and get over yourself?" Hunter sneered. "Who the hell do you think you are getting all crappy because Hannah has dared to find some companionship after all this time? Did you bother to stop and think of her? Think how she has lived with no one to love her but Dee. Did it ever occur to you that she would never forget you, or try to replace you, but that maybe just maybe she has paid for loving you long enough? That maybe after all this time she is allowing herself to care again. To open herself up to being hurt again. And you, butthead, she has picked one of your best friends and you should feel grateful to him because you know he will not hurt her or leave her or abuse her. So what the hell do you have to be all hurt for?" Hunter's chest heaved after his little speech, as he stood his ground with eyes blazing and muscles ready in case Jaxon took a swing at him.

"Get away from me," Jaxon fired back at him. "Get away from me and stay away, if you know what's good for you!"

"I won't," Hunter stated, "because I may need you to help with Dee, and Hannah may need you if the Dark comes after her. So you need to be ready. We need you. I need you to snap out of wherever you are stuck and get back to normal. Pull it together for your family, if for nothing and no one else."

Jaxon's eyes saw red. He wanted to put his hands around the neck of this Immortal smart ass and choke him until he was no more. He had no idea what it felt like to love someone so much and have to watch him or her turn to another for love because you could not. It hurt so badly that Jaxon felt like a ball of something was lodged in his throat. He couldn't get it to go up and he couldn't get it to go down, it just hung there like a lead weight. And it was killing him.

"If you need to scream, do it! If you need cry, do it! If you need to take a breath and collect yourself, then do it! But do it soon because the Dark is not going to wait around for you to get your poop in a group before they strike. As fierce as you are now, you are not invulnerable." Hunter ran out of taunts and could do no more. Now it was up to Jaxon to make the next move.

The air grew still and nature grew quiet, as all waited to see what would happen next. Jaxon took a step back from his daughter's protector, and then another, putting distance between the Immortals and himself. He felt like he was going to explode, literally. Saul reached out his hand and held Hunter back, as he made to follow Jaxon as Jaxon retreated.

"I thought you brought me here to help," Hunter said, looking at the powerful hand that held him in place.

"You've done your part," Saul said, looking at Jaxon as he spoke. "Now it's his turn," and he braced himself for what he hoped was coming.

And it came!

Chapter 64

Jaxon stumbled to a stop as feelings grew inside until he could not move. His eyes opened wide and his head reared back before he opened his mouth and roared. With clenched fists and corded muscles, he roared!

The sound was ugly and raw and came from the bottom of his soul. He fell to his knees and then to all fours, digging his hands into the earth, leaving deep gouges as his fingers curled into claws and then anchors, keeping him in place. Keeping him attached to the ground as his body heaved and his spirit purged.

Jaxon gagged as great gouts of oily, brown sludge spewed from his mouth and curled on the ground like living things, twisting and roiling until they lay still. Each dying coil was a part of Jaxon that had no place inside him. Jealousy, hurt, betrayal, rage and envy could not live outside the body, and it did not take but a few seconds before they sank into the ground, seeping below to the dark places where those feelings belonged.

Jaxon panted as he hung his head, sweat dripping from his hair and watering the mountain. He still had one more emotion inside him that didn't belong and it was the one he most loathed to reveal. He didn't consider it a weakness, but the one that he knew was going to hurt the worst as he rid himself of it.

He tried to hold it back but was not able to, as a lone tear rolled down his cheek. First one and then another escaped his eyes until they and the ones that followed made tracks down his face, until he cried out his sadness. Sadness at the emptiness of his arms that wanted, still, to hold the one he loved. Sadness for all he had lost and would never have again, sadness at not being able to take care of the ones he loved, and sadness at the loneliness his dying had forced on Hannah. She deserved happiness and he could not deny her this simple human necessity. But letting go hurt so badly. "It hurts, Saul," Jaxon whispered, as he felt like his guts were being ripped out by their roots.

"Yes," Saul said simply.

"Will it ever get better?" he wondered out loud and to himself.

"Yes," Saul said again.

"When?"

Saul moved to sit beside Jaxon, waiting until he wiped his face and drew a deep breath. "Better?" he asked, laying his hand on his friends shoulder.

"I guess," Jaxon said, feeling empty and detached.

"Just because we are Immortal does not mean that we are without feelings," Saul began. "It does mean, though, that we handle those feelings differently than the humans we give guidance to." He waited for Jaxon to say something, but he did not, so Saul continued. "I want you to do something for me," he said, waiting until Jaxon looked into his eyes before he told him what. "I want you to close your eyes and think of Hannah," he said.

Jaxon's face showed pain, as he was being asked to go right back to the place he was trying so desperately to leave.

"It's okay," Saul said his voice soothing. "Now take all the good things you remember, all the good times you shared, and hold those memories in your hand." Saul waited, until Jaxon held out his hand and smiled. "Now take your hand that is full of this goodness and place it on your chest, over your heart." Again Saul waited until Jaxon did as he was asked. "Can you feel it?" Saul asked.

Jaxon's face became peaceful and his being glowed softly as his memories and feelings of love were stored in his heart, always with him but now locked away until Hannah and he were together again.

"Nothing can take away your love," Saul said, "but it's just a little bit more manageable now. Carry it with you, but don't let it be your all."

"You couldn't have done this before?" Jaxon wanted to know, thinking all this could have been avoided.

"I couldn't. Hannah had a part to play in this and until she was ready there was nothing I could do. You would not have believed you needed help before this, so it had to wait." Saul replied.

Jaxon was quiet for a moment, as he seemed to be rolling something around on his tongue. Tasting it, trying it out before taking a deep breath and looking at Saul. "Thank you," he said. "I feel better. Pretty much normal," he said, and grinned at his mentor.

Saul nodded his head and rose to his feet. "Good," he said, and dusted off his hands as if to say all was finished.

"We need to get back," Hunter interrupted. "I need to get back. You two can stay here and finish if you're not done, but I've got to go."

Jaxon looked at Hunter and nodded his head. "Thanks for your help," he said cocking an eyebrow in his direction. "I'll be seeing you."

Hunter grunted, and without a backwards glance leapt into the air and was gone.

Chapter 65

Dee and Callie spent the morning cleaning up some of the areas that looked a little shaggy, and when the work was completed Dee took a few steps back to examine the end results. Everything looked beautiful and radiated peace. Exactly the look and the feel to which Dee had been aiming.

"Looks good to me," Dee said, bending down to brush the kitten at her feet. Callie stayed by her side wherever they went and Dee was glad for her company. Standing up straight, Dee prepared to call it a day as she told Hunter she would. There were no pressing issues and she was glad to have a few hours to herself. Maybe a nice long bath was in order with some candles and soft music to relax her. For the last couple of days, Dee had been on edge without knowing why. She had the feeling that something was coming or going to happen that was not going to be welcome. She had a bad feeling. Shaking her head to get rid of the direction her thoughts were taking her did the trick, as she gathered the few items she had brought with her this morning and began the walk back towards her home.

Following the rock path through the cemetery brought Dee and Callie to one of the benches she and her mother had painted not that long ago. She stopped short, as sitting on the bench was a little old lady dressed in what looked like her Sunday best, all alone. Alone and sad.

Dee approached the bench before setting down her tools and joining the woman.

"Can I help you?" Dee asked, wanting to reach out a comforting hand but not daring to.

The woman turned her head to look at Dee and Dee had to smile. She was indeed dressed in her Sunday finery, that being a filmy, flowery dress with a straw bonnet and pastel pink gloves. Her white hair haloed her head, her cheeks, though wrinkled, held a healthy pink glow and her blue eyes sparkled with life.

"I've come to visit my Martin," she said, her voice a little bit shaky.

"I see," Dee said. "I won't bother you then."

"No, stay," the woman said, raising a hand to keep Dee beside her. "I would welcome the company. My name is Adelaide, Adelaide Ester Picket to be exact. What's yours, dear?" she asked softly.

"I'm Dee, Dee Priest and I'm the caretaker here," Dee provided to complete the introductions.

The thin shoulders sagged at Dee's statement and the blue eyes clouded over. "I see," she said, turning her head to look out over the headstones.

"My Martin used to be the caretaker here," she said, her voice turning hard, seeming to come from someone other than the fragile being at Dee's side.

Dee didn't know what to say so she said nothing, giving Adelaide the chance to enlighten her or not.

"Yup, for over ten years we lived here and everything was good, really good. This place has a way of seeping into your soul and making you not want to leave it. Have you noticed that yet?" she asked, again looking at Dee.

"I've only been here a few months," Dee supplied for an explanation.

"Not long," Adelaide said nodding her head. "Do you know the story behind this place?" she asked, again averting her eyes from Dee's.

"Well, if by story you mean the legend of the Omen Lake, then yes, yes I've been told. The man who hired me told me the belief that a lake appears to people here and it means that person or someone close to them was going to die."

"Do you believe what he told you?" Adelaide asked, her voice tense.

Dee wasn't sure what to say because she sort of believed and, then again, she sort of didn't.

"Where is this man that hired you?" the old woman asked. "Was he a caretaker here also?"

"Yes, David was the caretaker here before me," Dee said, not wanting to give any details to this woman.

"Where is he?" Adelaide asked, finally looking back at Dee, letting Dee see that she already knew the answer to the question she had just asked. But hoping she was wrong.

"He died shortly after I took the job." Dee said, watching as the old woman's eyes teared-up, as if she had just been told an old friend had died instead of a stranger.

"He told you he saw the lake, didn't he?" she asked as a formality.

"He said he saw the lake for the second time, and that this time it was coming for him," Dee admitted.

"Still you have doubts about the truth of the Lake, don't you?" Adelaide asked, forcing Dee to look inside herself and decide once and for all about the legend.

"There's an undertone here," Dee admitted. "I can feel a sort of darkness lying beneath the beauty of this place. I don't know if that means the legend is true or not, but well, it's hard to explain."

"The lake got my Martin," Adelaide said, her voice hard and angry. "They told us about the legend when we were hired, but we were young and it just didn't seem possible for such a far-fetched tale to be true. But it is," she admitted. And before Dee could pull away, she grabbed a hold of her hands and pulled Dee into her memories.

Pulled in and drowned.

Chapter 66

Dee saw a young couple holding hands and laughing as life opened up for them and held all the possibilities in the world. She saw them accepting the job at the cemetery that looked different, but still it was the same as the one she now took care of. She witnessed the day Martin came in, pale and shaken, sitting in the kitchen as he finally told his wife of the lake that had appeared before his very eyes that day. How he had been scared of its meaning, wondering what were they going to do now?

Dee's face paled as she watched a young Adelaide bending over her husband's dead body, wailing out her grief and sadness. She stood with her as they lowered his coffin into the ground and she felt her rage at her loss to this damn place.

Finally, she saw Adelaide pack up her belongings and tell a man that she would not stay here another minute. Declining the offer for her to stay and continue the work Martin and she had been doing. Dee heard the man tell her that no matter where she went she was tied to this place, and she would eventually come back, come back and join her husband.

Dee pulled her hands out of the desperate clutch of the old woman's, panting with the knowledge she had witnessed. Her eyes glowed a deep red as she was given evidence that she could not deny. The truth behind the legend.

"You saw, didn't you?" the old woman asked, as she watched Dee struggle to come back from the memories that she had seen. "I'm not going to ask how you did, but I know you saw. So now you know the truth. You need to get out," she said, her hands wadding the silky material of her dress until it was clutched into balls in her fists. "Get out before this place takes from you what it did from me. It took my life!" Adelaide said fiercely. "It took the only thing that mattered to me, and it spit me out when it was done!"

"What are you doing back here?" Dee asked, confused as to why this woman would come back to a place that had robbed her of her happiness.

"I came here to die," Adelaide said. "I've lived my life as fully as I could and I'm tired. Tired and old and I want to be with Martin again. So, I came back here to wait."

"For what?" Dee asked as expected.

"For the lake, of course," Adelaide answered, arching a white brow in Dee's direction. "I'm waiting for the lake to come for me. I don't think I'll have long to wait."

Dee swallowed hard and felt a fear that chilled her all the way to her soul.

"Maybe you should come to the house with me," Dee coaxed. "I could make you something to drink and we can get you a ride back into town after that. How about that?"

Adelaide smiled softly at the beautiful young woman at her side. She opened her mouth to speak but no sound came out. Her cheeks turned ashen and her eyes began to water.

"Do you see it? "She asked. "Can you see it?"

"See what?" Dee asked, not wanting to turn around and follow where the woman's eyes stared.

"The lake," Adelaide said, her voice far away and weak. "It's right there."

Dee turned slowly and looked out over the cemetery that only a few minutes ago had looked pretty and restful. The sun still shone brightly and the grass was still as green as ever, but the shadows, the shadows seemed deeper, darker and more sinister than before. But she saw no lake and she was glad she didn't.

"No," she said, tuning back to Adelaide. "I can't see the lake."

"That's okay," the old woman said with a sigh. "It's here for me, after all. Not you, not yet." She finally stood up and took a few wobbly steps before turning back to look at Dee. "I have all the arrangements made so I guess this is the last time I'll be seeing you. I'm going to see Martin again and that makes me happy. Get out," she said, all signs of a sweet little old lady gone. "Get out before the lake comes for you. Go today," the rough voice instructed, "and don't come back. If you don't, it'll take everything from you and leave you empty and alone. Get out!" the gruff voice said one more time before the weak old body that the voice had come from turned and followed the rock path, until she was out of sight.

Dee sat on the bench and rubbed her thighs trying to return warmth to them. The hair on her arms stood up and a creepy feeling slithered up her back and settled in her gut. Something wanted her to turn around and look behind her but Dee fought it, standing up to leave.

"Callie," she whispered. "Let's get out of here."

Callie jumped into the arms held out for her and peered over her human's shoulder as they headed for home. She saw what Dee refused to look at. She saw the lake. She saw the lake coming for them.

She hissed!

Chapter 67

A be had listened to the exchange between Dee and the old woman from the deep shadows under the old trees. He knew the old woman spoke the truth when she said it wouldn't be long until the lake came for her. He could smell death on the old woman and knew she would be getting her wish and be joining her husband soon. As he watched, the lake did come for her, calling to her, letting her know her time was short. Abe smiled, because he knew that for all Adelaide's saying she was ready, he knew she was scared. Scared of the unknown, of dying and what came next.

He also knew that she would not be joining his team of Dark Minions. She was one of the good ones who would be claimed for the light. Abe wrinkled his nose as if he detected a foul odor and was offended by it.

He watched the old woman walk away and was about to walk into the light and approach Dee before she could return to her home, but was held in place when the lake again appeared. His heart beat faster in anticipation of Dee's death, but was once again surprised when it was Callie who saw the lake and not the human.

"What did that mean?" he wondered. The lake did not show itself to animals, so why did that stupid cat get to see it? He touched his cheek as he remembered how the feline had clawed his face the first time he had spoken to Dee, and he started to smirk. It did not mean that the lake had come for her really. It could still mean that the lake had been there for Dee. Either way, Abe decided that he was finally going to get to have some fun. One way or the other he was going to get to take a life and, to his way of thinking, it didn't get any better than that. He stayed hidden until Dee had passed by him, making her way with that damn cat towards the house. He stayed hidden, trying to figure out what his next play should be.

"Hmmm, interesting," Abe decided, as he faded back into the shadows. He would wait until one of them was alone and he would know which one to take. And if he was lucky, he would take one or both of them to hell before the Guardians knew their lives had been stolen and it was too late to save them.

"Oh, yes," he thought. It was a win-win all the way around, and he decided it was going to be a beautiful day after all.

That thought alone was enough to make him gag.

Chapter 68

Callie stayed close to guard her charge as Hunter instructed. All had been quiet and calm until the time for them to return home had come. With every step they took towards home, Callie could tell something was not right, she could smell it. The stench of the Dark was strong and she knew one was close by. Before she could warn Saul, Dee had stopped to talk to a female sitting on a bench. Callie sniffed the ankle of the new female but the smell she detected was not coming from her.

"There must be another," she thought and, crouching down, she let her cat eyes search as far as she could see. Her eyes grew black as she searched and finally found a shadow that was darker, denser than was normal. Her ears laid back, a growl rumbled deep in her chest, as she prepared to go hunting for the threat. It was as far as she got, as the elderly female stood up and, after a few words, walked away. Dee rose too, and called for Callie to come to her.

Coming from underneath the bench, Callie gave one strong leap and was caught and held in arms that needed her. Callie gave what comfort she could by purring her approval and was satisfied when they began the journey towards home. Callie did not let down her guard, and would not until the door was safely closed behind them and the Guardian had returned. Peering over Dee's shoulder, Callie watched for danger, but what she saw was more than danger. What she saw was death coming.

Dark grey water was rising to cover the grass and headstones until the only thing she could see were the angry white caps that lapped at the edges of the water. Edges that crept ever closer to Dee's heels as she walked, but not fast enough, as the water gained on them, closing the distance until it was almost upon them.

Callie dug in her claws and, with all her might, called out to the Immortals for help. "Danger!" she cried. "Help!" Over and over she called as her small heart beat fast in her chest and her breathing became pants. She was scared, but scared or not, she would do what she needed to keep her friend safe. One more time she nuzzled the neck of the human she loved, before wiggling free and, giving a mighty lunge, she ran towards the Dark.

Ran towards death.

CHAPTER 69

Saul prepared to leave Jaxon and follow Hunter, but before he could the call from Callie came, hitting him like a ton of bricks. Saul staggered back a couple of steps, taking the full force of Callie's call square in the chest.

"What is it?" Jaxon asked, knowing something was very wrong. Not many things could make the most powerful Immortal Guardian of them all falter under its weight, and Jaxon was ready to help.

"Callie," Saul said, as he leapt into the air and put all his power into slicing the air with his mighty wings.

That was all Jaxon needed to tap into his rage and fly beside Saul. It only took a moment for the two to catch up to Hunter as he made his way back to Dee.

"What the hell are you two doing here?" he asked, sure that they meant to hang around when he reverted to human form and joined Dee.

"There's trouble," Saul told him, never slowing down.

Hunter glimpsed the looks of determination on the Guardians' faces and he questioned no more. He too, dug deep, tapping into the power it took to keep up, as the three shot across the sky, fire trailing them as they burned the air with their speed.

"Callie," Saul called. "Callie, where are you?"

"In the cemetery," Callie's voice roared in his head. "I'm in the cemetery, hurry!"

Saul tasted the fear his small protector was feeling, but he also felt her courage and determination as she battled for her human's life. "Hold on!" he sent to her. "Hold on! We are almost there!"

"The cemetery!" he spat out to his companions, and all three zeroed in on the battle that now reached their ears. Moans and shrieks from a Dark Being could be heard coming from the trees bordering the grassy expanse, along with roars of a lion on the attack.

The earth bucked and heaved as three Immortals landed and circled the fighting pair. They saw claws of steel flashing in the shadows leaving trails of fire as they sank deep into the smoky flesh. They smelled that same black flesh burn as it fell in chunks to the ground.

Three voices roared as they joined the fight, but they were not able to lay their death dealing hands on the smoking figure before it disappeared from their sight.

The quiet that followed was eerie, as the only evidence of the fight were patches of charred grass and earth where the evil ones blood had spilled and its flesh had been torn off, burning until all that was left was foul smelling ash.

Saul scanned the area looking for, but not finding, the small protector that had fought so bravely.

"Callie," he called. "Callie, where are you?"

A small bloody body crawled from under a bush where it had been tossed when the Guardians had arrived.

"I'm here, Saul," Callie spoke softly. "I'm here."

Saul picked up the kitten and cradled it in his arms trying to take her pain into himself. Trying to give her a chance to heal. But he was too late.

"I tried," the small voice said to him. "I fought for as long as I could."

"You have done well," Saul whispered, giving Callie peace of mind. "You have saved your human and we will be forever in your debt."

Saul closed his eyes. When he opened them again Sam stood before him with his hands held out. "Take her," he said, as he passed the small body to his Guardian. "Take her with you and give her the immortality she has earned."

Callie purred one last time before her body stilled and her voice was silenced. Her spirit rose into the air to sit upon the shoulder of her new guide, where she was once again healthy and whole.

"Guard her well," she said to Hunter, turning the tables, as it was she this time giving the order of protection.

"I will," Hunter said. "Thank you." With that, he watched as Sam and Callie rose to begin her new life. Saul, Hunter and Jaxon remained standing in the now peaceful cemetery. But the peace was not to last. "I want him," Hunter said, his eyes blazing green fire. "I want the Dark piece of crap that did this."

"You have to stay with Dee," Saul said. "Jaxon and I will hunt the one that did this. If we can't find it, then you will have to stand between it and Dee. Do not let your guard down."

Hunter did not like being sidelined from a hunt he so desperately wanted to be in on, but he could not fault the reasoning behind it. "Very well," he said, preparing to leave to rejoin Dee. "But should you need me, call." With that, he left to get the pickup and return to his human form. Shooting one last glance at the silent Jaxon, he left.

Saul stood where he was for a few seconds, trying to get the pure rage that he had held back under control. He wanted to shout out his anger at the life that had been taken, and he wanted revenge. He wanted it now!

A small chill crept up Saul's spine as his eyes fell on Jaxon. He almost pitied the Dark Being that he was about to set his hunter on, yet he remembered the small broken body that he had just held in his hands. Death poured from Jaxon in a black, ominous wave, promising that Jaxon's retaliation would be painful.

"Go," Saul said. "Go and find the one responsible."

Jaxon turned cold, dead eyes on Saul and smiled in anticipation.

"Find me when it's done," Saul said, as Jaxon spread his wings and prepared to leave.

"I won't need to find you," Jaxon said in a cold voice. "You'll hear the screams." He leapt into the air and was gone.

"Good," Saul said. His need for revenge was bone deep.

"Good."

Chapter 70

Hunter drove into the yard and turned off the motor. He sat for a moment trying to figure out how he was going to tell Dee that Callie was dead. How was he going to explain to her how he knew what had happened? As he opened his door, he could hear Dee calling Callie's name. His heart hurt, before his anger took over, as he remembered the kitten that had become such a big part of their lives. He was going to have to pretend to go search for the little one, and then he would have to come back and break Dee's heart. "Damn the Dark," he growled, under his breath.

Walking to the steps he took them two at a time, bringing him to Dee's side and her into his arms. "Hey, baby," he said, as he nuzzled his face in her soft neck. "I missed you."

"Umm, I missed you, too," she said, wrapping her arms around his neck and lifting her lips to his. Their kiss was warm and sweet, and it made Hunter's gut ache with what the night was to hold. "You didn't happen to see Callie when you drove up did you?" Dee asked, letting her glance sweep the empty front yard yet again.

"I've been calling her ever since we came back from working today. She jumped out of my arms when we were heading home, and I thought she was following me. But when I got to the house she wasn't with me, and she's not coming when I call."

Hunter let his eyes travel the yard also, but he knew he would not find the bundle of fur, as much as he wished he could. "Nope," he said. "I didn't see her. Would you like me to take a look around while you fix some dinner?" he asked, preparing the way for his lie.

"Would you?" Dee asked, giving Hunter's hand a tight squeeze.

"Sure, honey," he said. "I'll see if I can find her." With that, Hunter moved down the steps and began calling Callie as he walked. He waited until Dee went into the house before he stopped calling the kitten's name. He walked to the place where her life had been taken and his eyes grew damp with the loss he felt.

Lifting his face to the sky, Hunter sent a message to Jaxon. "Find it," he called. "Find it and make it pay." The only response he got back was a bone-chilling laugh.

Hunter nodded his head and sighed before he gathered the most beautiful rocks he could find and made a mound on the spot where Callie had fought. He would tell Dee that he had buried the kitten there and take her pain into himself, as she grieved for her lost friend. Hunter headed back to the house and opened the door to the smell of chicken frying and corn on the cob cooking.

"Smells good," he said, as he closed the door at his back.

"Did you find her?" Dee asked, going to the cupboard to get a can of food, knowing that Callie would be starving by now.

"Yes," Hunter said. The tone of his voice caused Dee to turn with the can of cat food unopened in her hand.

"Hunter?" she asked. Her heart picked up speed at the look on his face.

"She's gone," Hunter said, not able to make the word dead leave his mouth. "I found her out by the cemetery, so I picked a real pretty spot and covered her with some of the prettiest stones I could find. I'm sorry, sweetie," he said, as he gathered her to his chest and let her tears wet his shirt. He let her mourn for a few moments before putting his lips to her hair and taking her feelings into himself. His chest squeezed with her pain that was now his, and he hoped Callie knew how much she was loved.

Hunter did not take all her feelings, he left her with all the love and goodness she had in memories of her much loved friend. When she thought of Callie she would remember her with a smile, not with the gut-wrenching tears that tore at her soul.

Dee pulled out of Hunter's arms and a small wet smile curved her lips. "I'm okay," she said. "I'm okay." She walked to put the can of food back in the cupboard.

"Would you like to go out for supper tonight?" he asked, even though the food was done and waiting to be eaten.

"No, let's just stay in," she said, and again told him, "I'm fine."

So it was a quiet pair that picked at the food on their plates and cleaned up after the meal was completed. And it was a quiet pair that stood on their porch to watch the stars that came out when the sun had set. Dee found one that seemed brighter than the others and she named it Callie, giving her a point of reference to speak to when she wanted to talk to her kitten.

"I miss you," she said in her heart, *"but I'll see you again,"* she promised.

"I'll see you again."

Chapter 71

Abe hid in the dark, licking his wounds, raging at the damage the little beast had done to him. So the Lake had come for the animal after all, and he was glad that he had been the one to take its life. If he could he would do it again and again, until he felt vindicated for all the wounds the devil's spawn had inflicted on him.

"I heard what happened," Roman said, as he slithered into Abe's hiding spot. "Really," he sneered, "beaten by a cat? I never would have imagined it."

"I killed it, didn't I?" Abe asked, wanting to strike out, but not daring to do so. "Leave me alone," he said, turning his back to his Master, as he battled to deny his shame.

"Very well," Roman said, satisfied that he had rubbed salt in this upstart's ego. "I shall be getting another to take over this mission," he said, before turning to leave.

"No!" Abe shouted, reaching out a claw to detain Roman. "I am more than capable of seeing this to the end. You owe me this," he hissed.

"I owe you nothing," Roman said, flicking off the hand that dared to touch him. "You are not worthy, having gotten you ass kicked by a mortal feline. Really, how weak."

Abe wanted to show his Master just how weak he was by ripping his head off and crowing over his shriveled up, decaying, dead body.

"I'm begging you for another chance," he said, bowing his head in submission. "Please," he groveled, "please?"

Roman needed to see Abe broken and on his knees before him. He needed to see this before he could consider letting him continue to try to dispatch this Dee Priest. As he looked on, he made the decision to allow Abe one more try. Not because he believed he could accomplish his goal, but because he knew the Guardians would be hunting for him. They would be hunting hard and he, Roman, had no doubt as to the outcome when the Guardians discovered the identity of the one after their human.

"Very well," he said, after giving the impression of considering the request. "You may try one more time. But should you fail, I will choose another to take your place."

"Thank you, Master," Abe said, as he backed away to keep himself from trying to kill the one he was supposed to follow. "I will be successful this time, I'm sure of it."

Roman left to see to other matters. He was sure the Guardians would kill Abe within the mortal week. He didn't care though, as he just wanted his problem eliminated. Maybe he should drop Dee's father a hint as to the identity of the Dark one who was responsible for this horrible act.

Roman giggled, as a plan came to mind and he went off to put it into effect.

"*Yoo-hoo, Jaxon,*" Roman thought. "*Calling Jaxon,*" he repeated.

The deep growl that came as an answer made what passed as a smile cover the black-fleshed face and Roman skipped off to set up a meeting.

"*Don't you just love it when a plan comes together*"? Roman was ecstatic as this thought crossed his mind over and over.

"Don't you just absolutely love it?"

Chapter 72

As Jaxon met with the Dark Leader, even Roman kept his distance, seeing the way the Guardian Hunter carried death with him. Jaxon did not come simply carrying death as a cloak, but instead he wore it as his armor. Dark and deadly was what Jaxon needed, so dark and deadly was what he had become.

"What do you want?" Jaxon asked, his voice raspy with rage.

"A simple meeting is all," Roman said, wary of the hunter. "I have some information in which I think you will be interested."

"Why would you want to share information with me?" Jaxon sneered, finding it hard to believe his enemy was trying to be his friend

"I am willing to share the name of the Dark One with you, the one who killed your human's pet."

"Why?" Jaxon spat out. "Why would you want to do that?"

"My reasons are my own," Roman said, not willing to share all with the Guardian. "If you are not interested, then this meeting is a waste of time."

"Talk," Jaxon said.

"The name of the one you seek is Abe," Roman supplied. "He takes the form of a human man and is trying to get close to your daughter. He means to do to your daughter what he did to the feline. He means to kill her."

Jaxon's wings slowly spread with his anger, both black and intimidating, until Roman retreated in fright.

"I have given you what you need, so there is no reason to kill the messenger. I believe it is now time for me to go." Before the growl had a chance to leave Jaxon's mouth, he had vanished.

Jaxon stood alone, but he still growled his anger. "Saul," he called, and in the blink of an eye the mighty Guardian appeared at his side.

"What?" Saul asked his eyes sweeping the area. "What?"

"The scum, Roman, requested a meeting, so I came," Jaxon started.

Saul cocked an eyebrow at this strange turn of events. The Dark did not call meetings, so he was curious as to what it was all about.

"He gave me the name of the Dark One who killed Callie," he said bluntly. He paused only a second, as Saul's muscles bunched and his lips peeled back in a sneer.

"Who?" he asked.

"Something called Abe," Jaxon imparted. "This Abe is appearing as a human man. He plans on doing to Dee what he did to Callie."

"Why tell us?" Saul asked. "Surely he knows we will kill this Dark threat. What does he have to gain by sharing this with the Guardians?"

"He wouldn't say, and before I could wring the information out of him, he vanished," Jaxon said, with his hands clenching empty air.

"We have to tell Hunter," Saul said. "We need to have him watch for strangers hanging around the cemetery."

"I agree," Jaxon said, "but I hope I get to this Abe before he does. It would be my great pleasure to tear it apart, piece by piece, until it has screamed its last."

Saul knew the feeling, but he was happy to let Hunter and Jaxon take care of dealing out death to the Dark Minion. He would be on the look out for other Dark plans in case this turned out to be a distraction. "I will meet with Hunter now and warn him of the danger."

"We will go talk to him together," Jaxon said, not willing to be left out of the conversation.

Saul nodded his agreement and the two Guardians took flight, arrowing their way to the cemetery where they had just lost a friend.

When they arrived, Saul lifted his handsome face to the wind and called out to Hunter. "We need to talk," he called, and waited for Hunter to come.

He came.

After the day before, he came ready to fight.

Chapter 73

"Easy, my friend," Saul said, as Hunter landed with a roar.

Hunter rose from his fighting crouch and pulled his sharp wings in tightly. "What is it?" he asked, impatient to be gone.

"We have just learned the name of the one Callie fought," Saul began.

"Who is it?" Hunter demanded, before Saul had a chance to continue.

"His name is Abe," Jaxon supplied. "Not that that will do us any good, but we have also found out that this Being has taken the form of a human male and means to attack Dee, as it did Callie."

A picture of the small broken and bloody body flashed through Hunter's mind, and he could see exactly what Dee would end up like if they were not able to stop it before it happened. Hunter's fists clenched and his muscles corded as he anticipated getting the scrawny neck of this Abe between his hands and squeezing until its eyes popped out and its black tongue bulged with death. He just might let the pressure lessen a few times to cause more pain and drag out the torture, before burning the foul creature to ash. His smile turned icy with anticipated pleasure.

"Have you seen any strangers in the area lately?" Saul asked, bringing Hunter out of his fantasies.

Hunter opened his mouth to give a negative reply, but closed it as an incident came to mind.

He remembered the night he got home and the door had been locked against him. He remembered having to drag it out of Dee about a strange man in the cemetery who had given her the creeps. He knew this had to be the one they were seeking.

"Yes," Hunter said, and told them the tale.

"Ah, yes," Saul said, as he too remembered the story the spunky young ghost, Jesse, had told him about a man stopping before Jesse's headstone. How she thought this man was bad. He also recollected how Callie had scratched the man, and how Callie described the dripped, black blood all over Jesse's headstone. "I believe this Abe has already been here," Saul said. He filled Jaxon in on the events, as told to him.

"What's the plan?" Hunter asked Jaxon, knowing Jaxon's human background in fighting wars and killing.

"Saul and I will go looking for this Abe, but I think our best bet of finding him will be when he shows himself at the cemetery again. We'll question all the Dark Minions that we encounter to see what they know of this Abe before killing them. Yet, we must do it quietly, so as not to alert him that we know about him or his plan. If he gets wind of us, he may change his tactics and then we will be in the dark again."

"And me?" Hunter asked again. "What do you want me to do?"

"Staying with Dee will be the top priority for you!" Jaxon barked. "If you have to leave her side, then one of us will be called to stay close by until you return. If Abe can't find an opening to strike, then we can end him before he lays a hand on my daughter."

"If he slips by us, we have a huge problem. And I don't like huge problems!" Jaxon ground out, his eyes going from dark brown to black with the thought. "Unless either one of you can think of a different plan, then I think we all know what to do. We need to keep this simple."

Saul and Hunter turned the plan over in their minds and thought it sounded simple enough. On the other hand, they knew it would be hard to hunt the Dark and keep Dee protected without her wondering why Hunter never left her alone.

"What happens when we find this Abe?" Hunter asked, wanting to nail down all the details.

"Which ever one of us corners the Minion will have to call the other two, and we will come. We can't give Abe a chance to escape. By all three of us attacking, he won't stand a chance." Jaxon replied.

"I want an update every day from both of you as to the progress of your hunting," Hunter said.

"Agreed," Saul and Jaxon said together. After a few more minutes all that had to be said was said.

"I need to get back," Hunter said, as he took a running leap and was gone.

Saul looked at Jaxon and nodded his head to the left. "I'll go this way," he said, "and I will meet you here tomorrow unless you call sooner."

Jaxon nodded his head once and remained still while the Guardian took to the air. Left alone, Jaxon sniffed the air and did the same to the ground where the Dark One had bled. He pulled its scent deep into his lungs. When he finally rose to his full height, he knew exactly who he was looking for, and when he found him he was not going to wait for the others. He had only said that for their benefit. If he found Abe first, he was going to make sure there was nothing left for the others to fight. All that would be left would be piles of ash where fallen chunks of flesh landed. He had a goal in mind, and it was time to get started.

"Here piggy, piggy," Jaxon whispered into the wind, as he took flight.

The wolf had been set free to hunt. And when Jaxon had run his prey to the ground, he had every intention of letting the wolf in to feed him.

Feed on death!

He howled!

Chapter 74

Saul and Jaxon covered the earth from end to end, having no luck finding the one set on killing Dee. Though Saul had had to jet off many times to handle situations as they arose, Jaxon did not. Jaxon looked under every rock and in every shadow for the one whose scent he carried with him. The few Minions he did find could give him no new information on the location of Abe.

Their screams reached into the corners of the Dark. Try as he might to keep it quiet, the Dark Hoards were made aware that Jaxon, the fierce Guardian Hunter, was on a rampage, but they knew not why this quest was being made. They ran from him and hid, with the exception of the stupid and cocky ones. These were extinguished when Jaxon got his hands on them. After wringing every ounce of information from them that he could, only then did he burn them alive, scattering their ashes into a wind that he powerfully and wrathfully caused with his powerful wings. Try though as he might, his hunger for revenge and death were not fed. The one he sought was not found.

Days passed and the meetings of the three Immortals ended the same, with none of them gleaning any news about their enemy.

"Maybe we scared him off," Hunter said, hoping.

"Not likely," Jaxon said, trying to put himself in Abe's place. "If I had to guess I would say the coward is hiding until his wounds heal. I think Callie did some serious damage to him. He deserves more," he added, his voice getting lower as his anger rose.

"There really isn't anything different we can be doing," Saul said. "We must continue to stay vigilant until the situation is resolved."

Hunter nodded his head and gave a run down on what Dee and he had planned. "Hannah will be coming out to stay for a few days," he said, shooting a sideways glance in Jaxon's direction to see how he would react at the mention of Hannah's name. Only a slight tensing of his shoulders was all the indication he gave in hearing his lost love mentioned. "I think I can spare a few minutes away from them as long as Hannah is there. She can see if any monsters approach and I think she will protect Dee until I can get there. I will just have to stay tuned in to her and jump when she calls."

"You would leave both Hannah and Dee alone? By themselves?" Jaxon demanded. "Are you crazy?"

"No," Hunter bristled, "but I'm tired of playing cat and mouse with this Dark threat. And if he thinks that we, or I, have left them alone, he just may make a move. I want this over."

Jaxon clamped down on his objections and calmed himself enough to think about this new plan objectively. "It might work," he said, hating to even think about placing his two most important girls in harm's way. But if they worked it right, it just might bring the Dark One out into the light.

"So should we try it?" Hunter asked, wanting a decision.

"I'm in," Saul said, siding with Hunter.

"We can try it," Jaxon said. "But if anything happens to either one of them…."

He let the sentence hang without finishing it, but neither Hunter nor Saul had any doubts as to what punishment Jaxon would deal out if harm came to his loved ones

"Then we do this," Saul said. Looking at Hunter, he asked, "When?"

"Hannah will be here this weekend. By that, I mean she will get here Friday night and be here Saturday and leave Sunday. I think I will be gone all day Saturday and we will see if this Abe takes the bait." Hunter laid out Hannah's schedule.

Jaxon and Saul looked at each other before giving their consent to the plan they would all follow.

"It sounds solid," Jaxon said. "I will be covering the cemetery," he said. "Hunter, you should probably stay by the house, but not too close or Abe will see you. And Saul, I think you should cover the other end of the cemetery, away from me. That way we know when and where he shows up."

"IF," Saul said. "IF he shows up."

"I would," Jaxon said, "But I would also be wary of a trap, so we will have to stay hidden until he comes."

"Very well," Saul said, and prepared to depart. "We will meet here at dawn on Saturday morning and get ready before Hannah and Dee awaken."

"Will Brandon be here?" Jaxon asked, his gut doing a flip as he thought of the reason why he would be coming.

"No," Hunter said, resting an understanding hand on his friend's shoulder. "That's why I picked this weekend. He will be out of town. If anything goes down that Hannah and Dee witness, being who they are and what they can do, I figured they would be able to handle it."

"Thank you," Jaxon whispered, grateful that he would not have to see Hannah with someone else. "Thank you."

Hunter nodded once and the subject was forgotten, as finishing touches were put in place and each was satisfied that all the bases had been covered.

Hunter left first, and then Saul, leaving Jaxon to walk the cemetery, unseen by human eyes. He checked out all the spots that could be a problem, planning his strategy down to the last letter. Nothing could go wrong, and he was going to make sure of it.

All he had to do now was wait.

Chapter 75

Abe took his time healing. He needed to be in perfect shape for his plan to work. He hid in the shadows, spying on his prey, being careful to leave no trace of himself for the Guardians to detect. It would not do to have them discover him before he was ready.

And yes, he was not stupid enough to think they would not be waiting for him. But if he was sly enough, he would be able to sneak in and kill the human before the alarm could be sounded and his enemies could arrive. He just needed an opening to present itself, and he would strike.

He listened to Dee and Hunter as they lived each day. It was not long before he learned that the man was to be gone for a whole day. He jumped in glee when he learned that not only would Dee be unprotected, but also her mother, Hannah, would be without Guardian protection as well. To have them both in the same spot for him to dispatch would be a shining feather in his cap. His bid for leadership of the Dark would be cemented when he and he alone did what no one else had been able to do. Kill the two mortals that could detect and hamper plans the Dark had made for chaos and destruction.

The when was set, the how was easy. Abe sharpened his skills, practicing cutting, slicing and burning with his stick-like fingers. The where, he decided, was to be in the cemetery. How fitting was that? To die where you were going to be buried?

He was sure the Lake would come to them, but it would be too late to do anything about it once he began his killing. Up until that point, he had no doubt that the humans would stay close to the house and have no forewarning of the death that was coming. "Surprise, surprise, surprise!" he chanted, as he did his happy dance in the dark. It wouldn't be long now before all the Dark and the Guardians, too, learned that he, Abe, would be the one with whom no one messed with at any time. His puny chest puffed up in anticipated importance and his slithering became more of a strut. Yes, his time was coming, and he would show everyone just how bad he was. He was finally going to get what was coming to him.

His time had arrived!

Chapter 76

Friday night came, and Hunter tried to keep his mind off what the next day would bring. But it wasn't working. He kept busy getting things ready for Hannah's visit, even raking the yard and washing the vehicles.

Abe had been right when he assumed the humans would stay close to home. Hunter wanted to make sure that nothing happened before they were ready for it, even though he knew Jaxon was camping out at the cemetery to insure all went as planned. He never saw him, but he knew he was around. Small animals that usually were so careful coming out into the open came out and played in the sun, knowing they were safe from harm. That only happened when a Guardian was near by. Hunter welcomed the extra security.

Saul appeared in corners and Hunter, knowing where to look, had seen him a few times hovering over the yard, keeping out of sight but still staying close. He had good friends.

Hunter grabbed Dee's hand and together they met Hannah as her car rolled to a stop at the front porch.

Before the motor was turned off, Dee had the back door open and was passing luggage to Hunter to carry into the house. Hunter was amazed at the amount that the back seat produced, as his arms became loaded and he had to put some muscle into carrying the load. *"Wasn't she just supposed to be staying for a night or two?"* he wondered. Looked more like she was moving in to him.

Hannah and Dee walked in, just as Hunter was coming out to see if maybe he needed to bring in the kitchen sink. To him, it looked like that was all that had not been packed and brought along. He stood back for a moment and enjoyed the sight of seeing Dee laugh and her eyes light up with happiness. Sometimes, he figured, you just needed your mother.

Supper that night was easy, as Hannah had thought to bring along take out from Dee's favorite deli. All that was needed were paper plates and silverware to allow them to dig in and fill their bellies.

As the night wore on, it found the trio sitting on the porch, enjoying the cool evening breeze, sipping wine and just enjoying being together. When the girls began to yawn and the conversation lagged, Hunter stood up, declaring that it was time to call it a night. Dee and Hannah agreed, hugging each other closely while saying their good nights and their 'I love you' before Dee went into her bedroom and prepared for bed.

"Thank you for having me out for the weekend," Hannah said, her unusual eyes locking with Hunter's. "Is there anything you want to tell me?" she asked, having gotten the feeling that there was more going on than what was actually meeting the eye. Not that she didn't want to spend time with her daughter and Hunter, but she just needed to know the agenda. She didn't like surprises.

"No, Hannah," Hunter lied, breaking eye contact. "We just missed you, and since I have to be gone tomorrow, I thought it would be the perfect opportunity for you girls to spend some time together. You know, without me hanging around."

Hannah was not satisfied and, looking at Hunter, she used her powers to try once again to see if what she saw before had changed.

Hunter knew exactly what she was doing and he stood still, not letting her know he was aware.

Hannah once again saw the golden aura surround Hunter and, as before, it shone as bright as the sun. But this time she did not look away. She stared hard, and as she did, a figure began to emerge in the center. However, it wasn't of the man standing before her. In fact, it wasn't anything she had ever seen before. What she saw was what could have been Hunter, but this being had a pair of beautiful golden wings growing from his back. Streams of fire dripped from his hands, and his hair lifted as if from a wind. Hannah knew that it was power coming from him that lifted his hair and blew it around his beautiful face. "What are you?" Hannah whispered, pulling her power back until she could look only at the man in front of her.

"Someone who loves your daughter," Hunter said, not ready to let Hannah know everything. "If you have any doubts about my intentions, I can tell you that I would die protecting Dee from anything that would harm her. She is safe with me."

Hannah was far from satisfied with his answer, but knew he would tell her no more when he crossed his arms over his chest and stood before her with legs apart and eyes hooded. "Does this have anything to do with why I'm here now?" she asked, trying to get a little more from him.

"Good night, Hannah," Hunter said, and stood aside inviting her to go to her room.

"Good night Hunter," she said. But as she passed Hunter to enter her room, the tall man reached out a hand and stopped her. He took her in his arms and hugged her close. Hannah got the scary feeling that he was trying to say good-bye to her without words.

"What is it?" she asked, fear edging her voice.

"Nothing," Hunter replied, releasing her and stepping back. "I'm just glad you're here."

"You lie," Hannah said. She was unable to get any more from Hunter before entering her room and closing the door behind her. She changed her clothes and brushed her teeth, but her heart refused to slow its fast pace. Climbing into bed, she punched the pillow, trying to shut her mind off and be able to sleep, but nothing she tried worked.

Jaxon stood beside her bed and watched. He saw her beautiful hair spill across the pillows, and remembered the feel of it in his hands, on his face, and on his body. He wished with all his heart that he could feel it again. "Sleep," he whispered softly into her ear, as he touched her warm cheek and took the feelings of fear and dread from her. "Someday," he promised her now sleeping form. "Someday we will get to hold each other again. I love you. I love you so much," he vowed, as he kissed her lips and made her smile while sleeping peacefully.

He stayed for a while longer, looking at his love and drinking in her beauty. But as the sun began to rise, he left her side and returned to his post in the cemetery. Things were about to get ugly and he settled down to wait. He was not good at waiting, but for this he would be still. Still and patient.

The monstrous black wings unfolded from his back, wrapping around his body, cloaking him in the dark in which Abe was so accustomed. Abe would not see what was coming, until it was too late.

The last thing Abe would see would be death in Jaxon's eyes.

His!

Chapter 77

The next morning dawned bright and clear, with only a gentle breeze to kiss the dew-laden trees. Everything was washed fresh from the day before, and the canvas of a new day waited to be painted. Hunter had not slept. Instead he had fed his need to hold Dee in his arms. If things went wrong, it could very well be the last time he felt her warmth and smelled her scent. He did not waste the chance to store up memories by sleeping. He would sleep when all this was behind him.

When Dee finally began to stir in his arms, he held her tighter, not wanting the moment to end. But he had no say in the matter, as her eyes opened and she smiled into his handsome face.

"Mmmm, morning," she said, stretching before snuggling for a couple of more minutes in Hunter's arms.

"Morning, love," Hunter said, giving in to the urge to kiss her lips and drink in her taste. "How did you sleep?"

"Like a baby," Dee said, before getting up to use the bathroom. "What time are you leaving?" she called through the closed bathroom door.

"After breakfast," he responded, putting on his clothes and donning his shoes.

"I'll miss you," she said, coming out and beginning to dress also.

"Me, too," he said, standing by until she finished and they could head to the kitchen together.

Out of habit, Dee reached for the cat food but stopped when she remembered there was no longer a need.

Only Hunter saw the shadowy figure sitting at her feet, only he heard the soft purring as Callie jumped on the counter and rubbed her head on the hand that now lay idle with sadness. "You're not supposed to be on the counter," he said to the cat, with a smile in his voice that only she could hear.

Callie turned her bright green eyes towards Hunter and he could have sworn she smiled. "How is she?" the feline Guardian asked, missing her human.

"I've made it easier for her to deal with your death," Hunter said, "but she still misses you and thinks of you often."

"Why don't you get another kitten for her?" Callie asked. "Being what I am now, Saul said I could be its Guardian and I could make sure it is safe from harm. Dee would not have to lose it before its time. I think she would like this idea," the kitten said before jumping to the floor and wrapping itself around Dee's legs.

"Maybe," Hunter said. "We will have to see what the day brings."

"Yes, I've heard what is to happen today," Callie said. "Saul told me. I shall be by her side and warn you of danger if it comes. Saul knew I would want to be here and help," she explained, at Hunter's surprised look.

"Thank you," he said, glad to have the help of one that loved Dee as much as he did. "I will hear you and be close by if you need me."

"Go ahead with your plans," Callie said, making herself comfortable on a chair. "I'm not going anywhere."

Hunter gave the cat a wink and made himself comfortable at the table as Dee set the morning meal down. Cinnamon rolls from town, juice and coffee were on the menu, and he served Dee before nabbing some for himself.

Only a few bites were taken before Hannah made an entrance and took a chair at the table. "How did you sleep, Mom?" Dee asked when Hannah had gotten what she wanted and settled.

"Surprisingly well," Hannah said, cocking an eyebrow at Hunter. She had not forgotten what had happened the night before, and she let him know it.

"Well, I've got to take off," Hunter said, before Hannah could bring up last night. He took his dishes to the sink and kissed Dee's raised lips. "You two have a great day," he said. "Relax and enjoy your visit." With that, he headed to the door and locked eyes one more time with Callie, before going out and driving away.

"Well, what do you want to do today?" Dee asked, as she rinsed the few dishes breakfast had created.

"Oh, nothing in particular," Hannah replied. "Maybe we could go for a walk and you could show me what you've done in the cemetery since I was last here."

"That sounds good," Dee said. "Just let me go grab a long sleeved shirt and I'll be ready."

Hannah waited for Dee to return before grabbing a bottle of water and heading out the door.

Hunter stayed by the house as planned, scanning the shadows for any signs of Abe. He knew that Saul would pick up the women as they walked out of the yard towards the cemetery, and then Jaxon would watch over them there. They would stay hidden so no signs of their presence would or could be detected by the Dark. He hoped it would work.

It had to work.

It must work.

Chapter 78

Hannah and Dee took their time walking to the cemetery, stopping many times as Hannah commented on 'pretties' that she noticed along the way. Neither one was in a hurry so consequently, they took advantage of their time alone. It still didn't take them long before they reached their destination and began to wander the grounds.

Dee pointed to all the work she had done, and Hannah praised her for the beauty of the lawn and the flowers that bloomed in strategic spots. "I'm proud of you," Hannah said, putting an arm around her daughter's slim shoulders. "You even have a pretty good tan going," she said, as she looked at Dee's sun kissed face.

"I know," Dee giggled. "I didn't even have to be bored by just laying in the hot sun waiting to bake."

Hannah dropped her arm and they continued to meander the morning away, catching up on gossip and just talking.

It wasn't until they were well into the cemetery that their alone time was interrupted. "I don't mean to intrude on two such lovely ladies but I just couldn't help coming over and saying hello," a voice said behind them. Both Dee and Hannah jumped as neither one of them had heard the man's approach.

After a few heartbeats, Dee collected herself and stepped forward to greet the man.

"Abe," she said. "Abe Black, right?"

"Yes," the blonde man responded, sending a dazzling smile in greeting out to Dee. "I wasn't sure you would remember me," he said, shifting his gaze to Hannah.

"I'm sorry," Dee said. "This is my mother, Hannah Priest. Mom, this is Abe Black. His aunt is one of our guests here," Dee supplied, preferring not to say that the aunt was buried there. It just sounded nicer to call those buried here, guests.

"Mr. Black," Hannah acknowledged, taking in his appearance as she stayed back a step or two.

"Just Abe," he said, and again smiled as he spoke.

"Abe, it is then," Hannah said, and waited for the man to explain why he was there.

"Just thought I'd stop by and say hi to my aunt," Abe said, satisfying both women's curiosity.

"Well, we won't keep you," Dee said, backing up a few steps.

"No, that's fine," Abe said, reaching out a hand to halt her retreat. "It isn't everyday that I get to be in the company of two such beautiful women. Please stay. Maybe we could sit on the bench over there and talk for a few moments."

Dee's eyes followed Abe's hand, as he gestured towards a bench under an old tree. A bench out of the sun, a bench in shadows. She didn't know what was wrong but she was getting that same feeling that she and her mother should get out of here. Now!

Hannah shrugged her shoulders and turned as if going along with the suggestion. That is until Dee did not move. Hannah looked back at her daughter and immediately noticed the ashen color of her cheeks and the way the red streaks in her eyes had turned to molten streams of lava, glowing hot and bright. Spinning to face the man, Hannah unleashed her powers, and her own eyes grew bright as fire. Dee might have sensed something wrong, but Hannah knew exactly what it was.

The handsome blonde man standing before her changed and disappeared. The mask of humanity dissolved and his true being was revealed to her. The golden blonde hair fell from its head, leaving a black oily pate shining wetly in the sun. The blue eyes that had smiled at them turned to black holes that stared with a cold dead light out of a mask of black and grey oozing flesh. Where his mouth had been only a black-lipped, drooling hole remained, and the smile it now showed revealed grey rotting teeth, jagged and foul.

Hannah reached out blindly with her right hand, grabbing the closest one of Dee's to her own. The left one. For the first time, Dee saw what her mother saw. She saw the tall human body shrink and change, until it looked like black sludge taking form and undulating before them. It dipped and swayed, as more black drool slid from its mouth and burned the grass where it landed.

"Dee, I think it's time we went back home," Hannah said, trying not to alert the beast before her that his mask of flesh had been ripped off. They were alone in a deserted cemetery, and if this thing decided to attack they had no hope of surviving.

Dee stood frozen to the ground, unable to obey her mother's suggestion. She wanted to scream but her mouth would not open. She wanted to run but her feet would not move.

Hannah swung her gaze to her daughter and saw that she was going to have to help if she was to get her moving. She would do whatever needed to be done to protect her daughter and make sure she got to safety. Jerking her hand free, Hannah put it on Dee's back and shoved, making her move or fall.

When the contact was broken, Dee tumbled forward before looking back at her mother. She saw Hannah's eyes and knew they had both seen the same image, and that her mother was still seeing it.

"Go home, Dee," Hannah said, her eyes back on the monster before her.

Callie jumped onto Dee's shoulder and whispered in her ear. "You must do as your mother suggests," she purred.

"I can't leave her," Dee's mind screamed. "I can't leave her here alone."

"She has help," Callie purred, giving Dee the strength to admit that she had no choice but to head home. "Walk," she encouraged. "Walk fast." Dee did.

Hannah never took her eyes off the thing before her, but she tracked Dee's progress, until she was out of sight and heading for home. She took a step backwards, and another, before an ugly laugh made her stop. Her body began to tremble and she felt a scream build in her chest.

"First you, then," the Dark gurgled out." First, I will kill you, and then I'm going after your daughter."

"You leave my daughter alone," Hannah said, and prepared to fight this thing until Dee had a chance to get inside to safety. Her fingers curled into claws and her lips thinned into lines of determination. "Come on, then," she taunted. "Come and get me!"

Before Abe could strike, the ground shook and the wind screamed, as Jaxon came to earth beside Hannah.

Hannah saw him. She saw him! For the second time that day, she was stunned. Stunned and scared. She remembered the Jaxon that had held her in his arms and made love to her. The one that protected her and made her feel loved and safe. The Jaxon that stood beside her now had wings on his back that were as black as night and his hands glowed with fire. He was death!

Jaxon reached out with his hand and touched the cheek of his love. The fire did not burn. Hannah could see the deep love he still felt for her streaming from his dark eyes, covering her and calming her. "I love you," he said, in the voice Hannah for so long had only been able to hear in her dreams.

"Jaxon?" she asked, reaching out a shaking hand until she touched his chest and it felt real. Alive and strong. "Jaxon?" she asked again, as her tears of blood dripped down her cheeks.

"I love you," he said again.

"How very sweet," Abe interrupted, "both of you together. The great Guardian Hunter Jaxon and his bitch of a human. I should thank you for making my job easier. Now I can kill you both. You can watch her die first," he gloated, as he raised a sharp-clawed hand to cut Hannah down.

Jaxon touched her cheek once more before looking into her eyes, and with all the love he still carried for her glowing in those dark sweet eyes, he commanded, "RUN!!!"

And she did!

Chapter 79

Jaxon waited only seconds to make sure Hannah obeyed, before putting her from his mind and facing the Dark beast before him. "You must be a special kind of stupid to believe I would let you harm either Hannah or Dee," he taunted Abe. "I told you all that they were under my protection and I would kill any who did them harm. It seems you have a short memory and I must remind you of my promise of protection."

"I remember," Abe squealed in anger at having been put down by the likes of Jaxon. "A keeper of the do-gooders in the world. I remember your worthless words and I am not afraid."

"You should be," Jaxon said, as he slowly spread his wings, until they reached wide and glinted like black diamonds in the sun.

"Well, call me impressed," Abe sing-songed at Jaxon's display of power. "If you're done talking and showing off, maybe we can get on with the killing," he said, tensing as he prepared to strike.

"By all means," Jaxon said, and mocked him with a bow. "I will give you one chance to leave this place and forget you ever heard of Dee and Hannah. But if that's a problem, and you're still feeling froggy, go ahead and jump."

Abe shrieked out his rage at being made fun of and he attacked. He came at Jaxon with his sticklike claws slashing, his teeth bared, meaning to cut the Guardian Hunter in half with one mighty swipe.

Jaxon easily stepped to the side, avoiding the rush. Using his fists he landed blow after blow to the black flesh, causing the acid they called blood to spew in all directions, and the stumps they called teeth to break and fall. Jaxon laughed at the feeble attempt, and bunching his muscles gave a mighty leap, meeting the next rush head on. As the two collided, the ground shook and the trees moaned.

Saul and Hunter heard the sounds of fighting, and in less time than it takes to blink, they arrived at the cemetery ready to aide their friend. Hunter wanted to plow right in, but Saul held him back with a grip of steel.

"No," he said, when Hunter turned his head with a growl of frustration. "We will leave this to Jaxon. If he begins to fall, only then will we step in to help."

Hunter didn't like this plan at all. He wanted to feel this Dark One's bones break under his hands for even thinking he could harm Dee. He wanted Abe to pay for taking the life of one so brave and true, though much smaller, such as Callie. He had issues.

"Just wait," Saul commanded. "Jaxon fights for his family and we must allow him this."

Hunter had to agree with Saul's reasoning, so he stood down, but remained vigilant in case the fight began to favor the Dark.

No thunderstorm had ever caused the air to tremble like the sounds of the two Immortals locked in battle. Each time fists connected with flesh, the thunder rolled. And as the Dark felt pain, the wind would shriek with that pain until it sounded like the most violent of storms had been let loose.

But Jaxon was not the only one to cause damage to his opponent. Abe had been able to reach in with his razor like claws and open wounds on the Guardian's body that ran red with his Immortal blood.

Both panted as the fight wore on, until Jaxon stopped playing and went in for the kill. Using the sharp edges of his wings, Jaxon cut chunks of flesh from Abe until the Dark One's mouth hung open in exhaustion and he could lift his arms in defense no more.

Jaxon walked in and finally wrapped his hands around the slimy black throat and squeezed, watching the eyes bug out and the black snake of a tongue loll out until it dangled and squirmed down on its chest.

"You dared to threaten my family!" Jaxon ground out, his brown eyes turning black. "It will cost you your life!" he said, as fire grew from his hands and began to ignite the Dark Being.

"You think you've won?" Abe choked out, as the pain of fire ate at him. "Well, you may win this round, but I'm going to have the last laugh."

"What are you talking about?" Jaxon demanded, shaking Abe's body like a rag doll. "What are you talking about?"

"You'll see," Abe said, before a scream of pure agony and pain erupted from his mouth. "You'll see." Then he was gone. Nothing but smoking ash remained to give evidence to the Immortal battle just waged.

Jaxon stepped back and dusted off his hands before wiping the sweat and blood from his eyes. Saul and Hunter landed beside the victor and, as the wind died down, each heard the cold laugh before it was carried away and disappeared.

"What was that?" Hunter asked, not liking the sound one bit.

"He said that it wasn't over," Jaxon said. "He said it wasn't over and that he would have the last laugh."

"What did he mean?" Hunter asked. When he got no response, he asked again. "What did he mean?"

"I don't know," Jaxon said. "I don't know, but it can't be good."

"It seems we have one more surprise to deal with, and I'm betting we're not going to like it."

Chapter 80

Saul and Jaxon stayed behind, as Hunter returned to his human form and went to check on Dee and Hannah. He didn't want to be away from Dee any longer, and he knew he was going to have to deal with what Dee and Hannah had seen.

"What should I do?" Jaxon asked Saul, as they sat on the ground and talked. "She *saw* me. Hannah, she saw me. What do I do?"

Saul was quiet as he weighed the options as he could see them. "I guess the only thing to do is talk to her," he said, finally. "Go to her and talk to her. She's already seen you, so you may as well speak to her face to face."

Jaxon's heart beat fast, as he would finally get to see Hannah and hold her after all this time.

"Have Hunter get her out on to the porch and talk to her there. It will be up to you to convince her to say nothing to anyone about you."

"If I can't?" Jaxon asked. "What then?"

"Then I would suggest you take the memory from her mind to save her the pain of knowing you are still here. Take all the memories of today from her if you must, and give her the peace of mind to go on with her life. I fear if you don't she will, again, isolate herself and always be waiting for you to come back to her."

"You can not. You know you can not let her keep seeing you, right?" Saul asked.

Jaxon hung his handsome head until the dark hair fell about his face, hiding his pain. "Will I have to lock this memory away with the rest? "He asked, not wanting to know the answer, but knowing he must.

"Yes," Saul said, hurting for his friend. "Don't forget that you will still carry the memory with you, but it will not cause you pain this way. It's for the best."

Jaxon sighed. He wished with all his heart that he could have Hannah by his side, and not just as a memory. All in good time her journey as a mortal would end, and then he would get her back. But until then, he would have to let her life take its course.

"Very well," Jaxon agreed, "but it doesn't mean that for this night, for this time, I can't enjoy being with her and holding her for a few moments."

"Enjoy the time you have," Saul agreed and stood to go. "My work here is done, for now. If you need me, call." With that, he took his leave.

Jaxon, too, stood, and brushing his hands down his legs, removed all traces of the fight from his person. He couldn't go to Hannah looking like he had just been rolling in the dirt now, could he? Opening the wings that had stood him well in battle, Jaxon made the short trip to Dee's house. Lifting his face he called to Hunter, "I need you to get Hannah out onto the porch," he said. "Alone."

"What for?" Hunter asked, being nosey.

"I need to speak to her, if you must know, and then I will need to wipe the events of the day from her mind. You, I trust, will do the same for Dee." Jaxon explained.

"I'm taking only the ones dealing with the Dark," Hunter said. "The rest, I will leave. Do the same for Hannah."

"Very well," Jaxon said, and stood in the shadows until Hannah slowly opened the screen door and moved out onto the darkened porch.

"Hannah," he called, barely above a whisper. "Hannah, my love, can you hear me?"

"Jaxon?" Hannah asked, standing tall and looking around. "Jaxon, is that you?"

Moving into the dim moonlight, Jaxon showed himself to Hannah and waited for her reaction. If he had any doubts about how she would react to seeing him, he should have known better. Hannah let the tears flow, as she ran down the steps and jumped into his arms, holding on for dear life.

"Is it really you?" she cried and laughed at the same time. "Is it really you?"

To prove he was real, Jaxon cupped Hannah's lovely face in his hands and lowered his hungry lips to hers. After all the years apart, he feasted on her lips, tasted her tongue and buried his hands in her soft hair, never seeming to get enough of her. Never enough. If he could, he would have taken her inside himself to carry with him until it was time for her to join him. But that was not possible and, with a heavy heart, he knew it.

"I've missed you," they said together, laughing at their timing.

"What happened today?" Hannah asked, knowing it was the reason he had come to her.

Jaxon walked to a chair and, after sitting down, pulled Hannah onto his lap. He wrapped his arms around her and thought his heart would break as the love he felt for her filled him to bursting.

"I have something to tell you," he said, and began his tale of becoming a Guardian. He told her everything, because he knew, in the end, she would remember nothing. By the time he was finished, the light from a new day had begun to chase the shadows away, making room for the sun. He knew it was time for him to go.

"I have to go," Jaxon said, kissing her lips until she had no breath left.

"Will you come back?" Hannah asked, not sure she could remain sane if he did not.

"I love you," Jaxon said again, as he walked her up the steps to stand with her in his arms one last time.

"Don't go, Jaxon," she begged, her voice low and cracking with her pain. "Please, I don't think I could live without you again. Please don't go," she said one last time before the tears clogged her throat.

"I'll always be with you. And when your time comes, I will come get you and we will be together for all time," Jaxon promised, as he prepared to leave her. "Just remember, I will be watching over you, and if you need me, I will come."

"Don't go," Hannah sobbed into his chest, hanging on with her hands, refusing to let him go.

Jaxon lifted her face and let his own tears fall as he kissed her, and with that kiss took her memories.

He took her memories, but again, left her his heart.

Chapter 81

Jaxon spoke briefly to Hunter before he could stand to stay no more. Just long enough to verify that Hunter had done the same for Dee and her memories.

"I'm sorry," Hunter told Jaxon, as they stood shoulder to shoulder out of sight of the house.

"What are you sorry for?" Jaxon asked, itching to get away from this place.

"I'm sorry that you can't be with Hannah," he explained. "I know you love her."

"More than my life," Jaxon said, as a sad smile curved his mouth. "I have to go," he said, and clasped Hunter's hand in farewell. "Remember what the Dark said, something else is coming, so be alert. Take care of my daughter."

Hunter squeezed the Guardian Hunter's hand, before letting go and giving his promise to remain vigilant.

"If you need me, call," Jaxon said, before leaping into the air and was gone.

Hunter looked up at the empty sky for just a moment and felt pity for Jaxon. He wondered if he would be able to handle the separation from Dee as well, when the time came for them to part. He doubted it. Heading back inside, Hunter joined Dee and Hannah in their everyday conversation. Neither one remembered the events of the day, so it was weird for Hunter, as he still remembered it all, but could not talk about it.

He helped Hannah carry her bags to her car when she was ready to leave, standing with his arm around Dee's waist, waving until her car drove out of sight.

"That was a nice visit," Dee said as they walked side by side up the steps. "It seemed to go by so quickly, though," she voiced, as she walked ahead of Hunter into the house.

"You know they say time flies when you're having fun," Hunter said, and received an elbow in the ribs for his effort.

"What?" he asked. "What was that for?" he laughed, as he followed her inside.

Hunter kept his promise to Jaxon and stayed vigilant for any signs of danger, but all seemed to be going smoothly. That worried Hunter almost as much as the danger they had just put down. If much more time went by without incident, Hunter knew he would be pulled off protecting Dee, and returned to his other charges that needed his guidance. He liked the help he was asked to give to his mortal charges, but he loved Dee. It scared him to think that before long he would be taken from the only woman he had ever loved. He didn't know what to do. So he did nothing.

He lived his life one day at a time, pushing the future as far away from him as he could. He spent all of his time with Dee, helping her with the upkeep of the cemetery, repairing things when they broke and making love to her in the deep darkness of the night, each and every night. He needed her like he needed air to live in his human body.

He hoped his luck would not run out. But time was against him, and the last thing that Abe alluded to was about to come true.

But Hunter didn't know that.

Chapter 82

"What's on the agenda for today?" Hunter asked, as he walked out of the bathroom, a towel around his waist, still damp from the shower he had just taken.

"Umm," Dee said, as she got caught up with the wide expanse of male chest in front of her.

Hunter smirked as his ego got a boost because he could leave her speechless just by showing off his chest. He turned his back and really smirked, thinking of what he could do to her when he held her captive with his body, under his body. Hunter pulled his mind away from those thoughts, before they ended up spending the day romping under the covers and saying to hell with work. *"Maybe that wasn't such a bad idea,"* he thought, warming up to the idea, as he got to thinking about it some more.

"Oh, yes," Dee said, clearing her throat. "Work, right. I was thinking I still have an area towards the back of the cemetery that could use a little work, so I figured I'd kind of clean it up today. What about you?" she asked, glad that Hunter had finally covered himself up, which allowed her mind to focus on something else besides the way his body felt under her hands and her lips. Absolutely, without a doubt, addictive.

"I'll tag along and do the heavy lifting, if you need help," he said, buttoning up his last button, before turning around.

"I think I can manage but there are a few rocks that need moved away from the trees, if you could handle that," she said, stopping to stand on her tip toes to reach his lips. Hunter obliged her and things heated up fast before Dee pushed back and smiled with her whole body.

"I love you," she said.

"I love you, too," Hunter replied, and wished she knew just how much he really did.

"Let's get going," Dee said. "Maybe, if we get finished at a decent time, we could rent a movie tonight, with popcorn and everything. Would that be okay?" She asked, not wanting to take for granted what she wanted to do, was necessarily what he would want to do.

"Yup," Hunter agreed. "That sounds nice. I'll even make the popcorn," he offered.

"Deal," Dee said, and floated on air to the kitchen. She was in love.

After a quick breakfast, Dee set out some pork chops to thaw for supper and the two headed out to the cemetery in the pick up, with Hunter driving. She pointed out the rocks she wanted removed and Hunter started on them. Meanwhile, Dee got a hoe and shovel and headed towards a tree at the back of the property. It was the last spot that needed her attention, and by hoeing and pulling the weeds here the ground would be as smooth as the rest of the cemetery. A few hours work and she should be finished.

Dee propped her tools against the big, old tree and slipped on her work gloves. She smiled. She had bought the gloves new, but looking at them now you would never know. They were worn, soft and comfortable now, just the way she liked them. They were like old friends.

Bending down, Dee pulled the weeds away from the tree, keeping at it until she could finally find the base without wading through knee high trash. "*Much better,*" she thought, dusting her gloves off on the seat of her pants. "*Much better!*"

She was about to turn away, when something in the grass caught her eye. Curiosity got the better of her, as she bent down and snipped at the grass until she was able to make out the object hidden. It was a gravestone. Not a seriously old one in fact, fairly new compared to some of the others in the cemetery. Using her gloved hands, she brushed the stone clean until she could read the name clearly. Dee slowly rose to her feet and had to hang on to the tree to keep from falling.

"*It couldn't be,*" she thought. "*It's not possible.*" But the proof lay at her feet, and she could not deny what was chiseled in the dark marble.

Hunter Gunn
Born May 19, 1952.
Died July 5, 1981.
Only the good die young

Dee screamed!

Chapter 83

Hunter heard Dee scream and ran. He got to her in time to catch her as her legs buckled and she started to fall. "I got you, Dee," he said, holding her to his chest. "I got you. Are you okay?" he asked, when her screams finally calmed down to whimpers. "Are you hurt? What happened?"

Dee wouldn't answer his questions, so Hunter propped her up against the tree and walked around to the other side. When he saw what Dee had seen, he groaned and hung his head. That's what Abe had been talking about, Hunter realized. Hunter stood looking at his headstone, as time stood still and his heart broke.

"Is that you?" Dee asked, coming from the other side of the tree. Her face was white and even her lips held no color. Only her eyes still held color as they looked at Hunter in shock and denial. "Is that you?" she whispered again.

Before he could think of an answer, Saul appeared at her back and held his hands out, palms up. "It's over," he said to Hunter. "It's all over."

"It can't be!" Hunter screamed in his head. "It can't be!"

Saul put his hand on Dee's shoulder and took her memories. Took the memories of finding Hunter's grave and replaced them with a story she could believe. One in which Hunter had to leave because of a family emergency, one in which she would resign herself to his departure, and him never coming back.

Hunter's human body disappeared, and he was once again an Immortal Guardian of mankind, invisible to the human eyes. Golden wings on his back opened wide and he leapt into the air, leaving Saul to clean up the mess.

Hunter flew trying to outrun his pain. But the pain flew faster and would stay with him until Dee joined him in death.

Hunter's tears flew behind him and fell to earth as a torrent of rain.

A torrent that lasted for days.

Epilogue

Jaxon and Saul stood before the Window to the World, neither saying a word, neither moving.

"Are you sure about this?" Jaxon finally asked, his voice low and sad.

"Yes," Saul said. His voice, too, rifled with grief.

"Why?" Jaxon asked. "This isn't fair."

"No one said fate was fair," Saul declared.

"Bull!" Jaxon said, willing to fight for what he wanted to happen. "Do something. Change destiny."

"I can't," Saul said. A thread of anger weaved its way into his voice.

Jaxon whipped his hands through his dark hair and began to pace, grinding his teeth in frustration. Before he could get another argument past his lips, the air rumbled and fire flew as another Immortal joined them.

"What did you do?" Hunter yelled, with a voice that shook the ground. He reached out hands that were curved into claws and grabbed Jaxon by the shoulders. He shook him and Jaxon did not resist. "What did you do? Why? Why?"

"I did you a favor," Hunter growled. Tears welled in his eyes.

"You knew what was going to happen, didn't you? You knew I was going to fall in love with her, didn't you? Answer me!" Hunter demanded, when Jaxon and Saul remained silent.

"I was hoping was all," Jaxon finally said.

"Hoping?" Hunter said, in disbelief. "Hoping? You were hoping that an Immortal Guardian and a human would fall in love? What were you thinking? Is it okay to cause this kind of pain to two beings? Is it okay to do this to me and to your own daughter?"

"I wanted you to watch over her. That is all I asked of you," Jaxon pointed out. "But I will admit that I knew if feelings grew between you two, you would move heaven and hell to protect her."

"What good did it do me or her?" Hunter asked again. "I am here and she is there. We can't be together and she will be in danger again. I can't protect her."

"Your job is over," Saul said.

"My job, "Hunter said, whirling until he faced the mightiest Immortal Guardian of them all. "It was more than a job and you both know it. Send me back," he demanded, falling to his knees, his golden wings lying limp at his sides, his cheeks streaked with his tears. "Send me back. I don't want to exist without her. I love her."

Saul moved to Hunter's side and drew him up to stand with him. "Come here," he said, and led the way until they stood before the Window to the World. "You too Jaxon," Saul invited.

"I don't want to watch her live her life from here," Hunter said, his black hair blowing back from his handsome face. "Am I being punished for some wrong I have done to you?"

"What is this, Saul?" Jaxon asked, as he wondered what the Guardian had wanted them to see.

"There is no punishment here," Saul said, sadness in his voice again. "I show you this to ease both your minds. All you have to do is watch."

The Window grew clear and the scene they watched was Dee sitting underneath a large tree looking out at nothing. Each could feel her loneliness, each could feel her pain at loosing a love she so desperately wanted and needed.

"No more," Hunter pleaded with Saul. "Please, do not make me watch any more."

"Watch," Saul said, clearly leaving no option in his voice.

All three grew quiet, all three for their own reasons. It only took a few moments before it was clear to Hunter and Jaxon why Saul had wanted them to watch. To be here and see.

Hunter drew in a sharp breath, as hope bloomed in his wide chest.

Jaxon, too, drew in a deep breath, but his was one of disbelief turning to white-hot anger.

"No damn it, no," he wailed.

As they watched, Dee raised her head and slowly rose to her feet. She stood still as the grass beneath her feet changed. Changed and disappeared. Where grass had been but a few seconds before, there now was water lapping in slow grey waves. Where there had been a sea of green before, a lake now resided.

The Omen Lake.

The omen of death had come.

But for whom?!!

Printed in the United States
By Bookmasters